RICCARDO BRACCAIOLI

THE SCENT OF DEATH

The Barcelona Serial Killer, A Gripping Crime Novel

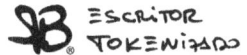

First published by ESCRITOR TOKENIZADO 2023

Copyright © 2023 by Riccardo Braccaioli

All rights reserved. No part of this publication may be reproduced, stored or transmitted in any form or by any means, electronic, mechanical, photocopying, recording, scanning, or otherwise without written permission from the publisher. It is illegal to copy this book, post it to a website, or distribute it by any other means without permission.

This novel is entirely a work of fiction. The names, characters and incidents portrayed in it are the work of the author's imagination. Any resemblance to actual persons, living or dead, events or localities is entirely coincidental.

Legal deposit: 2304264153136

First edition

Translation by Eva Alton
Editing by Julia Slack

This book was professionally typeset on Reedsy. Find out more at reedsy.com

To Lluís Estragués Carratalá, Sergeant of the forensic police of Barcelona, who taught me many of the investigative techniques present in this book.
To all law enforcement agencies and their investigators: thank you for your work keeping crime at bay.
To you, my readers, for without you none of this would have been possible.
To my parents.
To Eva.

"Wanting people to listen, you can't just tap them on the shoulder anymore. You have to hit them with a sledgehammer, and then you'll notice you've got their strict attention."

> KEVIN SPACEY - John Doe, SEVEN

Before The Scent of Death, there was

Learn the story of what really happened in Inspector Alex Cortes' first investigation in Barcelona.
An EXCLUSIVE PREQUEL, completely free for everyone who joins the Alex Cortes Readers' Club!
JOIN HERE!

"Write about death, to talk about life."

Riccardo Braccaioli

MAIN CHARACTERS

- Alex Cortes: Sergeant/Inspector of the Mossos d'Esquadra Barcelona Police Corps
- Karla Ramirez: Corporal of the Mossos d'Esquadra Corps
- Alfonso Rexach: Lieutenant of the Mossos d'Esquadra Corps
- Alba Guevara: Coroner, Chief of the Morgue
- Mario: Sergeant of the Mossos d'Esquadra Corps
- Alan Martínez: Agent of the forensic police, forensic IT division
- Rafa: manager of the cafeteria opposite the police station.

This novel is a work of fiction. Any resemblance to reality and people's names is purely coincidental.

1

Barcelona.
Tuesday morning.

When Barcelona's bloodiest criminal screeched to a halt at a crosswalk, he couldn't have imagined that he was about to cross paths with the only man capable of stopping him.

He drove a simple, anonymous-looking white van that perfectly disguised his disturbing cargo.

He braked just in time, avoiding running over police officer Alex Cortes. The latter was surprised that the driver was hidden behind a pair of sunglasses, despite the rain. He would soon regret not having thwarted his diabolical plan.

The van had entered Avenida Diagonal half an hour ago, but the great urban artery had become a river of cars paralyzed by the deluge. The driver's stiff leather gloves creaked loudly as he gripped the steering wheel. The load he was carrying couldn't wait, and it was too late to retreat.

Life in the city had stopped, and he drummed his fingers

incessantly, waiting for the traffic light to change. The spring rain amplified the traffic on a day that seemed like any other.

Umbrellas jostled for space on the sidewalks of Barcelona, creating a flow of passersby. Black, blue, checkered and spotted, in all directions and to multiple destinations. None of them escaped the persistent rain that was lashing down.

The vehicle was at a standstill, and despite the continuous flick of the wipers, the view through the windshield was blurred and tinted by the red lights of the cars in front. The only sound inside the van was the metallic clang of rain beating down on the roof.

The weather forecast was a critical variable that had escaped his attention while preparing the plan. The GPS instructed him to take a right. He turned onto Travessera de les Corts and was now just a few yards from his destination.

He drove past the hotel entrance but kept his eyes firmly focused on the road and continued along a side street where the traffic was smoother, even though the rain was still pouring as hard as ever.

He pulled down his glove to check the time on his watch: half past eight in the morning. The plan had been delayed by half an hour, enough time to blow the whole thing out of the water.

The man took a deep breath.

He had almost arrived at his destination. He stopped at the last red light on the left and saw an empty parking lot where he could leave the van.

The traffic light turned green. He put the van into gear and pressed the accelerator, narrowly missing two pedestrians running the red light. He slammed on his brakes and ignored their indignant yells. As his eyes followed the men, he

1

remained impassive, as cold as an iceberg.

Alex Cortes, a Barcelona police officer, was one of the two men, but the driver didn't know it. They locked eyes, and an invisible beam penetrated the windshield, sending a shiver down the driver's back.

Once the men had stopped protesting about his driving, they walked away. The man spotted a parking spot in front of a cafeteria and quickly reversed in. Then he took a bottle out of the glove box and sprayed it all over the dashboard: he couldn't leave any traces.

He climbed out of the vehicle just as the two men reached the cafeteria. When he looked up, he was in front of his target and narrowed his eyes as he stared at it for a moment. Then he locked the van and pulled up his hood. He disappeared into the rain and made his way to the nearest subway station.

Barcelona had been cleansed by the rain that morning. The dirt and pollution from its streets washed away down the city's sewers.

The man had left the van outside the entrance to the central police station. It was only a matter of time before its contents would ferment and mature, forever changing the neighborhood and the city itself.

The city engulfed the man, but not the truth. That would soon shatter.

2

Barcelona.
Saturday, one month later.

Alex Cortes sat in his car, waiting. Waiting for the perfect moment, confident that the tip-off was genuine.

His new vehicle stood out in the rundown neighborhood. It was clean and shiny, its black and white stripes attracting attention. The Mini Cooper had been a whim that had pleased him and annoyed his girlfriend. But Alex had always been stubborn, which was why he was sitting here in his Mini and not watching the Champions League final on TV. It would have been better to be in an undercover patrol car, but none had been available that day, and Alex didn't have time to wait for another opportunity to present itself.

As he listened to the *Barça* match on the radio, he sipped a takeaway coffee without taking his eyes off the entrance to the building. The sporting event was worldwide, and the Barcelona streets were quiet. The information had reached him that afternoon, and he couldn't ignore it for something as trivial as a soccer final. Alex felt it was his duty to determine if the tip was accurate.

The door to the building opened.

Time was running out, and the final whistle would blow in a quarter of an hour.

The *Blaugrana* team was leading after a goal from their Argentine star.

Alex slouched in the car seat, hiding behind the dashboard.

The suspect exited the building, closed the door behind him and looked around. After lighting a cigarette, he set off walking down the street.

The police officer got out of his car without being noticed and trailed behind the suspect. A few meters away, the man entered a grocery store.

Alex followed. Even though he was an experienced officer and accustomed to facing danger in operations, his heart drummed.

A young Asian man sat behind the counter, following the game on his cell phone, oblivious to the customers. There were a few aisles of food on old recycled shelves, and a cooler buzzed in the corner.

Alex picked up a bag of chips, trying to act casually, and watched as the suspect put his shopping in a basket. When the suspect placed the basket on the counter, Alex grabbed a soft drink from the cooler and stood behind him.

The man was the same height as Alex. He reeked of acid sweat, and his clothes looked old and worn. His hair was so flat and greasy that it looked like it had been pasted down with gel.

The shopkeeper scanned the products while keeping one eye on the game.

"Hey, how long until the end?" asked Alex from behind the suspect.

The suspect turned to look at him, but the policeman didn't return his gaze.

"The end of the game?" asked the shopkeeper.

"Of course, what else?

"Less than ten minutes."

"I'm going to miss it," said Alex, looking at the floor and shaking his head. "Is the score still the same?" he asked, checking what the man had bought: a 6-pack of beer, fast food and some cookies.

The shopkeeper nodded as he bagged the items for the man.

Alex scratched his eyebrow and ran his hand through his beard.

The suspect left the store. Alex put the bag of chips on the counter next to the bottle of soda, pushed some coins toward the shopkeeper, and hurried out.

He opened the bag of chips and began to eat them as he followed the man for the few steps that separated the grocery store and the man's building.

The suspect entered, and Alex waited for him to disappear. He leaned on the door so it wouldn't close, but it clicked shut.

"Damn," he thought.

He peered through the slits in the door, but the man had vanished. The landing was a long corridor that led to a narrow staircase. There was no sign of an elevator.

He looked back at the deserted street. The likelihood of anyone coming in or out was slim, and he had to act fast.

2

He pulled out his cell phone and checked the informant's message.

"Second floor, third door. It's dangerous."

Putting away his phone, Alex threw the half-eaten chips and the can of soda into a trash can.

Only minutes remained until the end of the match.

He pressed random doorbells, avoiding the suspect's, until someone answered. He pretended to be a neighbor who had left his keys at home.

The first man who answered was annoyed at being interrupted at the most crucial moment of the game and told him to clear off.

The second person, a lady, reluctantly agreed to let him in.

He raced up the stairs, taking two at a time. There was less than a minute until the end of the game.

When he reached the second floor, he found the third door on the landing.

All the doors were old and shoddy.

He took out his cell phone, but as he was about to press dial, the game ended. A roar of cheers resounded throughout the building. *Barça* had won the Champions League. The neighborhood suddenly came alive as Barça supporters shouted from their windows and threw firecrackers from the balconies.

Alex put his cell phone back in his pocket and took a deep breath. Mustering all his strength, he walked the few steps to the landing and threw himself against the door, knocking it down with a single blow.

He was in.

As his eyes became accustomed to the darkness, Alex took his gun out of its holster. In his left hand, he held a small flashlight. He crept down the hallway, feeling his way along the wall.

His heart was banging: it had been a long time since he had found himself in a situation like this.

The stench from the dozens of garbage bags that filled the hallway was disgusting, and he tried not to gag.

Finally, he checked the living room, but no one was there. He wondered where the man had gone.

The informant had told him that only one man would be on duty during the evening of the final. But right now, he couldn't even find that one.

Out in the street, the shouting and bangs of firecrackers grew more frenzied. Alex advanced in small steps, keeping his gun and flashlight pointing into the unknown.

The first bedroom was empty, but as he went down the corridor, he spotted a door ajar.

Moving silently, Alex peeked through the crack and saw what he was looking for.

A sense of relief washed over him; he had been scouring through Barcelona's underworld for several weeks in search of his target, but his relief was immediately replaced by fear.

The whole city was looking for *him*; all the media and, of course, the Barcelona police, *Mossos d'Esquadra.*

Alex had longed for this moment to come, and now it was finally in front of him. He stepped away from the door and breathed in deeply through his nose. He put his finger lightly on the trigger and barged into the room, pointing his gun.

The man he had followed to the supermarket was holding a gun to his hostage's head. The hostage he should have been protecting that night until the cops had discovered his hideout.

"All right, drop the gun. You have no way out," Alex commanded.

Sweat trickled down the man's forehead. He shook his head and pressed the gun harder against his victim's temple. The hostage, his eyes squeezed tightly shut, was no more than a kid.

3

The situation had gotten out of hand.

Alex had chosen to go in alone without informing anyone where he was, what he was doing there and, worst of all, that he needed backup.

The surprise effect hadn't worked, and now the operation was hanging by a thread because of his pigheadedness.

He stood in front of the man he had followed to the supermarket just minutes earlier, sensing his fear, cornered like a rat with no way out.

The boy's hands were loose, but his mouth was sealed with duct tape. His eyes were wide open, frightened. Long blond hair fell across his forehead. There were no apparent injuries, but he must have suffered emotional damage after so many days of being held hostage.

The policeman took a quick look around. There wasn't much—just a couple of threadbare armchairs in one corner and a table. Cobwebs floated in every corner, and the floral wallpaper, faded by the passage of time, was beginning to peel off the walls. The windows had wooden frames with green, weathered paint.

"Are you all right?" Alex asked the hostage. But the boy didn't answer. He trembled violently and stared blankly at him as if he didn't understand what was happening.

"Yani, we're leaving now, okay?" continued Alex.

The child was still in shock.

"Boy stays here with me," said the man, tightening his grip on the gun. "My friends are coming."

Alex kept the gun trained on him.

'The place is surrounded. You're not going anywhere," growled Alex.

The man glanced over his shoulder toward the window directly behind him. No patrol cars were on the street, only fans celebrating their team's victory.

Alex decided to play his only card.

"Hold it! Don't shoot! He's got the kid!" said Alex, pulling the collar of his leather jacket closer as the kidnapper's head snapped around to look at him.

The man was paralyzed.

His bluff had worked.

"What's your name?" asked Alex.

There was a deathly silence.

The man's eyes darted around as if looking for a way out.

"Hey, what's your name?" he repeated.

"Kai," mumbled the kidnapper reluctantly.

"Listen to me, Kai. You have no way out; the building is surrounded. See that window out there? In the building across the street?"

The kidnapper didn't turn around.

"Look at it," insisted Alex.

The kidnapper obeyed.

"Do you see that window on the third floor, with the shutter half down? A sniper is aiming his gun right at you. When I give him the signal, he will shoot you. But I'd rather not."

The kidnapper grabbed the child tighter and began to whimper, mumbling something incomprehensible. Alex got the impression that he was praying.

"Kai, nobody needs to get hurt. Do you underst—" But before he could finish, the kidnapper turned and hammered on the thin glass window: the din of shattering glass was hardly audible over the noise of the firecrackers, but the child's screams made Alex's blood turn to ice.

Time stood still for the policeman. This situation had gotten totally out of hand. They were two stories up, above a row of motorcycles parked on the sidewalk. With his elbow, the kidnapper smashed out the last of the glass and hoisted the boy up. Alex knew his career would be over if he allowed this to happen, and thanks to his reflexes, he managed to grab the child's feet. The child moaned in terror as he was suspended over the high drop.

Alex got a better grip and pulled the boy up, wincing as a jagged piece of glass pierced his skin. When the child was safe, Alex let out his breath. But the operation wasn't finished yet.

The back of the kidnapper's jacket was caught on the metal handle of the window, and he flailed helplessly, screaming at the policeman to help him.

Alex stared at him. Good and evil flashed through his mind. How sweet it would be to let him fall. But he wasn't a judge, and deciding on another person's fate was nothing to do with him.

3

He got down on his knees and gripped the man's legs. With a superhuman effort, he was able to pull him back through the window. The man fell to the floor, terrified and trembling. Alex found the duct tape the man had used on the child on a small table and wrapped it tightly around the man's wrists behind his back.

Alex turned back to the boy, who had curled up into a ball, sobbing.

"It's over, Yani, it's over," said the policeman, crouching beside him and pulling him close to his chest.

Then he took out his cell phone and, still holding the little boy, made the call he should have made before entering the building.

"Central, this is Officer Cortes. I'm at 34, Calle Diplomatica, second floor. You can inform the president of Barça that I've found Yani. He's alive. Send an ambulance and backup. I've got one of the kidnappers."

4

When he opened the door, it was already early morning.

He stood still. The fatigue was extreme, but the fear of not finding her there was even greater.

The hallway lights were still on, and four bulky suitcases sat by the door. They didn't belong to him, but he knew them well. He frowned, and his gaze drifted toward the kitchen door. Neon lights shone through the glass.

"Will you close the door?" came a woman's voice from inside.

Alex closed the front door and entered the kitchen. Sitting on a chair at the table was a woman with her legs crossed and facing the doorway. When she saw the man, she took a last drag of her cigarette and stubbed it out in her empty coffee mug.

The smoke from her cigarette drifted through the open kitchen window behind her.

"So you're leaving?" said Alex with a raised eyebrow.

The woman was his girlfriend, or at least she *had* been until he'd entered the apartment they shared and seen her packed cases. She was American, younger than him, with blonde hair tied in a ponytail and short bangs. A graphic designer and a rock nut. They'd met at a Miles Davis concert in the capital. He'd fallen in love with her, but she had fallen in love with Barcelona.

"Do I have a choice?" she replied in Spanish with a thick American accent.

"Just stay! Won't you even think about it?" said the policeman, leaning on the counter and giving her a wry smile.

The woman's smile was more like a sneer.

"I've given you time to change, but you haven't."

"If you love someone, you accept them unconditionally. Not want to change them," he said.

"Do you think this is an acceptable time to arrive home?" she asked, taking out another cigarette from the packet on the table in front of her.

"How many times have I asked you not to smoke in the house?"

The woman held the lighter, looked at it, and with a defiant expression, flicked it. There was a crackle as her cigarette burned, and she drew the smoke deep into her lungs.

The man didn't like that at all. He scratched his beard.

"I saved the child," he said quietly.

"Wow. Congratulations, cop!" shouted the woman in a mocking tone. "Are you getting a medal?" She took another drag of the cigarette and smirked at him. "Yes, a medal to the fool of the year."

Her words stung Alex, but he said nothing.

She remained silent for three puffs, and he respected her silence.

"My flight is in four hours," she snapped.

"We could have made this decision together."

"No, I have an incredible job opportunity in New York, and I'm not going to let it slip away," she said without looking at him. "If you want, you can come and see me there. Besides, I think we need a break from this," she said, squinting her eyes against the smoke.

"This?" he asked in surprise. "You call a two-year relationship... *this?*"

The woman dropped her cigarette in the mug and stood up. Before she could speak again, Alex had already left the room.

"What are you doing?" she said, puzzled. "Where are you going?"

"I'm going to take a shower and go to bed for a few hours because tomorrow I have a press conference."

"What are you talking about, man? Aren't you coming with me to the airport?" she asked, her voice dripping with resentment.

Alex stopped and turned to look at her.

"Call yourself a cab, Mary," he said, looking into her cold blue eyes one last time.

He left the kitchen, and as he made his way to the bedroom, he called over his shoulder.

"And leave your keys on the table on your way out."

5

Barcelona.
Sunday.

Justice never sleeps. Just because it was Sunday wasn't an excuse to take a break at the police headquarters. Since the president's son had disappeared weeks earlier, the serious crime department at the Travessera de les Corts station had treated him as a priority case. The father had pulled all the political strings he could, and his son had been the most sought-after child in Spain. He wasn't just an average kid; he was the *Barça* football team president's kid.

Now they had found him.

Nervousness was palpable from early in the morning. The press conference, scheduled for the afternoon, was to be attended by everyone from the top dogs down to the lowly junior officers.

A team of cleaners had worked for hours to restore the building to its former glory. The presence of all the staff gave the impression of a normal working day and not a day of rest.

Alex took it easy. He was the star of the show and would show up later than everyone else.

* * *

"How's it going, Juan?" said Karla to the man on her left.

Her subordinate gave her a sidelong glance and looked up.

"What do you want me to say? They want this report done before the press conference," replied Juan, sighing.

She raised her eyebrows and stared at him in surprise.

Karla Ramirez was an investigative officer in the same division as Alex Cortes. She had progressed quickly up the ranks because of her whip-smart intelligence and had just been badged for the first time. But life in the police station had begun to stifle her freedom and untamable appetite for adventure.

"I know, but there's a limit," she said, glancing out the window. "Hey, I was just going out for a coffee and a snack. Do you want to come with me?"

Juan raised his hands in surrender. He turned off the computer and stood up.

"Let's go, boss."

The two officers took the elevator to the first floor and crossed the access control booth. They went around the back, where the service entrance was, and came out onto the street. Right opposite the station was a cafeteria that was always full of *Mossos d'Esquadra* agents. It was styled on an

American franchise and served the best coffee in the area, with pastries designed for the local palate. The atmosphere was neat, with soft jazz music and armchairs to take a break between investigations and reports.

They went inside. The place was crowded with people making the most of their lazy Sunday morning. The rich aroma of coffee and freshly baked croissants permeated the whole place. Families sat on the green and brown couches, their buggies pushed against the wall. Most wore sports clothes, believing a Sunday stroll would burn a week's worth of calories and lighten their conscience.

The officers stood in line and waited for their turn.

"A coffee with oat milk and an *ensaimada*," ordered Karla, looking at the typical pastries. "Are they freshly made today, Rafa?"

"Of course!" replied the manager, grinning at her. He'd only come to help serve because of the mid-morning rush. "After all this time, you still need to ask?" he said, shaking his head with a smile.

"You're so touchy about this place! Juan, this one's on me. What do you want?"

They ordered their breakfast, and Karla took out her card to pay. Unable to contain her curiosity anymore, she leaned on the counter and addressed Rafa.

"By the way, Rafa. What's going on with the sewers? Every day it smells worse and worse in here. What are you throwing in there? Are you using them as a trash can?" she whispered, half-smiling.

"Don't even talk to me about it, please. I've been complaining to the council for days, but I'm still waiting to hear from them. See how crowded it is in here?" he said, flapping his hand towards the inside of the café. "Nobody wants to sit on the terrace because of the stink coming from the sidewalk. The tables are empty; nobody wants to be out there," he said, thumping the cash register monitor with both hands. I don't know what else to do!"

The woman scratched the back of her neck and glanced around.

"You're right. I hadn't noticed. Even though it's a lovely day, everyone's inside."

"It's only May, but it's warm today, and the terrace should be full."

"Karla, here you go. Where are you guys sitting?" asked the waitress coming out from behind the counter holding their tray.

The officer smiled at the girl and made her way over to a quiet table at the back of the café. Juan followed her.

"It's such great news about Alex, isn't it?" said Juan, handing Karla her coffee.

She snorted.

"Today will be an absolute farce! All the top dogs will be puffing out their chests and taking all the credit. The politician of the day will come in to praise the department and say whatever bullshit he wants. All this just because the elections are close," she said, stirring her coffee.

Juan glanced around to see if there was anyone they knew and lowered his voice.

"What are you talking about, boss?"

"I've been doing this for a year now, and that's exactly what's gonna happen. Instead of being at home on our day off, we have to be here and deal with all this." She shook her head as she dipped a chunk of *ensaimada* into her coffee.

"Have you seen that video of Alex's that went viral?" asked Juan.

"What video?"

"Boss, do you live under a rock?" said the subordinate, smirking. He took out his cell phone and showed her a video of the Barça celebrations in the streets. Suddenly, an upstairs window shattered, and a man appeared, followed by Alex hanging on to a child. The man was swinging from side to side. Alex dragged the child inside and then came to help the man. Triumphant applause and whoops of delight came from the shocked crowd watching from the street below.

"Alex is the hero of the hour. Everyone's talking about him," said Juan, putting his phone back into his jacket pocket.

The woman almost choked.

"I'm having breakfast, Juan. Don't put me off my food!" she said as she caught her breath. "It's way too early to mention Alex. He's already so smug, so finding the kid will make him unbearable. And this is just what the system wants you to see, that justice always has a winner."

Juan stayed silent, ate his chocolate muffin and put aside the subject that always infuriated his boss.

The two finished their breakfast, said goodbye to the busy manager and headed back to the station. As they walked through the door, she saw a man enter, carrying a local newspaper with a front-page photo of Alex Cortes. Karla pretended not to see it and turned her face away.

The sun shone brightly in the cloudless sky. Barcelona was waking up with a hangover from the previous day's victory in the Champions League, but the headlines didn't mention that. Instead, all the stories were about the shocking rescue of the president's son.

6

Alex didn't particularly enjoy fame, nor did he welcome heartbreak.

He jumped into the shower and turned the heat to maximum. The steaming water soon misted up all the glass surfaces.

He leaned against the sink and ran his hand across the mirror, staring at himself. The man looking back at him in the mirror wasn't the same person he used to know. Despite being a celebrated policeman, his life was a mess. He no longer liked Barcelona. He felt like a foreigner in a city with a plasterboard society, an outsider who had never managed to fit in.

When he'd first arrived in Barcelona, it was like arriving in Mecca. He thought it would be the land of opportunity, but it hadn't turned out that way. Life there was very different from what he had imagined.

He'd moved because of his job and because his siblings lived here. He was from a village in Tarragona and had always felt that Barcelona was too big for him. Mary was the only reason he'd stayed. He had little else to look forward to but her. Now that she'd left, everything else had faded away, and he was withdrawing into himself. He didn't see the point of living in a city that had become cold and unwelcoming.

The night was short, but his mind whirred with ideas.

Looking in the mirror now, he noticed that the forgotten dark circles under his eyes had returned, the same ones he'd had when he first met Mary. Back then, they were the consequence of midnight dinners, concerts and long nights of sex. Back then, it had been fun. Those were the times when he disguised hickeys with bandanas and accepted her scenes of jealousy in front of his workmates. He would accept anything because he was in love.

At that moment, seeing his face in the mirror, he no longer recognized himself.

The decline of the relationship they were forging led him to ask for a transfer to Tarragona. His bosses did not want to lose him, but he decided this would open a window of possibilities for him.

He had already decided to leave; it was just a matter of *when*.

Alex went into the kitchen and took an aspirin for his headache. Then he made coffee and sat at the dining room table.

He kept seeing the specter of Mary in front of him, with memories of the times when they laughed and made love on top of this very table.

Mary's favorite mug was still in the same place. Inside, he could see the last cigarette butts she had smoked in his kitchen.

He hit it with the back of his hand, and the cup flew across the kitchen, smashing into a thousand pieces. As it fell, ash scattered on the floor.

He felt a certain liberation. It was the end of an era, and when he walked out the door, another would begin.

He dressed in his uniform for the best occasions and went out, leaving the shards of the cup on the floor next to the broken pieces of his heart.

The press conference was held at the police station.

Politicians who were running for election appeared alongside the city's top officials. The press and TV stations fought over the best seats. The conference table had a plethora of microphones from various countries. They all wanted to cover such heartwarming news and have a picture of the man who saved the country's most wanted child.

When Alex arrived, the press jostled to get a photo of him, and he shielded his eyes from the camera flashes. He felt like an impostor: he was taking credit for a tip-off and a dare that could have cost him dearly.

His colleagues applauded him. Everyone in the department cheered, slapping him on the back as he passed and begging for selfies.

Meanwhile, in the background, Karla stood with her arms crossed, looking on with disdain.

The event began late. The Barça president was coming straight from the hospital, and his plane landed late.

The police spokesman and high-ranking officers hogged the limelight, leaving Alex with little opportunity to speak. While the televisions were broadcasting live, his cell phone kept vibrating. Finally, he took it out to see if it was the message he so desperately wanted, the one from Mary. Even though he knew she would still be on the plane, on her way back to her hometown, his heart clenched when he saw it wasn't her.

He stayed in the office until late, filling out the reports. Being a media sensation didn't exempt him from bureaucracy.

At dinnertime, he went down to the vending machine and bought a sandwich. He ate it at his desk, watching the sun set on another working Sunday.

The lights in the coffee shop across the street turned off.

He saw Rafa, the manager, come out with the garbage. When he returned, he was accompanied by two uniformed officers.

Alex didn't pay much attention to them.

He focused on his screen and kept working, determined to finish his report.

7

Café Sirena.

It was the name of a chain of coffee shops in Barcelona. There were several in the capital: comfortable armchairs and fresh pastries, all accompanied by good coffee. It was the most famous café in the city.

Years earlier, the original owner had read in the newspaper that a new police headquarters would be built for the entire province on that street. Without hesitation, he drove straight to the area. He looked for the best location and offered the owners of an old inn a reasonable price. They didn't think twice, signed the deed and retired. He soon had the largest cafeteria chain in the city, run by Rafa, one of his best employees.

That Sunday went by fast for Rafa, the cafeteria manager. Due to the lack of staff, his presence was needed throughout the day.

He finished the service and stayed to clean up. Once the cash register was counted, he sat down with a soda on the terrace. The stench was unbearable, and in less than a minute, he gave up and went back inside. When he took out the trash, he stopped and stared at the dumpsters. He knelt down and sniffed the sewer, which was only ten feet from the coffee shop. He couldn't smell anything. He walked back toward the establishment, perplexed. He stood in front of the glass door, and it opened automatically. But instead of entering, he turned around.

"This can't be right," he said aloud.

Not a soul passed by on the sidewalk. A few cars went past, probably returning home after the weekend.

Rafa approached the sewer, seriously pissed at the turnover he was losing by not having the terrace. He covered his nose with his T-shirt and walked over to the manhole in front of the coffee shop. Crawling between two cars, he put his nose right on top of the manhole, sniffed again and frowned. There was no odor coming from there. He was surprised: the stench was powerful, but it wasn't coming from the sewers. He shuffled toward a parked vehicle and suddenly reeled. The putrid smell almost took his breath away, and he gagged.

"Jesus Christ," he gasped, almost falling in his haste.

"Are you all right, young man?" asked a man walking his dog.

The barman, still coughing, mumbled as he held his t-shirt over his nose.

"Yes, I think so. Thank you."

The man gave him a funny look and left.

Rafa was still recovering from the putrid smell: it was crawling over him.

He stared at the vehicle and knew he'd found the source of the problem.

He looked at his watch; it was past ten o'clock at night.

"She's going to kill me," he thought, thinking about his wife.

Unfortunately for his wife, he couldn't let this matter drop and had to settle it once and for all. He locked the door and crossed the road. He had to do something about it, and it couldn't wait.

"Hello, guys," said Rafa entering the police station.

"Look who it is! Have you brought us some coffee?" asked the desk sergeant.

"No, I've closed up for the night. I'm sorry to bother you so late."

"What's going on? Shouldn't you be at home?"

"I wish... Do you remember how our terrace has been smelling weird for days?" The agent didn't answer, but he narrowed his eyes and paid more attention. "Well, I've been looking for the source because, with today's heat, the damn stink has increased."

"And?" The agent didn't seem very interested.

"I just found out where it's coming from: there's a van parked right in front of my coffee shop."

"Great detective work," said the sarge, his lip curling up into a grin.

"Yes, but... could you come and take a look?"

"Me? I can't. I can't leave the desk." The phone rang as soon as the words were out of his mouth.

"Police, Travessera de les Corts, one moment, please," he said and pressed a button. "Listen, if it's bugging you so much, I'll send a couple of officers to see what they can do."

Rafa nodded.

"Give me two minutes. They're on their way."

"Thanks," said Rafa, giving the officer a thumbs-up.

He waited at the door for a few minutes until the two men came out.

They wore short-sleeved shirts due to the unusually hot spring weather. They adjusted their hats and put on their truncheons.

They checked that no one was coming and crossed the street.

"So you think this smell is coming from the van, not the sewer?" asked the shorter man.

Rafa motioned for him to come closer and smell the vehicle from below.

One of the agents pursed his lips.

"Here, hold my hat," he said to his partner.

He took a cotton handkerchief from his pocket, put it in front of his mouth and approached the spot indicated by Rafa.

When the agent lowered the handkerchief and sniffed, he fell backwards.

"Are you all right?" asked the other officer.

"Shit, it smells like vomit!" he said, coughing and standing well back.

When he recovered, he looked at the vehicle with disgust.

"I told you!" said Rafa, shrugging.

"It's a hell of a smell," said the officer, wrinkling his nose.

"Whose van is it?"

The cafeteria manager shrugged.

"No idea. It's been here for a few weeks."

"Does it belong to one of the neighbors?" asked the other officer, glancing up and down the street.

"God knows. It's not right having to put up with this stench in the middle of the city. I'm losing money because no one wants to sit outside," said Rafa pointing to the sidewalk.

7

"Guys, please, can you help me?"

The two agents looked at each other.

"Something is rotting inside, and it's only going to get worse, I'm telling you," Rafa said, stuffing his hands in his pockets. "What if something has happened to the owner, and he doesn't come back to get it? I can't stand it anymore.

"Well, we can check out the license plate."

The shorter officer grinned at Rafa. "But only because it's you!"

"Thanks, but it's not just for me. It's for the whole damn area. We can't live like this."

The officers left. Without knowing why, Rafa turned the lights back on in the cafeteria instead of heading home. His instinct told him that the night ahead of him would be long, but he didn't imagine it would also be full of surprises.

8

Life goes by fast in the city.

There's no time to adapt; all you can do is run with it. It doesn't matter in which direction, or from here to wherever. Only one thing is important: running fast enough.

Slow living is not for city dwellers. It's the same for the thief and the policeman. Everyone must run in the giant hamster wheel that is Barcelona.

Rafa switched on the coffee machine. He filled a cup with fresh coffee and stood by the door, waiting for the officers to return.

He sent a message to his wife, warning her that he would be late, without going into detail. Half an hour later, the police returned, accompanied by a third man.

"Well? What did you find out?"

"How long did you say the van has been parked here?"

The manager grunted.

"I don't know exactly, but I'm sure it's been several weeks. I'd almost say a month," he said, puzzled. "Why?"

"There are no results on the traffic database," said an

officer, pointing to the third man. "This is Domenech, the commander on duty tonight."

Rafa shook hands with him and was surprised by his presence.

"Come, smell this," said the officer to the corporal.

The officer followed and noticed the strange odor coming from the vehicle. They took out their flashlights and inspected the cabin from the outside.

Nothing looked out of place. Not a piece of paper, not an object; everything inside looked brand-new. They walked around the vehicle, examining it, and realized it had no sticker, no plate or identification on the license plate. Nothing.

"What shall we do?" asked an officer.

"Do you want a coffee while you think about it?" asked Rafa

The men glanced at each other, nodded and followed Rafa inside.

"The van has been here for too long, as the gentleman says," said the commander, pointing to the cafeteria manager. "It's clear by the wheels, the dirt and rubbish accumulated around the tires."

"But it isn't a crime to leave a car parked for a long time in Barcelona."

"Of course it isn't, but the car is in the name of a company from Madrid. What's it doing here?"

"Isn't it better to wait and let the morning shift take care of it in daylight?" asked an officer, frowning.

They picked up their coffees.

"No. We can't leave it here; it's a breach of public health. I'll tell you what we'll do. You make a report and have it signed by the person in charge. In the meantime, I'll call forensics to come and open it up, and we'll take it from there. Whoever owns will be hit with a fine they'll remember for the rest of their life."

"Don't we need a warrant to open it up?"

"It's not necessary for a vehicle. Besides, we wouldn't have it until tomorrow," said the commander, heading for the van. "It smells like hell. Who knows what on earth they left inside."

Half an hour later, a guy from forensics turned up. He came out of a building on the right, one of only a handful that still had lights on so late on a Sunday.

Rafa and the two officers stood on the sidewalk, waiting. The coffee went down faster than the awareness of having found something important.

The CSI was carrying a heavy-looking bag. He leaned it against the side of the cafeteria and introduced himself.

"Evening, folks. I'm Joel from forensics. You just caught me in the nick of time. I was about to go out on another job, but they prioritized this. I was told there was a problem. What's going on?" he said, peering inside the establishment.

The officers pointed to the vehicle, and Joel frowned as he turned to look at the van.

"It's this van. You have to open it."

"I do?" he said, laughing. "You'd be better calling a 24-hour locksmith."

"My boss says you have to open it. We don't know what's inside, but it smells gross."

The officer who had just arrived dropped the briefcase and approached the van. Within seconds he had put a mask on. He glanced around and came back.

"Did you notice the locks?" asked Joel. "Come here."

They approached the side door.

8

"You see, the handle is gone. It's been replaced by a black metal plate that looks like a handle. And if you follow me to the other side, you'll notice the rear door lock is armored and impossible to open."

"So what do we do?" asked an officer.

"I don't know, but I won't be able to open it. It's pretty strange," he said. "Whoever owns it definitely doesn't want anyone to see what's inside it."

"Yes, you're right. It's weird as hell," confirmed another officer.

"I can't do anything here. I think you should call the fire department, and when they've opened the door, I'll come back," he said, picking up his bag. Before the police could protest, he walked back toward the forensic department without allowing the other two enough time to protest.

9

It was only when Alex turned off the computer that he realized something was happening in the street.

He'd finally finished the report on Yani's rescue. It had taken much longer than he'd expected. He had to skip part of it and recreate certain scenes so his career and reputation wouldn't be questioned.

During the press conference, the inspector had promoted him from Corporal to Sergeant.

Alex saw that as a problem, not a reason to celebrate. His only concern was that they would accept his request to transfer to Tarragona. He didn't care about moving up in the force.

Tiredness was clouding his mind. He needed to take a few days off. Perhaps see Yani again and see how he was doing.

He glanced out the window, his eyes widening at what he saw in the street. At first, he thought it was a bomb, or a drill, right in front of the police station.

From his window, the view was more befitting a movie set

than a city at nighttime on a Sunday. He had been so wrapped up in work that he hadn't noticed the flashing lights of the firetruck.

A patrol car was parked at either end of the street, preventing cars from passing. Neighbors were leaning out of windows and balconies, despite the hour.

A metal structure held up yellow plastic sheeting and blocked the view of what was happening around a white van parked in front of the coffee shop. Next to it, right in front of the police station, there was a fire truck and a few emergency cars.

Several corps units were huddled around as if they were assessing the vehicle.

He stood for a while contemplating the scene and then left. He was too tired to meddle in matters that didn't concern him. He turned off the office light and walked to where he had parked his Mini. He started it up, pushed the glass off the roof and drove home, enjoying the cool air on his face.

Back at the station, the fire unit was studying the vehicle. The smell became more unbearable by the minute, and they approached the van with gas masks on, the same ones they used to enter burning buildings.

"I'd take the radial saw and open it up like a can of sardines," said one firefighter.

"We can't. It's forbidden. We're in front of an official building, and there could be gas or explosives inside."

"What if we drill a hole and put a camera probe in?"

"It's still dangerous; we don't know what's inside. We'll

have to open it mechanically."

"But it has no handles—"

"Pass me the Halligan," said the fire chief, pointing to the truck.

He realized something was wrong as he approached the rear doors and ripped off the black trim. There was some strange material between the sheet metal of the doors and the bodywork, very unusual for a van.

He picked up a chisel and, after several attempts, tore a piece off. He picked it up and inspected it.

"What's that, boss?" asked one of his colleagues.

"It looks like glue. I don't like this at all," said the boss, a muscle twitching in his cheek. "This is incredible. You know what this is?"

The other firefighter shook his head.

"I think it's rubber boat silicone! It's used to seal hatches and cracks. Wherever you put this, not even light can get through. I've never seen anything like this in my career."

The chief was stunned. Although he was unnerved, he reluctantly ordered the van to be opened.

The two firefighters got to work with the tool they used to open the fire doors, and the fire chief approached the officers to explain what the vehicle doors were sealed with.

"For some reason, the owner has sealed the doors with boat silicone," said the fire chief.

"What? Why would someone do that?" asked one of the officers.

"No idea, but I think we'll soon find out, and I have a feeling we won't like it at all," he said, looking at his men, who were having trouble forcing the doors. "Have you noticed that it's not a normal van?"

"It's a delivery Opel," an officer replied with a shrug. "What's so special about it?"

"Look at the doors. This van is isothermal."

"Iso… what?"

"Isothermal. Vans like this are used for transporting frozen food."

"That makes sense," said the officer. "Apparently, the registered owner has a meat distribution business in Madrid. I mean, are we doing all this because of a delivery man who forgot a tray of out-of-date bacon?"

The fire chief looked at him, puzzled, but chose not to answer.

He approached his men. They had managed to drive the tool in, but it still wouldn't yield enough for them to open the vehicle: the filling was too hard.

After a while, they gave up.

"What the hell is someone hiding in there?" the fire chief asked, taking it as a personal challenge.

"All right, guys, give it up," he said, waving his arms. "Get the hydraulic clamps."

"But sir, we can't use them because—" said a fireman and was interrupted.

"If I say that's what we're going to do, then that's exactly what we'll do. Come on, guys, let's get the clamp."

They deployed the hose connected to the truck and started it up.

The neighbors, unable to sleep because of the noise, watched with morbid curiosity as to what the hell was going on in their street.

Columns of spotlights powered by generators illuminated the fenced area. The noise they emitted reverberated on the facades of the buildings, spreading several blocks. More and more neighbors from nearby buildings came onto the street in their robes to find out what was happening.

When the truck was switched on, the noise intensified.

The hydraulic clamp could cut through a steel beam as easily as a child could eat ice cream.

It was connected to the truck, and after a practice run, a firefighter climbed up a ladder and placed it on the van's roof. With the first snip, a jet of internal air came out. The fireman wore a mask and didn't notice the putrid air that had been fermenting for weeks. He continued to split the structure and, with each snip, looked increasingly satisfied.

When the man finished cutting the section where the two rear doors joined, he left the clamp and flashed his torch into the darkness. He couldn't see anything.

Another firefighter joined him, and they picked up the Halligan. Between them, they began to pry the doors open, trying to remove the hinges. After several attempts, they managed to open the door a couple of inches.

The firefighter closest to the gap looked inside.

He moved closer to peer through with his flashlight but suddenly jerked back as if he'd been punched in the face. A wave of putrid gas blasted him in the face, passing straight through the strong filters of his mask. He fell to his knees and, ripping off his mask, lay on the ground, coughing and struggling to breathe.

Those two inches had turned several weeks of putrefaction emanating from the vile package into an ecological bomb.

In between coughing fits, the firefighter crawled away from

the van just as a cascade of coagulated blood poured out of the gap, full of wriggling white larvae—small, light-colored, half-an-inch worms, the kind that proliferate in putrefying bodies.

Out of the top of the gap, a swarm of angry flies flew out into the air like a plague of locusts.

The horrified firefighter and police watched in shock, all taking a step backwards. The fire chief's jaw dropped. He'd never seen such a hideous sight. The larvae spilt out of the van, spreading along the sidewalk and down the sewer. Some of the men muttered in disgust, all moving further away from the grotesque spectacle.

The fire chief approached and, taking care not to step on the larvae, stood in front of the gap in the rear doors. But before he got a good look at the contents of the van, he, too, was forced back by the smell.

"Jesus Christ! Close it NOW," he shouted once his bout of nausea had passed.

But it was too late. Pandora's box was open, and everything inside flowed out: stench, blood, larvae and the terrifying truth.

An officer approached and patted the fire chief's back.

"Are you all right, buddy?"

The fire chief coughed, covering his mouth with his hand until he could breathe normally.

"Benito, what the hell is it?"

"Now I understand why they used the silicone. Don't come any closer, for God's sake. We have to get it away from here as soon as possible."

"But what's inside?" asked the cop.

The fire chief looked him directly in the eye and replied.

"Corpses. It is full of corpses."

10

Barcelona.
Monday.

Alex was woken by his neighbor.

He'd gone to bed last night without setting his alarm clock. He couldn't take it anymore; he really needed some rest. After the unexpected promotion, Alex had been granted a few days' leave.

He'd always wondered what his upstairs neighbor did for a living. Every morning around that time, the back of her bed hit the wall like a jackhammer.

He and Mary had had several theories. Her husband had left for work, and a lover, a client, or a neighbor came round to visit. Or it was the same husband coming back. Each theory was more daring and twisted than the last.

The few times they were both at home, listening to the woman, they were aroused and had ended up doing the same.

That morning was no different. When he opened his right eye, he noticed the sun was high overhead. He turned away from the bright daylight, but it was already too late, and he was wide awake.

He looked at the time: it was noon. His belly had been rumbling for several hours.

Alex sat up in bed and remembered the American.

He would have liked to call her, but he had to resign himself: Mary was part of his past, not his present.

He looked at his cell phone; he'd never had so many messages.

He overlooked them all and only looked for Mary's, but hers were the only ones that weren't there. There were some from colleagues, missed calls and a heap of social media messages from people he didn't even know.

He went to the washroom, and when he returned, a noise pierced the relentless headache he'd had for days. It was the doorbell.

Through the peephole, he recognized Mario.

He opened the door and went into the kitchen.

"Finally, I thought you were dead," said the guest as he closed the door. "Do you know how long I've been knocking?"

"I didn't hear you. I was woken up by the woman upstairs, with her…" Then he thought and waved his hand. "Nah, forget it. It doesn't matter. What are you doing here?"

"Hey, we're friends and all, but standing here in your underwear is a bit too much, don't you think?"

"If you don't like it, you know where the door is," he said, jerking his head toward the hallway as he made himself a pot of coffee.

"Where's Mary?" asked Mario, pulling out a chair.

"Mary?" he said with a bitter laugh. "She left Saturday night."

"Oh, I didn't know. When's she coming back?"

"I hope never," he said as he turned away.

"What? Your Mary? Impossible! What have you done to her?"

"Mario, what are you doing here? Have you come round to wind me up?"

"I came to check on you because you don't answer messages."

"Mario, I have a few days off. Could you leave me alone? I'm not asking for much, just a few days."

The man looked at him as he shook his head.

"Haven't you heard?"

Alex was about to swallow an aspirin and glanced at Mario,

"I just woke up, Mario. Why don't you go to hell and leave me alone?"

Mario was an officer of the Mossos d'Esquadra who worked closely with forensics. He was in charge of document fraud and dealt with forgeries. He worked on the second floor of the same building as Alex, who worked on the first floor.

The guest took out a newspaper and showed it to him.

"Look what they found tonight."

Reading the headline out of the corner of his eye, Alex whistled under his breath.

The Van of Death
Dead body found inside a van.

Yesterday at dawn, in front of the police station on Travessera de les Corts, a corpse was found inside a parked van. According to initial witnesses, it was in an advanced state of decay.

"Now I understand about last night," he said, scanning the rest of the article.

"Did you see it?" asked Mario excitedly.

"No. I saw something was going on, but when I'd finished the report, all I wanted to do was to go home."

"The lieutenant sent me."

"Why?"

"He told me to come and get you. He needs you on the case. He needs all the manpower he can get."

Alex shook his head.

"Not happening. I need to rest. For Christ's sake, we're not robots," he said, pouring himself a cup of coffee.

Mario sat at the kitchen table.

"What's all that glass doing on the floor?"

"It's a long story," he answered without looking and sat down with a huge cup of coffee. "I'm sorry, I didn't ask you. Did you want some, too?" asked Alex, raising his eyebrows.

"Coffee? No, not at this hour. I've had too much already today."

They were silent for a moment before Mario added:

"The lieutenant is right. What you see in the newspaper is nothing compared to the truth. My guys did the initial checks. We had to take the van to the outskirts of Barcelona, to a military hangar," said Mario, chewing the inside of his cheek. Then he picked up the newspaper and put it back in front of him, pointing to the headline. "Luckily, not all the information has been leaked. They don't know anything yet. What we found in that van is shocking, and I'm telling you, I've seen a lot of things. We need you to come and see. Trust me. It's the van of horrors."

11

It was raining that morning.

Fat drops showered down onto the palm trees with force, and the wind rattled the billboards. Motorcycles weaved unsteadily between cars. Traffic was at a standstill, the city's arteries almost completely blocked.

The two policemen listened to the radio, exchanging few words.

Alex looked out the window. His headache was killing him.

As Mario drove, Alex flipped through the newspaper, remembering the images he'd seen from his office window. The firefighters, the van, the lights, the chaos and the neighbors leaning out of their windows.

The newspaper article had no photo; it only showed the police building. It was a conglomerate of conjectures that did not imply anything concrete. There was little data. A lot of fluff and journalistic creativity solely to sell more copies.

He put the newspaper away.

When they arrived, Alex understood why Mario had wished him luck at a traffic light earlier.

A dense mass of journalists stalked the entrance to the

building.

"Let me go first," he said, hoping to distract the journalists.

The TV news cameras and journalists were patiently enduring the persistent rain that was falling heavily.

He got out of the partner's car and approached the entrance, covering his face with the newspaper so he wouldn't be recognized. But five yards from the entrance, one of the guys from El Pais spotted him and tried to shove his mic in Alex's face. But he was too late: the automatic station doors opened, and Alex took refuge inside.

He swiped his identity card and went up in the elevator.

The door to the boss's office was closed. He knocked and entered.

Behind the desk was Lieutenant Alfonso Rexach, and seated across from him, Corporal Karla Ramirez was writing in a notebook.

"Come in, Cortes. Sit down," Rexach said, getting up.

Even though they were no longer of the same grade, Karla Ramirez didn't stand up to greet him. She gave him a sidelong glance, but he ignored her.

"How are you, Alex?" asked his boss.

"Do you have any aspirin?"

The man opened his desk drawer and tossed him a box. Alex took it and swallowed a pill without water.

"You don't look so good."

"Why did you call me? It's my day off. I think I deserve a break."

"But did you hear what happened?"

The younger officer held up the newspaper.

"Only what the papers are saying, but if I'm honest, I don't care. It's not my case. I told you yesterday. I need to rest."

The chief settled back in the armchair, turned to the window and sighed deeply.

It was still raining heavily.

"Cortes, I know perfectly well what I told you yesterday, but things have changed. I wouldn't have called you if it hadn't been important. The whole corps is on alert because of what has happened. When you see it, you'll understand."

"When I see it? No, no. I'm leaving," he said and got up. "I'm not staying. I kept my promise, boss. I saved that kid. Now you keep yours."

The woman hadn't said a word, but when the officer got up and put his hand on the door handle, a satisfied smirk crossed her face.

"Alex, wait!" Rexach said. "If this wasn't a matter of life and death, I wouldn't have called you. I need all my troops. I need your intelligence, your experience. More than ever."

"If he doesn't want to stay, let him go," the woman replied. "We're here. My team is fully staffed and can handle the case perfectly well. Chief, we don't need him."

"Wait a moment, Ramirez," said the chief, extending his arm toward her.

"Boss, forgive me for insisting, but just let him go. I'm at your complete disposal."

"Will you shut up, Ramirez?" he snapped, imposing his authority.

Then he stood up, walked around the desk and stood in front of Alex.

"When you see it… you'll understand. I'm asking you as a personal favor. You know I wouldn't ask if I thought I could do this without you on the team."

Alex's hand was still on the door handle, and he shook his head without speaking.

There's something else, isn't there?" said Rexach, narrowing his eyes.

Looking down, Alex blew out and then looked at his boss.

"Chief, I'm sorry, but I'm accepting the transfer to Tarragona."

The lieutenant took a step back, and his eyebrows shot up. That decision, coming from one of his best men, hit him like a bullet.

"Don't mess with me, Cortes. Have you already decided?"

"It's better if he leaves, Boss. Give me the case." said the woman, getting up. "You know my homicide team is more than competent."

"Sit down and shut the hell up!" he shouted at her and turned to Alex. "Couldn't you wait a little longer? When are you going?"

"I don't know, I haven't made it official yet, but I would like it to be soon. For personal reasons."

The chief nodded and sat down heavily in his chair. There was an awkward silence.

He fiddled with the fountain pen his wife had given him when he had received his third stripe and suddenly blurted out.

"Can you at least sit down for a minute?"

Alex's shoulders slumped. He closed the door and sat down.

"What do you think about this: while you're still here, you give us a hand with this case. Listen to me," he said in a conciliatory tone. "Before any transfer, you always need a few weeks to move house, settle in, and so on. I promise I'll only ask you this one last favor. Stay for a few days to help us. Just a few days." He stretched out his hand to Alex. "What do you say? One last favor?"

Alex glanced at the woman, who was listening in dismay. Then he held out his hand and said:

"What about Ramirez?"

"I need all available officers. You'll have to work together these days," he said, looking from one to the other.

"I still don't think I need Cortes," Ramirez said, cutting the boss off.

"Ramirez, the day you have the grades of lieutenant, then you will decide. For the time being, I'll decide. And until Cortes leaves, you will investigate the case together. Is that clear?"

The woman felt intimidated but held his gaze and nodded. "Understood."

"Okay, you can go. I have every confidence in you both."

They both stood up, and Karla Ramirez was the first to leave.

Alex followed her and closed the door.

"Hey, wait for me," he shouted after her.

"What do you want? Couldn't you have left without any fuss or bloody attention? No! You've got to stay here and piss everyone off until the very last day."

Alex was surprised. What the hell was she talking about?

"Look, I have zero desire to argue, okay? It's only for a few days. I'm sure we can put up with each other for a couple more days. Anyway, I don't give a damn what you think. I'm doing this for the boss," he replied, his eyes hardening.

The woman barely let him speak. She hoisted her bag up her shoulder and started walking toward the elevator. The man followed her.

"This is going to be worse than the Battle of Troy. I wish I'd stayed in bed!" he thought.

They entered the elevator, and he asked:

"Where are we going?"

"To see the van."

"To the warehouse?"

"No, there was no room for it."

The man turned around quizzically.

"What do you mean? It didn't fit?"

The woman pressed the button on the first floor and sighed.

"We're going to a military airport. You'll soon understand why."

12

The camouflaged patrol car left the parking lot.

Even though they'd chosen an undercover vehicle, the journalists still jumped on them as they pulled away from the station. The rain hadn't deterred them, and they continued to besiege the police building.

They surrounded the car, taking pictures and recording with video cameras.

When the traffic light turned green, the woman glared at the vultures and angrily honked her horn.

"Come on, guys, what the hell are you doing? Are you stupid or what?" she said through gritted teeth.

Alex frowned and turned away.

"They're only doing their job."

"Let them do it somewhere else. Ours is more important."

"You're wrong."

"Are we going to argue already? Do you think you're better than everyone else?"

He didn't like the way she was talking to him, but he was too tired to reprimand her.

"Hey, don't speak to me like that. Firstly, because I'm a

colleague and, secondly, your superior."

"Jesus Christ, Alex! You've been a sergeant for less than twenty-four hours, and you're already being an officious jerk."

Alex turned to look out of the window and dropped the subject. He didn't want to argue with her. He wasn't in the mood.

He was silent the rest of the way.

They left Travessera de les Corts and headed south along Avenida Diagonal.

Alex was pensive as they passed El Corte Ingles, university faculties and two landmark bank buildings. Society went about its life under the apparent umbrella of security. It was thanks to the police who brought order and returned things to normal whenever chaos reigned. People had to remain calm and follow the flock. Working, living, shopping and watching television. But reading the newspaper or watching the news on TV had the opposite effect. It scared people into staying with their herd life. The authorities didn't want their herd out of control. But occasionally, the flock lost control because a sheep thought it was a dog or, worse, a wolf.

Alex had no idea what to expect. If he had, he probably wouldn't have agreed to go.

They went along the Ronda de Dalt, the ring road that circled the city on the north side. It was also backed up with traffic at a standstill. They advanced slowly, as they did daily in the rush hour and in the rain.

Alex only had to put up with this woman and one last investigation in Barcelona for a short time. His head was already in Tarragona, his hometown, close to his parents and

12

childhood friends.

After almost an hour without speaking to each other, they reached Sabadell, a town on the outskirts of Barcelona.

"How much longer?" he asked.

Turning on the radio, she gave him a sidelong glance and ignored him.

At that moment, a well-known news program was reporting about the van. The reporter was doing a great job of scaring the masses.

The biggest radio station in the region was spreading panic and suspicion among the population. Until the police had more information about what was happening, they couldn't issue an official statement.

They arrived at the exit for "Sabadell Sud - Airport".

"Can you tell me where we're going?"

She drove in silence until they arrived at Sabadell airport, a state-owned company belonging to Aena and dedicated to private and leisure flights.

They drove past the "Barcelona – flight school" offices and continued along the perimeter, but the car didn't go through the main entrance.

Almost on the opposite side of the space, red and blue lights began to reflect in the rain on the windshield.

A long gate was guarded by two Mossos patrol cars. Karla stopped in front, lowered the window two inches and flashed her badge.

A Mosso in a raincoat approached and carefully studied it. Then he went to the long rusty gate and pulled it open.

The car continued to a nearby warehouse. An army tank was parked in front of the massive doors, and two soldiers with machine guns poised held their posts despite the heavy rain.

Civilian cars, police cars, fire engines and ambulances were parked next to what looked like an access gate.

Alex cleared the mist from his window to see what awaited him. The closer he got, the less tired he felt and the more his curiosity grew.

Karla parked and turned off the engine.

"What is this place?" asked Alex.

"An abandoned army hangar."

"Abandoned?"

"In disuse."

"So why not do it at our headquarters in Sabadell? At the corps' headquarters next door?"

"Let's go," said the woman, pulling up the hood of her raincoat and climbing out of the car.

Alex did the same, grabbed the newspaper to protect his head and followed her.

They stood under the porch, in front of a side door.

Karla pressed a doorbell, and after identifying themselves, the door opened.

As soon as Alex walked in, he shuddered at the sight before him.

13

It smelled like a mixture of wet cement and cadaveric putrefaction.

The air was thick with what appeared to be dust, and when Alex looked up, he saw the roof was formed by gabled interlocking iron beams.

The space was large enough to fit two planes. The floor was of light cement, stained by dark puddles where the rain had leaked through the roof.

Uniformed people from different teams were walking around the perimeter zone. In the center, spotlights connected to external generators were aimed at the van, which had all its doors open.

The woman nudged Alex in the chest. In her hand, she carried a mask and a canister.

"Put it on. You'll need it."

Alex obeyed: these were the same masks the CSIs wore. Then he applied camphor ointment under his nostrils to neutralize any smells.

They put on boot covers, white coats and caps and then

approached the center of the hangar. Forensics were standing in small groups around the vehicle. The closer they got, the more he realized how strange the van appeared.

The rain was heavy on the high metal roof.

"We brought it here because its cargo is full of larvae, and the smell can't be tolerated in an enclosed space. They decided on this location because of the structure. They say that when they opened it here, they had to remove three bags of *Sarcophaga carnaria* larvae and leave several hours of oxygenation of what was inside. It was unbearable. The smell went through the filters of the firemen's masks."

"Do we know whose van it is?"

"It looks like it's a company from Madrid, but it doesn't make sense."

"What about cameras?"

"I'll explain later, follow me," said Karla, and they continued walking.

As soon as Mario saw them, he came over.

"You can't even imagine. This is crazy. Come on," he said, strangely upbeat, almost as if he was enjoying the show.

They went to the cabin area.

"There's not a print, not a trace of DNA. This guy is a master," he said admiringly. "And look at this." Mario pointed with his blue gloves to the floor, where a test number appeared. "It's a bleach and hydrogen peroxide spray to cancel all organic traces. So we wouldn't be able to find out who it was."

"What else did you find in the cabin?" asked Alex.

"Nothing! It was clean. In the glove compartment, there was only that and nothing else. No papers, no tickets, nothing," he said as he put the plastic container back on the ground and walked around the van.

The other two followed.

"We haven't been able to understand much, but, as you can tell, the smell knocks you over. It's hard to get close."

The two approached, and as soon as they peeked into the box, they understood.

"The plastic walls are impregnated."

"What kind of van is this?"

"It's for the delivery of fish, meat or refrigerated food. Look at these plates?" Mario indicated the vehicle's walls, which had a thick, pink-colored substance over the white metal sheet. "This was originally white and washable, but it's impregnated with gases formed by evaporated blood. I guess it's because of the heat."

Alex watched silently.

"As you can see, the door is gone." The officer pointed to the cut edges of the sheet metal. "The door has been glued with a mixture of rubber boat silicone and a super-strong industrial glue. Once sealed, it couldn't ever be opened. Look at these cuts; the firemen had to cut it with hydraulic clamps."

Alex turned to see the fire truck still standing to the side.

He put on his gloves and leaned against the outer plate. He stuck his head out, covering his mouth, and looked inside, holding his breath.

"What is that?" he said.

Mario walked over and looked at the ceiling.

"Oh, yes, we don't know. It's a rail, and a strange contraption is held with a pin at the end. We assume it was meant to blow up these balloons that you see here. But we have no idea what they are for. We've passed the photos to the forensic team so they can evaluate them."

"Where are the two corpses?" asked Alex.

"Next door, in the basement," said Mario, stepping away from the van to breathe better. "The lieutenant said you should go there once you've finished here."

"What have you done with all the larvae?" asked Alex.

"One sample went to the forensic laboratory, and the rest, about three bags, were taken by a pest extermination company."

Alex looked around.

"What are you going to do now?" he asked.

"We have a lot of work to do. We're waiting for the expert from the manufacturer to come and dismantle the passenger compartment and the rest of the vehicle. We will take it apart piece by piece and analyze everything to see if we can find any traces."

"Shall we go?" asked Karla, taking control of the situation.

Alex didn't answer. He wandered over to look at the objects the forensics had laid out on some folding tables. He observed them, walking slowly with his hands behind his back. The hum of the generators was almost camouflaged by the pounding rain on the roof from the storm. The doors already cut from the van were on easels, and a policeman was flicking black powder on them with a paintbrush. He was looking for the prints of the monster who had devised and carried out such a heinous act.

He came back to stand beside Karla.

"We should go. But I just have one more question," he said, turning to Mario. "Luminol? What results did it give you?"

"Do you want to see it?"

Alex nodded his head slightly.

Mario pulled out the ultraviolet light fixture and turned

it on. A few fluorescent spots appeared on the walls as the cargo space was illuminated.

"It's funny, Alex, the bottom is full of them," he said as he shone the light on the base of the van. Then he raised the light and continued. "There are very few stains here, almost none. That means the corpses were put into the van when dead. They weren't killed in here."

He switched off the light and turned to face Alex with a serious expression on his face:

"By the way, there aren't just two corpses, Alex. There are five."

14

Alex and Karla got back into the car, and Karla drove to the Mossos headquarters. After identifying themselves, they entered through the main door and drove around the building. At one end, there was an access point down to the basement. The car went down a ramp, and a huge space opened up. Karla parked in the first free spot she saw, and then they walked down a flight of stairs.

Alex followed. Not being in charge was new to him, but it didn't bother him. His mind and hopes were already set on his new, more peaceful life in Tarragona, the police station with the lowest crime rate in the region.

On the double metallic door was a sign: "Morgue, central laboratory".

Karla pushed the door open and entered first.

They continued down the glassed-in corridor. To the sides, there were dark spaces that looked like laboratories.

Reaching the last door on the right, Karla opened it and went through.

Inside, several people in white coats and masks examined a

body, discussing the remains on the gurney.

As soon as they became aware of his presence, one of them approached the two officers.

"Alex Cortes?" said a woman holding out her hand.

She looked down, saw her gloves were stained with blood and took them off, turning them into a ball. She squeezed his hand, and he felt her sweaty, talcum-powdered hand. He grimaced in disgust.

"I'm Dr. Alba Guevara. The lieutenant informed me that you were coming accompanied by..." she said, looking at his companion. "Ah, hello, Karla."

Alex sensed friction, a magnetic force between the two women like two forces of the same pole repelling each other.

Alba was a medical examiner that he'd heard of on numerous occasions. In the corps, she was colloquially called *"Madame Death"*.

She was attractive, with strong features and wrinkles that crisscrossed her forehead. While working, she gathered her blonde hair in an informal bun using a toothpick. She never talked about her personal life, but rumor had it that she only had sex with the corpses of the Central Morgue.

Alex cleared his throat, glanced at Karla and focused on what they had come here to do.

"Guys, give us a moment. Go and rest, and come back in half an hour. We'll continue later," called out Dr. Guevara.

The other doctors left.

The room was a cold space meant for corpses. In the middle of the room were steel tables, side by side, illuminated by lamps hanging from the ceiling. On four of the tables, there were blue zippered bags. On the nearest gurney was a naked corpse, illuminated by a white light.

Alex moved closer to the steel table, the M. E's voice growing faint.

As he approached the corpse, he felt a lump in his throat. His heart raced, and he began to feel a pressure in his chest at the sight.

The lifeless body was female, her small breasts crushed by gravity.

She was covered in blood and half-eaten by larvae: some were still crawling out of the wounds on her body.

But what struck him the most was the amputations.

The head had been severed at the base of the neck. The arms were intact, but the hands had been severed at the wrists.

The legs were missing the feet at the ankles.

Larvae were still emerging from the sectioned area, and the cuts in the bones were clear.

The skin suggested that the process of decomposition was advanced, nearing mummification.

Despite the mask and camphor he'd applied, Alex began to gag. He pulled away and sat down on a stool.

"Sergeant? Are you all right?"

He began to take slower, deeper breaths. Karla subtly turned so he wouldn't see her amusement.

After a few minutes, Alex recovered.

"Do you want to call it a day? Would you prefer to continue some other time?"

"No, thank you, Doctor, the killer won't wait," he said, swallowing. "Please go on."

Alba Guevara turned to the corpse.

"Well, all the other four are in the same condition. But, let me tell you, the surprises don't end here."

15

Whenever an image or a situation is associated with a smell, you only need to perceive it again for your brain to remember the associated memory and reproduce the same sensations.

Alex didn't doubt that, from this moment on, the smell of camphor would forever be associated with the corpse of this decapitated woman.

He had smelled camphor several times in his intense career. It was a substance with a characteristic odor, extracted by distillation from oriental trees for medicinal use.

That day, it took on a new meaning for him.

"Sergeant Cortes, let me tell you that in my whole career, I have only seen this kind of thing in university manuals or FBI reports," Alba said.

"I believe you," he replied.

"Have you been able to move forward with anything else, Doctor?" asked Karla.

"Yes, let me show you."

The coroner walked over to the corpse, picked up some

photos taken before removing the bodies from the van, and came back.

"When we find ourselves in front of a corpse, we ask ourselves five questions: Who is it? When did they die? Where? How were they killed? And who did it? We're a bit lost in this case because we don't have many clues. But we'll soon find out many more things," said the woman.

She then pulled out a laser pointer.

"We can't know who this person is because ... I think that much is obvious. The only thing we can do is record the DNA and enter it in the biobank in case of a match. The cause of death could have been exsanguination. We assume so because of the amputations. I haven't yet confirmed this, although I will give a hypothesis after seeing the blood test results. But you can see here..." she said, pointing to the lumbar area.

On the back and on the areas of the body that touched the ground, a purple stain had appeared. The doctor lifted one arm of the corpse, revealing a purplish expanse of skin.

"What I mean is that once dead, she was left in this exact position. Here are the lividities. See? These are red-violet. The blood gathered on the lower part of the body because of gravity."

Alex took a breath.

"The where and when we can't know yet. We're still waiting for some tests," she continued.

"Given the degree of decomposition, Doctor, could it be days, weeks since she died?" asked Alex.

"I think several weeks, although it's true that with the van being in direct sunlight, it was like a greenhouse, and consequently, decomposition was accelerated," she replied. After a pause, she continued.

"Another thing that stands out is how he killed them. The cut is too perfect. I think it was an electric saw or a chainsaw. The section is perfect, which is impossible to do with manual tools. These sections remind me of the types of injuries typical in carpentry accidents."

The doctor stared at the body and shook her head.

"I don't think I've left anything out. That's all we know for the moment. We're awaiting further analysis, and the lieutenant has asked me for a detailed report as soon as possible."

"Doctor, do you believe the victims may have suffered some kind of abuse?"

"Sexual?"

Karla nodded her head in agreement. That was the first sign of interest that she'd shown.

"It's difficult because it's been a while, but we know that no sperm or lubricant was on any of the three women. Either in the vagina or in the rectum. At the moment, I'd rule out a sexual psychopath, but we'll see in the test results."

"What about other types of violence?" asked Alex, feeling the blood returning to his cheeks.

"Well, I don't believe so. The bodies don't show any physical violence other than amputation."

"You said there are three women and two men?"

"Haven't you seen the photos, Sergeant?"

"Please, call me Alex. It's less formal."

"Of course, of course, Alex."

Karla glanced sideways at them, sharpening her gaze.

"Look, these are the others."

Alex took the photos and flicked through them while the

doctor continued talking.

"We have three women and two men. One woman has darker skin, and the others are very light-skinned. One of the men is fair-skinned, and the other one is darker. The women have some tattoos. You'll see them in the reports that will be ready tomorrow."

As he listened to her, Alex noticed how the five corpses had been crammed into the small space of the van, arranged like in a photo of a Nazi concentration camp.

"Have you analyzed the larvae?"

"These tiny demons are more voracious than lions. They are *Sarcophaga carnaria*. They only show up in the first two weeks of decomposition, indicating that they could have been in that infernal vehicle for only a few weeks, but I'm not sure."

Karla walked away, took out her cell phone and called the lieutenant.

"Rexach."

"Ramirez here. We're almost done here. What shall we do now?"

"Come back to the station. We have a lot of work to do."

The two policemen said their goodbyes and headed to Les Corts, stopping to grab a sandwich and fill up the tank.

The rain continued to fall with the same intensity.

"Hungry?" asked the woman as they reached the tiny room used as the station canteen.

"I haven't eaten anything since last night," Alex replied.

"Can you believe something so awful like that could happen in Barcelona?"

The woman scratched her forehead and swiped her napkin across her mouth before drinking from the soda bottle.

They were sitting at a high table next to the vending machines.

"I can still see those images in my head. It's inhumane."

"Well, you were spared from seeing it live. The boss called me this morning, and we went to see the bodies being removed. That would have really turned your stomach. Officers were dropping like flies, throwing up in the bushes!" she said, smirking at him.

"I can imagine."

Alex stood up and shoved some coins into the machine. Another sandwich dropped down, and then he got another coffee.

Stirring the sugar, he suddenly remembered.

"Wait a minute. I remember that van. Son of a bitch! Oh, man. He almost ran me over, the bastard. I saw him! I looked right into his eyes," said Alex, a shiver causing the fine hairs on his arms to stand up. He sat down heavily, shaken by the emotion and then by the rage of not having stopped that sick fuck when he'd had the chance.

"I was going for a coffee with Mario. It was a day like today, rainy. I remember because we ran a red light to avoid getting wet. Of course! It was him!"

"What did he look like? Would you be able to make a sketch?"

Alex set his coffee down on the table and closed his eyes, rubbing his eyes with the palms of his hands.

"I can remember his face. Inexpressive, but I couldn't draw it. He was wearing dark glasses, like aviators. The rest is blurred, and I don't remember anything."

"Well, at least it's something."

"Wait, what about the cameras in the central office? It has

to be recorded, right?" he said, cracking his knuckles.

"My officers are looking into it. Do you remember what day it was?"

"What day was it? What day was it? Wait… Why did we go for coffee?" Alex squeezed his eyes shut, racking his brains.

"Of course! It was the day the Champions League games were announced. I mean, wait…"

Alex looked at his cell phone and did a quick search.

"I got it, Karla. It was the fifth of April."

She began counting on her fingers. "What the fuck? I can't believe it!"

"What's wrong?"

Thirty-two days ago!" she spat, hands on hips.

"Why? What is it, Karla?" he snapped impatiently.

"This guy knows us better than we think. He's way ahead of us."

"Will you tell me what's going on?"

"Thirty-two. Every thirty days, the surveillance cameras are wiped."

16

The Ronda de Dalt was still backed up with stalled traffic.

It seemed like a curse: the rainiest days of one of the wettest springs on record.

The undercover car was moving at a snail's pace. Alex took advantage of Karla's driving to think. Seeing the road from the passenger side was a privilege he couldn't enjoy very often

He turned for a moment to look at Karla. He realized he no longer had any idea who she was. If he stayed, she'd be under his team from that day forward. But that would never happen.

Her long, thin, brown hair poked out from its messy bun. He got it; she tried to disguise her femininity in such a male-dominated environment. She wasn't stupid; she needed sharp claws to get ahead in the force.

A warrior soul and feline eyes. Rebellious.

The tight jeans made her more feminine than he suspected she wanted to appear.

What was this woman hiding? Why was she so arrogant? From a lack of affection?

From childhood? From nonconformity with what she was

currently going through?

She wasn't the same person he'd known before he'd left her just before he met Mary.

He was looking at her obliviously until she noticed him staring.

"What are you looking at, Cortes?" she asked, looking back at the road. "Admiring my beauty?" He felt his cheeks warm up; she wasn't far off the truth. "I was just thinking about the traffic."

They turned into the street leading to the station and then down into the underground parking lot of the building before the press spotted them.

In the lieutenant's office, Alex informed him of everything they had discovered, with Karla adding the odd detail here and there.

"You look pale, Cortes," interrupted the chief.

Alex nodded and turned to look out of the window. He cricked his neck and ran his right hand over his face.

"Must have been those sandwiches from the gas station."

"No one said a policeman's life is a walk in the park."

"What we've just seen isn't easy to digest."

"Our job isn't easy, Cortes. You should know that by now."

"But this is different. I don't think I can handle this."

"Can't or won't?" asked the chief, pinning him with a sharp look.

"Look, Rexach, I don't know how long I'll be here, so why don't you give this case to Ramirez? I have enough chaos in my life without this," he said, turning to his partner. "She's perfectly competent. Besides, I managed to solve the kidnapped kid case. That's more than enough, right?" he said, turning back to the window.

Karla tutted.

"Ramirez, leave us alone for a moment."

"But boss, you heard him. I can handle the case."

"Ramirez!" Rexach insisted. "You have a lot of work to do. Now go."

The woman turned to Alex and looked resentfully at him. Their eyes met. She stood up and, muttering something under her breath, slammed the door shut behind her.

Alex raised his eyebrows.

"That girl has character. She'll be a good substitute for you," said the boss.

"Do you think so? Maybe she has too much character," Alex said, watching Karla stomp down the corridor through the glass partition.

"Alex, I don't want to convince you to stay; that ship has sailed. I just want you to know that we need your help for a few days. And that's all. Do you want to help us? Look, go home now; it's late. I'll see you in the morning, right?" he asked pointedly.

Alex nodded and, without another word, walked out the door. As he was about to close it, he poked his head back around it and said:

"I'll think about it."

Alex walked through the office. After grabbing his jacket, he left the building through the back door. The reporters had already left, but the rain continued.

He walked to Diagonal and took the first cab he managed to flag down. He didn't want to take the subway.

Out of habit, he gave directions to a couple of streets before his home address, ever fearful for his safety, and then laid his head back on the headrest.

The cab driver drove quietly through the streets. When Alex opened his eyes, he noticed the driver glancing at him in the rearview mirror from time to time.

As they pulled up outside the address he'd given, the cab driver plucked up the courage to speak to him.

"It's you, isn't it?"

Alex lifted his head from the backrest and sat up.

"What do you mean?"

"Who saved the president's son."

At that moment, he realized the cab was full of Barça memorabilia. *Oh shit*, he thought.

"Yes, I guess I am," he replied, looking out the window.

The bad weather made the city even darker than anyone but a cop could ever imagine.

"You're a hero!"

That's what worries me, he thought. *What if I stop being the hero and turn into the villain?* But it wasn't the sort of thought to share with a stranger, even if he'd wanted to.

"Don't believe everything the newspapers say," he said instead.

"The video of how you saved the child has already been sent to me five times," he said, looking in the rearview mirror. "You know, there are days when you think this city is a shit hole and people are rats. I don't know if I'm making myself clear. Man, in this job, sometimes you see things that would make you cry. Every once in a while, you have some joy. Hell, it gives you life. You think there are still good people in this city. You know what I mean, right? Since Messi left, the joys are few."

Alex didn't answer and stuck to thinking.

"We both have the same job; we serve the community in different ways. Anyway, we're here. I'm sorry, the cab isn't mine, otherwise, I wouldn't charge you."

"Don't worry about it; you have to eat. Thank you."

Alex paid the cab driver and disappeared into the crowd.

As he entered the building, his phone pinged with a message from his friend, Mario.

"Alex, we have news about the van. Rexach has told me something interesting. See you tomorrow."

Alex closed the app without opening the message. He sank down on the couch; the house felt empty without Mary. Life had changed so much for him, and he missed her more than he wanted to admit.

He realized that escaping to Tarragona was just a band-aid and that he would miss her there too. He wouldn't leave his problems in that apartment.

He closed his eyes briefly, thinking about her and the beautiful moments they had shared: those lived in his head and would never leave him to return to New York.

He fell asleep on the same couch where he had fallen asleep so many times in Mary's arms, but now without her, all he had were the bittersweet memories that peppered his dreams.

17

Barcelona.
Tuesday.

The first light of day came through the cracks in the shutters.

Alex's building faced the sea and was among the first to see the dawn break.

The razor-thin cracks in the blinds woke him up. He was in the same position he'd fallen asleep, with his head twisted on the couch, and his neck cricked painfully.

The first thing on his mind was the brutally amputated female corpse.

Clouds continued to cover the city, casting a dreary gray tinge on the horizon.

He looked at his watch, feeling drowsy. He couldn't be bothered to go for a run, though he knew he'd feel better if he did.

He got dressed, his neck still stiff after almost twelve hours of sleep. He went down in the elevator and down toward Paseo de Barcelona.

Exercise and the salty breeze helped clear his mind as he went over the most pertinent problems he faced—the move to Tarragona, Mary, the kidnapped child and the corpses in that van.

He got rid of all the stress he'd bottled up inside him, and when he returned half an hour later, he felt lighter.

He took a shower, made a pot of coffee and picked up the pieces of the cup that were still on the floor.

He went down to his car and headed to work, weaving through the busy morning traffic.

As soon as he set foot in the station, his team welcomed him with a round of applause for the promotion. Grinning at everyone, he shook hands with several of the team and then sat down at his desk. Karla appeared from behind.

"Feeling better?"

Alex grimaced and nodded.

"Morning. Team meeting in five minutes?"

"Okay," she responded and left.

As she walked away, his eyes followed her, admiring her pert ass. He shook his head, glancing around to see if anyone had noticed him staring so overtly. Then he turned his attention to his computer and opened his e-mail.

He addressed it to the chief commissioner of the police station, copying Lieutenant Rexach.

The subject was: *Relocation*.

He began the e-mail by thanking him for his time at the Travessera de les Corts station and emphasizing his gratitude to Chief Rexach, but that he'd decided to accept the transfer to Tarragona. He wanted to make it official; he would stay an extra week to assist with the current case.

When he'd finished, he hovered the mouse over the "send" button and looked around. He was homesick and knew that the e-mail would change everything. But he was determined.

He took a deep breath and clicked 'send'.

Then he got up, grabbed an espresso and entered the team meeting room, where most of his team was already seated.

Karla walked past Alex, leaving a trail of shampoo scent. Alex sniffed, and warm memories stirred in his mind.

"Okay." Alex put one leg up on his desk. "What have we got? Let's start with the van. Karla, do we know whose it is? Mario said there was news, right?"

"So, the vehicle is in the name of a company based in Madrid. But yesterday, some colleagues from the Guardia Civil visited the site and confirmed that the real van with that license plate is still in Madrid and hasn't left the capital. They have recordings to certify this. It's an isothermal van, just like ours. It's a dead end."

"How could our man have done it?"

"We believe he looked for the same model, an Opel Vivaro with the same spec, and copied the license plates. It's almost identical, and even if the police pulled it over, no one would ever spot the difference."

"Is it that easy to forge a license plate?"

"I understand it is," she replied.

"I have some friends who own a workshop producing plates and sending them by post. The customer e-mails the paperwork, and they make the plates. They could have sent counterfeit documents or had a friend make them," replied an officer.

"Understood. So the license plate is a dead end."

"This guy is smart and knows what he's doing," Alex confirmed, crossing it off the list he'd written on the board.

"What about the VIN?"

"The VIN has been filed off with a radial saw; it's unreadable," Karla replied.

Alex crossed it off the board.

"How could we find the owner, then?"

"I have two officers tracking the surveillance cameras. But the problem is what I told you yesterday. It's been longer than thirty days, and it's been erased." The woman shook her head grimly. "The guy has covered all angles."

"Well, the recordings from our headquarters can't help us either, but I'm sure there are some from the school and the hotel opposite the station."

"Check if anyone has touched the van or got close to it. Check everything, every little thing. Do you understand me? Karla, who's in charge of that?"

"Eleonora," she replied as an officer raised her arm at the back of the room. "Check all the angles and all the shops in the street to find suspicious movements around the van, okay?"

The woman at the back of the room nodded her assent as she jotted something down in her notebook.

"Alvaro and Maria are dealing with the cameras at the police station, so I'll let you know as soon as we have something."

Alex turned to the board and put a tick next to 'Cameras'.

"Is there any news about missing persons?" asked Alex.

"Miguel, what do you have?" said Karla.

The young agent stood up.

"Relax, sit down," Alex told him.

But Miguel stayed where he was. He was so thin that he'd earned the nickname *Fideo*—noodle

"As soon as we have the forensic reports, we'll have more

data, but there's no one on file which matches the initial characteristics, at least not here in Barcelona."

"How can someone be missing without anyone noticing?"

"We haven't found anyone within the past four to six weeks," Miguel said.

"Okay, not in Barcelona. What about the surrounding area?"

"No, nothing. In fact, within a radius of twenty miles, that is, the entire province of Barcelona, we have no record. But I'll keep investigating," he concluded and sat down.

Alex turned, underlined the word "*missing*" and then stared at the board.

"Anything else?" he asked.

Someone put up their hand at the back of the room.

"Yes?" said Alex.

"Is it true that you saw the murderer?"

Alex looked at Karla. She was the only person he'd mentioned it to, but she was reading a message on her cell phone. He scowled and then turned back to the team.

"Yes, it looks like it. I'll get a likeness drawn up, and tomorrow I'll let you have a copy."

"We can also pass it on to all stations in the city, as well as to other police forces, borders, airports, gas stations and the media."

"Not to the media for the moment. Rexach doesn't want us to. Everything except the media is a good idea. But I don't think our man cares about escape; I don't think he's staged all this madness to simply disappear. He wants to see the result of his work, and I think this is just the beginning of what could potentially be a long game.

"The problem isn't so much 'when'," said Karla, "but 'how'."

Alex nodded.

"Well, we have a lot of work to do, guys. Thanks for now, and let's get to work. Karla, can you stay for a moment?"

The woman approached the board.

"What's up?"

"I think it would help us if we named our killer."

Karla frowned.

"If we give him a name, he would be more human and less of a serial killer. Looking for someone with a face and a name would help the team visualize him. You know, I think it would be better."

"Well… I guess so," she answered with a shrug. "Do you have any preferences?"

"I don't know. How about Valerio or Roberto, for example?"

"Whatever you say. Roberto is fine."

"Okay. He's Roberto from now on."

"So you are really leaving?" said Karla solemnly. "I've seen the mail."

Alex was surprised.

"I see the good news is spreading like wildfire," he said as he erased the four words he'd written on the board. "But that's what you wanted, right?"

"Are you doing it because of her?" she said, looking at him from under her lashes.

"What do you mean?"

"I heard you and your girlfriend broke up. Is that why you're leaving?"

Alex looked at her. She may be attractive, but his personal life was none of her business.

"I'm leaving for personal matters, Ramirez. What matters to you is that you'll get to keep this case. It's all yours, just as you wanted," said Alex bluntly. "I'll be here for a week, and then I'll be leaving for good. The rest is private."

"I didn't mean to get personal," the woman replied.

"Yeah, but you have. It must be great, standing on your pedestal, looking down on people, right?"

"Excuse me? You've no right to speak to me like that," snapped Karla, folding her arms.

"Maybe, but once you have nothing left to lose, you stop caring," he answered.

"Jeez. Do you think leaving here gives you the green light to be a total jerk?

"Nope. I just say what I see. You've always been that way. You're getting married at the end of this summer, aren't you?" said Alex, raising his hand with authority. "Marrying the son of that perfume magnate. Very neat."

"Butt out, Cortes. You can leave right now, as far as I'm concerned. We'll solve this case without you," she said stiffly, walking to the door. Then she paused and, after a beat, said, *"You shouldn't blame others for your own problems and spit your venom at those around you. I don't care if you leave. But running away won't help you heal,"* she said. Without looking at him, she quietly closed the door to the meeting room.

He knew she was spot on, but the wound was too fresh to see things clearly. He couldn't allow himself to sow hatred in the station that had given him so much. He remembered something his grandfather used to say: *"He who sows the winds reaps the storm".*

He walked out the door and went to get a coffee. He needed another fix before talking to the person who had opened that damned Pandora's box.

18

Alex crossed the street.

The traffic light was green.

As he crossed, Alex noticed a white van waiting to let him pass.

It was raining again, and Alex was soaked. It seemed to him that the driver was looking at him through those sunglasses he would never forget—aviator lenses, drop-shaped.

Who was he? Why was he gesticulating? He searched for his gun inside his leather jacket.

The van moved as if it were about to run him over.

Finally, Alex's eyes focused on what was in front of him. The driver began to honk, waving his hand. *Déjà vu*, a memory of Roberto that had blended with reality in the morning traffic. Alex realized he was still on the crossing, obstructing the traffic. He raised his hands in apology and stepped aside. The car's horn sounded for quite a while after he disappeared. It had awakened the old memory in his mind like a light bulb.

Alex entered the coffee shop and ordered a latte and a pastry.

"Hi, Rafa, how are you?" he asked the waiter.

"Hi, I was told you're in charge of—" said Rafa, but Alex stopped him with a gesture, understanding.

"Do you have a moment?" said Alex, jerking his head toward the quieter end of the counter.

"Of course!" he answered and turned around.

He prepared the sergeant's order and placed it on a tray. They went to the back of the shop and sat at a long table where no one could hear them.

"Congratulations," Rafa said.

"Congratulations?" replied the policeman.

"For the kidnapped kid case," he replied and shrugged.

"Forget about it. It's in the past. I wanted to see you to talk about the van."

When he mentioned the vehicle, the manager's face twisted in disgust.

"Do you remember the exact day the van was left?"

"No, Alex, I've got no idea. I only remember the day I noticed it and how it stayed there for several weeks until the smell appeared."

"Do you remember when that was?"

Rafa cleared his throat.

"About a week ago, it was abnormally hot and felt like summer."

"Go on…"

"The customers began complaining about the bad smell coming from the street. We noticed the sewer was behind the van and thought it was coming from there. But the complaints got worse and worse as the days went by. Until I decided I had to do something. Despite the nice weather, people were no longer sitting on the terrace. So I started to investigate. I'd already decided to call the estate manager and complain about the sewer. But then I noticed that the stench was coming from the van," he said and paused for a heartbeat. "That's all I can tell you."

"And you don't remember anyone hanging around the van, looking at it or anything else that caught your attention? Rafa, you're the one in charge, and you never miss anything," Alex said, eating the last piece of his pastry.

"I never saw anything."

Alex nodded.

"What about your cameras? Do they point to the street?"

"We used to have a camera aimed at the tables to see if customers left without paying. But with the latest data protection law, we decided to take them down. Now we only have them above the cash register and inside."

Alex finished his coffee and left the cup on the tray.

"Thanks, Rafa. I'll leave you my number. If you remember anything, any details, call me."

"I sure will," the manager replied, taking Alex's business card.

As soon as Alex stepped onto the sidewalk, his phone vibrated.

The screen showed a message from Karla.

"Come asap. The coroner's report has arrived."

Nothing else. He could guess Karla's mood just from that text. He looked up, gazed at the glass building, and returned to the office.

19

Memories.

Why did memories always have to come back at the worst times?

Were they a quick escape for the mind to divert our attention? A trick to take the focus away from what it didn't like?

Memories of Mary were present in the sergeant's mind, but now, older ones had been added—of Karla—memories from when he had started to work at the station and they'd first worked together. The first months of a relationship are always the most beautiful and passionate but also fleeting. Those initial moments always remain idealized in our minds. Alex's memories were no less.

The past can't be erased. Sometimes it stings more than a lemon squeezed into an open wound. Going upstairs to see what had arrived from the forensic lab, he wondered if his mind was providing him with a lifeline. Mary's sudden absence must have activated his survival mode. Alex's mind was like a hunter's; once his target had disappeared, he looked for new ones within reach.

He entered the homicide room and approached Karla.

"Shall we have a look at the report?"

"Whatever you say... boss," she said, sounding bitter.

They went to an empty office, locked the door and turned on the lights.

On one side of the room, the windows faced the street, allowing them to see the darkening sky. The rain dominated the city once again.

The report was about three inches thick.

They put two long tables together and stood one on each side.

On the whiteboard, they began to hang papers and photos. They added the license plate of the van, the images of the corpses, and below that, photos of the larvae and some other information.

They opened the coroner's report, which Dr. Alba Guevara had signed.

"How do we split the work?"

"One corpse at a time."

They added more photos to the board and numbered them from one to five.

Alex began to read the report on the bodies, and Karla applied the sheets and photos in order.

They only spoke if necessary. Underneath the photos of each mutilated corpse, they placed sheets of paper where the coroner had identified all the marks on the bodies, pre and post-mortem. There were tattoos, piercings and scars, but no scratches, bruises or signs of violence besides the amputations.

"These two will be more difficult to identify," said Karla, pointing at two corpses with no visible signs of violence.

Alex looked up. The board was a macabre collage. He stood in front of it, scanning it through narrowed eyes.

Above the photo of the van, she wrote: *"Who is Roberto?"*

"Did you notice that they were all quite young? I'd say they were in their twenties and thirties."

"Yes, it looks like that. Young, but they didn't seem to have struggled. I wonder if they knew their killer?"

"This is horrible," Karla said.

"Where do your parents live?"

The woman didn't like the question.

"You know that already. They live near Cadaques."

"And how often do you talk?"

The woman shrugged.

"I don't know, once a week, maybe twice?" she said without looking at him. "Why?"

"How long would you have to go without talking to them before they called the police or came looking for you?"

"I have no idea, *sergeant*."

"Karla, think. If you lived alone in a big city, how long would it take? One week? Two?"

The woman looked at him without understanding what he was getting at.

He stopped looking at her and looked at the pictures.

"How can five people be missing for a month, and no one has noticed?"

"Maybe it's because we're looking in Barcelona, and they're from another county or even other countries."

"Good idea. Tell your officer to widen the search. What else, Karla? What else have we missed?"

"What does the coroner say?"

"Nothing new from what she already told us yesterday. All confirmed. The lividities are because the bodies were already dead when they were put in the van. I don't understand why there was so much blood around the bodies. We need to clarify that with the coroner."

"What do you mean?"

Alex looked up from the documents.

"When you cut a body in more than five places, the blood pumps out of the holes. But, because there was so much blood, it would suggest that Roberto cut them inside the van. But then again, if you remember, there was no blood spatter on the walls."

"That's right. Mario showed me."

"I don't understand," he said, shaking his head and smoothing his beard.

Alex returned to the report and continued reading.

"The amputations were made with a metal saw. Alba has found some metal microparticles in the severed bones. Then she says that the *Sarcophaga carnaria* fly is viviparous and voracious. It appears after one week. It needs heat and oxygen." Alex looked at the woman. "Oxygen; doesn't that remind you of something?"

"Oxygen," the woman repeated. "The balloons!"

"Exactly. Those balloons that were bursting on the ceiling were releasing oxygen. Could they have been full of flies? Because how else could these bugs have gotten in?"

"Good point. We should ask the coroner that, too."

"Okay," said Alex and continued reading. "The doctor confirms that none of the bodies shows any clear signs of violence or any sign of sexual assault. Our guy isn't an opportunistic or sexual killer who has had a lapse of insanity. He's calculating and smarter than we think."

"Or maybe you're wrong. Maybe he's simply an insane person who has committed an act of madness."

Karla felt a cold shiver run through her body.

One of the decapitated women had a slender body and a beautiful chest. She recognized herself in the woman. It could have been her, on that stretcher, lifeless, her skin devoured by voracious larvae. But fate wanted her to be her, on the other side of truth and history, in that office, deciphering the message of a serial killer.

The press couldn't talk about anything else. In the newspapers and on the radio, self-proclaimed experts speculated and debated all possible angles but couldn't shed any light on the subject because even the police didn't know what had happened. All they did was to spread panic among the public. The news that there were five corpses was already public knowledge. People were afraid to travel on the subway, and there were fewer people at night than usual. Barcelona was immersed in a fog covering the truth, turning it into a gloomy and dangerous place

The judge ordered the summary proceedings to remain secret. Information sharing was blocked to avoid leaks. The press didn't know that the bodies had been mutilated, but going on the significant bribes offered to officers, it wouldn't take long for them to find out.

"Karla, look at this. The doctor says the bodies were sedated with a cocktail of drugs to keep them asleep. She's found

19

heavy doses of anxiolytics mixed with barbiturates and another unknown substance they're still investigating."

He continued reading quietly and then looked up.

"Goddamn it!"

"What is it?"

"The doctor says these substances are less present in some bodies."

The woman shrugged and asked, "What do you mean?"

"She thinks some weren't fully asleep while he amputated their limbs. Jeez, they would have felt everything."

20

It had been a long time since Karla and Alex looked at each other properly.

It wasn't exactly like the old times, but almost; now, they stared at each other in horror.

The two officers were only just beginning to untangle Roberto's mystery.

Alex took out his phone and called Alba Guevara.

On the second ring, she replied.

"Guevara."

"Doctor, this is Cortes."

"Alex, good morning."

"Do you have a minute? Can you speak?"

"Yes, of course. And please, call me Alba."

There was silence, and Alex saw Karla grimace.

"Yes… Alba. I'm on speakerphone, and Officer Ramirez is listening."

"Good morning," she said, changing her tone.

"Hello," called out Karla.

"I've read the report," Alex said.

"Already?"

"This case is a top priority," he replied, flicking through the pages.

"Of course. So what are your thoughts?"

"Well. The first thing I want to know is how the vehicle's walls had no splatter stains, yet the van was full of blood."

"I don't know. I've been wondering that, too. It's as if the corpses were placed inside and then sealed. It doesn't make sense. If the vehicle had been parked on a sloping road, then a certain amount of blood would have stayed inside."

"But there would have been splatter on the walls, and with the Luminol test, the front wall would be phosphorescent. But that's not the case."

"I know. It makes no sense. Also, looking at the microscope tests, the sections haven't been made with a handsaw. The cut is typical of a power disc saw with a wide diameter and high speed—the kind you find in a carpentry workshop. Perhaps the body was cut with that and then put inside while closing the door. But he could only do that with one corpse, not all of them. Which means that someone must have helped him."

"In theory, serial killers don't usually have an accomplice. They work alone. They're not social, most likely sociopaths," said Alex. "Have you extracted the DNA from the bodies? In case it matches any in the police biobank database."

"We're getting it done, but it will take a while, and I doubt we'll find any matches."

"One last thing, and maybe the most important: the analyses you sent us show a disturbing detail. You say that some bodies have a more consistent dose of drugs in their veins than others."

"Exactly, they're identified in the report."

"Yes, but... what exactly do you mean by this?"

"It can imply many things, but in my experience, I believe that the killer's *modus operandi* evolved. This is a theory, and if we knew the chronology of who died first and who died last, then I could confirm it," said the doctor and cleared her throat. "It's not a question of gender. At first, I thought it was, but now I think the killer changed his technique. I think he cut the last ones while they were still conscious. The amount of drugs in the body was insufficient to knock out an adult person. Do you know what I mean?"

"I see. Sometimes I wonder about the extent of human malice," said Alex. Then he took a moment, turned some pages, and continued, "Anyway, do you think we'll find out where the heads are buried?"

"I don't know, Alex. I was thinking about that last night. This morning I looked at some FBI documents, as they're more used to dealing with serial killers. I found an analogous case from the eighties in Connecticut. A year after the murders, some hunters found the buried heads. Every year, they went to the same out-of-the-way place in the mountains. The murderer knew when they were going and had left the heads there for the hunters to find. So when your man decides or wants to, he'll let you find them, too. Maybe a week from now or a decade. Who knows?"

"Or we might catch him first," said Karla, trying to counter the doctor's bleak prognosis.

"I might be wrong; you never know," Alba replied.

"Thank you, doctor," said Alex. We have no more questions. Thank you for your time."

"There's one thing I haven't told you," she said just as Alex was about to hang up. "One of the girls had a circular tattoo.

It's the logo of a rock band from Barcelona. I did a reverse online search. They play regularly in the Gothic quarter in a pub with the same name as the band. I think it's strange that a girl would have a tattoo like that, don't you?"

"Which one are we talking about?"

"I think it was woman number three."

Alex got up and went to look at the photo.

"Yes, Alba, I see it. It's a small symbol at the base of the ankle. Almost invisible."

"How strange that a girl from Barcelona disappears without anyone reporting her missing," said Karla.

"I only mentioned it because it could be an important lead."

"Well spotted, Doctor," said Alex. "We'll check all the tattoos in case there are any others."

"I've reviewed them, but I don't see anything else we could use. But you do it yourselves."

"Thank you, Alba. We will keep you in the loop. Thanks again."

"My pleasure," she said and hung up.

Karla looked serious, and Alex was overwhelmed by the work that awaited them.

He sat down and began scrolling through his phone, looking for the music bar that Alba had mentioned.

"The group Alba was talking about is playing tonight. I'm going to go and see if anyone has noticed that a super fan is missing."

"Alex, you're in all the papers. Your face is too well known. It'd be better if I go instead."

"I won't let you go alone. We can both go," said Alex grabbing the folders, "if that's okay with you?"

21

No Limits.

The place wasn't inviting, and the name even less so.

The bar in the Gothic Quarter was disturbing.

Alex arrived a little before midnight, the time he'd arranged to meet Karla.

The narrow streets smelled of history and urine. He'd never been there before, nor did he ever wish to go back.

"What was I hoping to find on a Tuesday night? Come on, don't be a jerk," he told himself.

It was a dreary weekday night. The grim street was crowded with somber individuals, each one stranger than the next.

The bar was in a rabbit warren of alleys, making him think of *Jack the Ripper.*

He wasn't used to visiting places like that, nor did he know much about hard rock, and he felt out of place.

Some people had fluorescent-colored Mohicans; many looked off their faces, and almost all had piercings. Leather, punk and heavy metal outfits. Tattoos and tangled dreds, and black t-shirts of bands with unpronounceable names.

Alex adjusted his leather jacket and looked for the gun in

its holster to reassure himself.

He did like rock, but only the commercial kind: it had been a point of union with Mary and his rebellious youth.

He looked at the clock; it was several minutes before he was due to meet Karla. He decided to check out the nearby streets and circled the ghetto block. He didn't understand the configuration of the neighborhood, which was so different from the rest of the city. The Jewish and Gothic quarters were the oldest neighborhoods in Barcelona. Their architecture followed irregular patterns, totally different from the grids that the Romans and Cerdà had created.

He found a back door that led to the bar, covered in stickers of the band. His phone vibrated with a message from Corporal Ramirez, telling him she was at the front entrance.

"Not bad," she said as he appeared.

"This place looks like a zoo," he whispered in her ear.

"Have you taken a look around?"

"Sort of, but this isn't what I expected."

"Look, it's the same as the woman's tattoo," she said, nodding at the sign.

It was a white illuminated sign. On one side, there was the logo of a famous brand of beer, and on the other one, the bar's round logo and the name they shared with the rock band.

"*No limits*? Interesting name," said Karla, looking around. "But not as much as the people around here."

"Shhh, they could hear you."

She raised her eyebrows and went inside.

Alex followed.

She wore a classic biker jacket, black pants and a black

Rolling Stones T-shirt.

As they entered, everyone turned around to stare at the new faces.

The two of them approached the bar and ordered two beers.

They sipped their drinks as they glanced around. The band was supposed to come on soon, but with bands one never knew in Barcelona—they always started late.

They felt out of place, but they pushed through the discomfort.

"Any ideas?" shouted the woman over the music.

"What a shit place to work," he shouted back. "They don't give you any receipts, the volume is unbearable, and the place is an absolute dump."

"Never mind that. Let's focus on our business. I have an idea," she replied and returned to the bar.

She waved at the barman, and he came over.

"Do you want anything else?" he asked.

"Where's the manager? I want to ask him something."

The barman stood quietly, looking at them.

"I don't know. He comes and goes."

"How can we find him?"

"No idea. I'm new. But I guess he'll be along in a little while. Probably when the band comes on."

Alex watched Karla chatting to the barman, noticing the curious looks she was getting from the dead eyes dotted around the bar. Suddenly, the barman pointed to someone, and Alex turned to see what he was pointing at.

"Look, there he is," the barman said to Karla and pointed.

The owner was on the other side of the premises, shaking hands and greeting people. He stopped when he saw the barman pointing at him. Karla glanced at Alex, and they both approached him.

The manager stared at them and, without warning, turned around and started running. Karla took off after him, dodging through the crowd of people. He slipped through a door into a room illuminated by red lights, full of couches with people stretched out on them and all kinds of drugs on the tables.

The man flew out the door on the other side, with Karla closely following him.

They entered a dark, elongated warehouse full of junk, and the only light was the faint green of the exit door.

The bar owner knocked things to the floor to slow Karla down, but she managed to keep up.

"Stop! Police!" shouted the woman.

The man closed the back door and slammed it behind him. They could still hear him running.

But when Karla opened the door and looked up and down the street, there was no sign of the fugitive.

That man was running as if his life depended on it. Karla reached the corner and saw him fleeing down a dark, narrow street, but just as he was about to disappear, an arm grabbed him. The man yelled as he was punched squarely in the face, and his nose shattered under the impact. He fell to the ground and covered his head with his arms, unaware of what had happened to him until he saw Alex. The man writhed on the floor, trying to escape, as his nose gushed with sticky blood trailing down his neck.

Karla came up from behind, and Alex grabbed the fugitive before he could flee again.

22

Karla was panting from sprinting after the man.

Half of the man's face was covered with blood.

His head was shaved, and he had tattoos around his neck and forehead. Others were visible under the sleeves of his black shirt.

His small, bloodshot eyes indicated that he must have consumed alcohol or drugs, and blood dripped off his long beard onto his shirt.

"What's your name?" asked Alex, grabbing the back of the man's shirt.

He slammed him against the wall.

"Let me go, son of a bitch! What do you want from me?"

"We just want to talk," said Alex.

"Why did you run away?" asked Karla.

The man looked from one side of the street to the other, avoiding their eyes.

"Listen to me; we just want to talk. Do you understand?"

"I'll listen if you let go of me!"

Alex loosened his grip, and the man shook his arm away and adjusted his shirt.

22

"How did you know we were cops?"

"Maybe we're a little rusty with this incognito stuff," Karla mumbled.

"I can smell you guys for miles."

Karla offered him a tissue, and the man wiped his bloody nose.

"You broke my nose. How am I going to sing today?

"Well, you shouldn't have run away," she said, pressing her finger to his chest. "Why did you run?"

"Listen," interrupted Alex, "We want to ask you a few questions. We're looking for a girl who's disappeared."

"Well, she's not here."

"How do you know if I haven't told you who she is yet? First of all, what's your name?"

The man tried to push past them, but Karla pinned him against the wall.

"My friend asked you a question."

The man looked at the ground.

"My name's Jerry, okay?" he replied, glaring at her. "Damn cops!"

"Yeah, and my name's Tom. Don't take the piss," said Alex, stepping closer.

He grabbed the man by the neck and smashed his head against the wall.

"We're investigating a murder, you dickhead. I could send you to jail for obstruction. That might refresh your memory."

"Or better yet, collaborating with a murderer!" added Karla.

"I'll repeat it for the last time. What's your name?" said Alex through clenched teeth.

The man took a deep breath.

"Manolo Mejías Pérez."

"That wasn't too difficult, was it, Manolo? I'll release you now, but I don't want any more jokes, understood?"

The man nodded.

"We're looking for a girl who must have disappeared about a month ago. We think she might be one of your fans."

"I don't know," he shrugged. "What's her name?"

"Do you think we'd be here if we knew?"

"She has a small tattoo with the name of your band on her right ankle. Is that ringing any bells?"

The man shook his head.

"I don't know. There are lots of crazy women with tattoos around here. Is she blonde, brunette?"

"We don't know. Do you have any female fans you haven't seen for a while?"

The man shook his head again as he stuffed the already-soaked handkerchief up one nostril and threw his head back.

Alex looked at Karla, and she nodded in reply.

"Manolo, we're going to let you go, but be reachable," he said. "We need you to let us know if you leave town or remember anything. You can contact me here at any time." He handed him a business card that still said *"corporal"* on it. *"Anything*, is that clear?"

The man took the card, smearing it with his blood, and put it in his pocket.

Thunder rumbled in the distance.

Alex looked up. He saw a few drops falling, illuminated by the street lamps.

They let the man go and watched him enter through the bar's back door.

"You went too far. He could report you," said Karla as they

22

walked away down the street.

"He knows something. He only has a broken nose for now, but next time we'll see," answered Alex.

As they reached the subway, the rain started to fall harder and harder.

"What a weird spring," she commented.

"I don't ever remember so much rain," he agreed.

"We needed it."

"I wish it would wash away all the psychos like Roberto."

"What do you think of this Manolo, by the way?" Karla asked.

"I don't think anyone runs away unless they're hiding something."

"Good point. Do you think he has anything to do with Roberto?"

"I'll tell you what I think tomorrow. I have a hypothesis."

The woman laughed, shaking her head.

"You're doing it again," she said.

"Doing what?" he asked.

"Leaving your sentences unfinished," she replied, smiling, then turned and walked away. "See you tomorrow," she said over her shoulder.

He nodded silently and took the subway in the opposite direction.

23

Alex woke up late.

He turned off the alarm clock and went back to sleep. The rain had a meditative effect on him: its sweet sound was therapeutic. He reached across the bed, but there was nobody there. Only cold sheets and an unused pillow. Mary's departure wasn't a dream; it was a nightmare that had already become part of his reality.

A new day was beginning under a slate-gray sky. As he opened his eyes, he remembered Roberto and the investigation.

He sat up and looked at the clock; it was much later than expected. He switched on his cell phone, and several messages appeared. One was from the boss, asking for an update on the investigation.

Alex showered and prepared a pot of coffee. He put on his raincoat and left for the station.

Journalists were still stalking the building, searching for juicy news, but he brushed past them with a *"no comment"* and went upstairs to his office. He peeled off his soaked raincoat and left it hanging on the window handle.

Karla was at her desk, speaking on the phone. As soon as she saw him, she ended the call and hung up.

"Alex, I've been trying to call you all morning."

"I was tired. I'm off to see Rexach."

"He's been waiting for you since eight in the morning," said Karla.

When he entered the boss's office, Rexach looked up from the computer.

"Where have you been? I've called you several times."

"I know, but I was done in and needed to sleep," he answered, leaning against the doorway.

"Have you got any news?"

"Come with me. I want to show you something," said Alex to his superior.

Rexach frowned and stood up.

Alex entered the briefing room first, followed by the boss and Karla. He opened the door and turned on the lights. Nothing had been moved since the previous day.

Alex updated the chief on the previous day's forensic report—all details, assumptions and considerations.

"Who's Roberto?" asked the boss.

Alex looked at Karla and gestured to her.

"We've decided to personify the murderer," Karla explained. "Since we don't know his name, for the moment, he's called Roberto. This way, the search will feel more real."

"Good idea, Corporal," the boss said.

Alex kept quiet.

"It was Alex's idea," she answered, staring at the floor.

"Anyway, it doesn't matter. You see, this one," said Alex,

pointing to the third row of photos. "It's woman number three. See this tattoo here," he said, pointing to the image. The chief approached, putting on his glasses. "Coroner Guevara found out that it's a symbol of a bar and a rock band, and we went there yesterday to check it out."

"And what did you find?"

"Well, we met the lead singer of the band."

"And how did it go?" asked the boss.

"Let's say we shook him a little," Alex smirked.

The chief glared at him.

"Did he know anything?"

"I think he knew something but didn't want to tell us."

"Could it be him? Could he be Roberto?" said the chief, turning around. "Shall we assign some officers to follow him?"

"No, we'd be wasting our time. He's a junkie and a two-bit musician. I don't think he knows anything about the murder, but that doesn't mean he doesn't know something about the missing woman."

"This is good," said the boss, pointing to the board.

"Lieutenant, you're wanted on the phone," said an officer poking his head around the door and glancing curiously at the wall covered with photos.

"I'll be right there," he replied to the officer, then turned to face Alex. "You're doing a great job, guys. It won't be easy, but if this son of a bitch has made a mistake, I'm sure you'll find it," he concluded and left the room.

Alex and Karla looked at each other.

"Come on, let's get back to business," said Alex.

"What are you going to do?"

"Right now, I'm going to take an aspirin and have a coffee. When I've checked my mail, I'll let you know."

The woman nodded and left the room.

Alex turned off the lights and closed the door. He walked over to the coffee machine and ordered an espresso. He stood looking out of the windows, staring blankly at the street down below.

He remembered the scene from a couple of nights ago when everything was fenced off and the spotlights that illuminated the white van.

A yellow delivery truck with three red letters on the side was parked up on the curb in front of the station.

People holding umbrellas scurried along the sidewalk. The coffee shop was open, with the tables regrouped but still empty, not because of the stench but because of the inclement weather.

A young girl was walking down the street in a pink raincoat. She entered a doorway and disappeared inside. Alex's mind returned to the corpses: Once real people who had walked along the sidewalk just like the girl, unaware they would end up decapitated and left to rot in a white van.

He returned to his desk, his whimsical philosophizing overtaken with thoughts of emails and returning calls.

From across the room, an officer called out to him.

"Sergeant, that arrived for you," he said, pointing to Alex's desk and returning to his computer screen.

Alex turned to see what it was. A box was sitting in the middle of his desk.

He took the last sip of coffee and threw away the plastic cup.

He approached the plain cardboard box sealed with regular

brown tape. The label on the top bore the logo of the shipping company: DHL.

He was the addressee, and they had written his first and last name and the station's address.

Alex glanced around: all his colleagues were busy with work. Nobody was paying attention.

He took a pair of scissors and set about opening the parcel.

24

The rest of the world faded into the background.

Until this moment, he'd enjoyed his job for the most part, even on the toughest days. But in all his years as a mosso d'esquadra, this was the first package he'd ever received.

No one was looking at him; the entire research group was working at full speed, all focused on their work.

He inhaled deeply, punctured the adhesive tape, and gently opened the cardboard wings.

Inside there was a white box. He touched it. It was a plastic-type material, like porexpan.

He closed it and looked again at the shipping company label; it had been sent from Barcelona, but he didn't recognize the sender's name. He frowned, worried.

Alex returned to the inner box: it was more like a Russian doll than a standard package.

The polystyrene box wouldn't come out, and nor could he remove it with his hands. He lifted it and estimated it weighed about ten or maybe twelve pounds. He couldn't separate the two wrappings.

He cut off one of the corners, and a crack appeared in the

white box. He repeated the procedure on all four sides.

A cold chill ran down his spine, and he shivered involuntarily.

What was inside it?

He separated the lid with the tip of the scissors, and a burst of fresh air came out of it.

It smelled aseptic, like a hospital, and very similar to bleach.

When he looked up, Karla was watching him with the phone cord stretched out.

He finished lifting the lid of the package and looked inside.

He felt a spike of apprehension unlike anything he'd ever felt. He'd heard stories from the traffic police when they explained how they felt when witnessing an accident scene. This must be how they felt.

He peeked inside and closed it again, unable to believe his eyes.

He held his breath and didn't dare speak in case it wasn't safe. But Karla knew him well. She hung up the phone and walked over.

"What's wrong?"

Alex didn't answer.

Karla tried to open the box, but he stopped her.

"Call the Lieutenant and follow me," Alex whispered. He carefully picked up the box and headed to the meeting room.

When they entered, raindrops played a strange, almost macabre symphony against the windows.

The boss came in, not sure what was going on.

"Alex, what is it?" he asked.

Alex didn't look at him.

"Close the door," he whispered to Karla, and she obeyed.

Alex exhaled loudly and felt a drop of sweat trickling down

24

his forehead.

Then he lifted the lid of the polystyrene box and put it to one side. After that, he grabbed the handles of a transparent plastic bag and lifted it out.

Once the bag was out of the box, both spectators shuddered.

"Son of a bitch!" the boss blurted out and turned his head away in horror.

"Jesus Christ, I can't believe it," said Karla and approached the bag. "This is the cruelest, most fucked up thing I've ever seen."

Alex didn't quite know what to do with the bag. He placed it gently on the table so it wouldn't roll off.

The plastic bag was sealed and vacuumed, and the plastic contoured its contents. Neatly arranged inside was a head, two hands and two feet.

The face wore a lopsided smile, with the mouth stretched by the force of the vacuum. One eye was open, and the other closed.

"Fuck!" said Karla, making the sign of the cross. "Looks like this is a game, and it's only just begun!"

25

Alex looked at Karla.

"How can you call this a game?" he yelled, pinning all his frustration on her.

She was puzzled.

"Your Roberto is dictating the rules of the game. First, he sent us a van full of corpses, and now this—"

"Shut up, you two," said the Lieutenant calmly, approaching the head. Between the plastic and the skin, diluted blood had created a pinkish liquid that moistened the contents. The head looked like a man's. He seemed young, with short dark hair.

"Let's focus. We're in front of a human being who has died," he said, going closer and peering at the grisly specimen. "Alex?"

"Yes, boss."

"Call Mario, tell him we're bringing them something. Tell him we'll meet him at the lab right away," said the boss, looking at the bag. Then he pointed his finger at them. "Don't even think of saying anything about this to a soul unless it's strictly necessary. Now put it back in its box, and let's take it upstairs."

"Damn it, Rexach. I was working on a documentoscopy report I have to deliver this afternoon. What's so urgent?" asked Mario, looking irritated as he opened the lab door for Alex. He was surprised to see the boss and Karla behind.

"Where can I put this?" asked Alex.

"What is it?" asked Mario impatiently, puzzled by the sudden incursion into his lab.

Alex looked at him and sighed.

"Can I put it here?" he asked, barely hiding his impatience, and rested it on a countertop.

Mario turned and glanced at a couple of his team analyzing samples of seized drugs and fingerprints on Coca-Cola cans from two unrelated cases.

The boss asked the two workers to leave the lab.

"No, they stay, they're on my team, and I can vouch for them."

"All right. Alex, open it," ordered the boss.

Alex removed the cardboard box, then the polystyrene box and finally took out the plastic bag with the corpse's remains.

The three lab officers stepped back as soon as they saw the contents.

"This research is of the utmost importance, and we can't let a single word about it slip out. Is that clear?" Rexach asked the laboratory staff. "The judge has ordered the investigation to remain secret."

Mario came closer to observe the macabre contents of the bag.

"Has anyone touched it?" asked Mario.

"Alex?" asked the boss.

"Well, I think it was just me and, I guess, the front desk officer who picked it up," he replied, turning to the other officer. "Karla, have you touched the parcel?"

"Negative."

"Well, just me then. Why?" asked Alex.

"Because of the fingerprints. We'll check if the killer has left any traces," he said, then looked at his fellow investigators. "So, what do we do with… this?"

"Hey scientists, a little tact, please. These are the remains of a person. It's *him*, not *this*," Karla scolded them.

"When did it arrive?" asked Mario.

"Half an hour ago."

Mario put on some latex gloves and walked over to the box. He inspected it and stopped at the label.

"What a surprise, look at this," said Mario as the others approached. "They sent it to you, Alex. This means something. It wasn't sent to the station in general. It's *for you*. This guy's targeting you for some reason."

"Have you received any strange calls in the last few days? Or has anyone followed you?" asked the boss.

Alex crossed his arms and shook his head.

"Nothing unusual, but I've been exhausted after the kidnapped child's case."

"Could both cases be related, boss?" asked Karla.

"I don't know, we'll see."

The boss frowned and looked at Alex, who was washing his hands. He'd just realized that he'd opened the box without gloves.

"We can't open it here," the chief replied.

"Do you think there's a chance we'll get any prints from the box?" asked Alex to Mario.

"Of course. We have the technology here. Don't worry about that. If there are any fingerprints, we'll find them. Both on the box and in the plastic bag," confirmed Mario.

"We should take it to headquarters to be opened by forensics," said Lieutenant Rexach.

"Let us get the prints off the bag first. We'll also need your prints, Alex, and those of the officer who received this.

"Okay, I'll call the judge to inform her and get her authorization to move the body. Well, of the remains," said the chief.

"I'll have one of my officers get the ones from the delivery guy, too," said Karla.

"I'll inform the medical examiner that we're coming," Alex added.

"Okay, I'm going downstairs, but I'll be right back," said the chief.

"Lieutenant, can I come with you?" asked Karla.

"It would be better if you stayed here to coordinate the investigation. The sooner we get started, the better chance we have of catching this sick bastard," said Alex.

"He's right. Your team, Ramirez, has to provide full support," confirmed the Lieutenant.

Alex approached the bag again and touched it. It reminded him of a baby cocooned within a placenta—a cruel and disgusting sight.

"Let's get going. We don't have a minute to lose," confirmed the chief and went out the door.

26

It was Wednesday in Barcelona.

There wasn't much traffic on the Ronda de Dalt, perhaps due to the never-ending deluge.

The wipers were still struggling to clear the water on the windshield. Rain streamed down from the roofs, flooding the sidewalks. The dark clouds had been hanging over the skies for days and showed no sign of leaving.

Alex decided to take a patrol car. A uniformed officer was driving, and he turned on the blue lights and siren. Cars parted for them as they sped through the flooded lanes.

Alex sat in the back with Lieutenant Rexach. The amputated remains were in the trunk.

There was a tense, tomblike silence in the car, and the officer driving seemed uncomfortable. Occasionally, he glanced at his passengers in his rearview mirror as if trying to guess what was happening.

"Do you think it's him?" asked Alex, snapping out of his thoughts and turning to the boss.

"Are you talking about Roberto?"

Alex nodded.

"Yeah, I hope we don't have more than one loco out there."

"I don't know. Do you think we'll get any clues from the box?"

"A guy who organizes this kind of show doesn't leave threads dangling or make stupid mistakes, like putting his real name on the return address," said Alex.

"What a can of worms... we weren't expecting this."

"Nobody expects a can of worms like the one we have in the trunk."

The driving officer furrowed his eyebrows, and his eyes widened slightly. Alex noticed it.

"This is fodder for the press, and I don't know how long we'll be able to keep it quiet."

"I just spoke to the judge. She warned us that nothing must be leaked," said the chief and sighed resignedly. "And she's right."

"My team won't say a thing."

"But journalists pay very well."

"Yes, but you can get a five-year suspension without pay if you're caught. The internal affairs people don't mess around," said Alex, staring in the rearview mirror until the officer looked at him.

Alex knew the driver had understood the message because he didn't look back for the rest of the trip.

After twenty minutes, they arrived at the central police station in Sabadell. Alex looked at his watch.

"Ten minutes less than driving in a camouflaged car. This is great!" he said as the car went down a ramp into the basement of the complex. "What's your name?" he asked.

"Herminio."

"Herminio?"

"Yes, like my grandfather."

"Good job, Herminio. If I was staying in Barcelona, I'd hire you as my official chauffeur," said Alex.

The wet tires began to squeal as the driver looked for a free space.

They parked next to the door. Alex got out, took the plastic box from the trunk, and walked toward the medical examiner waiting at the door.

"I've been expecting you," she said.

Alex and the Lieutenant followed her inside.

They entered the main area of the morgue, where another doctor was waiting, ready with a powerful light illuminating an empty gurney.

Alex laid the box on top.

"Please wait outside. There are some chairs just outside the door," instructed the coroner.

"No, I want to be here," said Alex.

"I'll watch from the outside," said the lieutenant.

Alex changed into white overalls and stayed a step away.

"Exhibit number seven in the van case," said the woman, knowing the camera was recording. Then she said the date and the time.

Alex looked up at the device, which was hanging from the ceiling. A red dot indicated its presence.

"Let's extract the bag. We confirm the presence of a human head, two severed hands and two severed feet. Everything points to them being from one of the victims in the van. The remains are in what looks like a large vacuum bag. It could be something used in a butcher's shop or meat factory. The thickness of the wrapping doesn't allow any odor to escape.

We're proceeding to puncture the bag."

Taking the scissors from a wheeled table full of utensils, the other coroner held the bag in both hands, and the woman cut into it.

With the first snip, the bag swelled, instantly losing its vacuum, and the perfectly symmetrical composition of the human parts fell apart, escaping from the assistant's hands. The second cut made the stench diffuse into the room. Alex coughed.

"Are you sure you want to stay?"

The policeman gave her a thumbs-up as he recovered.

"We'll continue," said the woman as she trimmed the perimeter of the bag.

He lifted the plastic flap, exposing the body parts.

"I think we're witnessing the first parts of the puzzle the murderer wants to show us."

She took the right hand and raised it in the air.

"We can see that the killer has left the deceased's fingertips intact. The section here, made by removing the hand, presents the same characteristics of the parts found in the van."

Then she examined the feet without saying anything. She tried to pick up the head, but the slippery liquid made it awkward, so she rested it on the table, on the base of its neck.

The hair, flattened as if freshly showered, covered the man's forehead. He still had one eye open and one eye closed. She bent down and kept talking.

"The head appears to be that of a young man with a dark complexion. There are no lividities, but there may be in the scalp area. The autopsy will tell us more. It may correspond to man number four. The nostrils are quite flat despite being unpressurized."

As she said this, she picked up a pointed utensil and opened his nostrils.

"The nostrils aren't obstructed," she said, putting the instrument between his lips. "Wait a minute; there's something here."

She prized apart the man's mouth to see what it was.

"Well, here's a surprise. Our man has sent us something. There's a piece of paper between his teeth."

27

Peaks and valleys.

The elements that create a unique structure in every individual's fingertips were the reason Mario first became hooked on science. Human evolution has conspired to make each of us different in both appearance and organic traces.

"Men may lie, but fingerprints never do," Mario always said.

Mario and Dr. Guevara enjoyed complex cases. The ones that fed them with challenges and took them out of the monotony of everyday life.

The lab staff focused on the cardboard box that had just arrived. They cut it into pieces and dipped it in the paper reagent, a red liquid called Ninhydrin. The light brown cardboard gradually became impregnated with the liquid and took on a pinkish hue. After several minutes, red fingerprints appeared against a lighter surface as if by magic.

Using tongs, they removed the cardboard from the tray until it stopped dripping. Then, they put it in an oven to dry.

They turned their attention to the porexpan box. First, they tried the black powder, but nothing appeared. Then they tried the cyanoacrylate system.

They inserted the box and lid into the hood, applied the reagent on a hot base and closed it. Vapors from the chemical base of *Super Glue* adhered to the walls, and only one print appeared. It was Alex's.

Once the cardboard had dried, they took photos of the prints and entered them into the computer. They compared them with those of the DHL delivery man.

Mario then called Karla.

"Ramirez here," she replied right away.

"It's Mario. It's not good news."

28

A deadly cargo.
The courier agency had no idea what they'd transported.

Karla immediately called the company's head office. She identified herself and asked to speak to the person in charge of logistics. She gave them the shipment number and asked for the exact route the package had followed.

She found out that the package hadn't been picked up at the customer's house—he'd taken it in person to the Calle Espronceda branch and left it there. He'd indicated it was a birthday gift and must be delivered a few days later.

Karla sent two men there to get more information. She pulled out her phone and looked at the photos she'd taken of the cardboard box.

She zoomed in, looking for clues. Then she transferred the photos to the computer and enlarged them. A mark was hidden under the seal that closed the bottom flaps. From there, she began to unravel the clues.

She analyzed the measurements and characteristics: places that sold it, if it was professional material, what it was for, and what it could contain, among others.

She started to browse online and discovered something interesting.
  She picked up the phone and called Alex.

29

The macabre game had begun.

The coroner's assistant held the head tightly, and Alba inserted the scalpel for leverage. The jaw was hard to open.

The human body is a perfect machine with a hydraulic system. When the heart beats, it irrigates the tissues, the muscles and the bones, and the whole body can move thanks to a constant blood flow. When the heart stops, the blood stops flowing, and the muscles stiffen. Moving a limb or a human part after blood flow has stopped is a titanic feat.

As soon as Alba managed to open the jaw, she inserted a dilator and was able to extract what was between the teeth.

"We've found a piece of paper inside the oral cavity. It appears to be laminated and folded. I'm opening it. Inside are a succession of black lines of differing sizes, otherwise known as a bar code. There are no numbers."

Once unfolded, she showed it to the camera and handed it to Alex.

As soon as he picked it up, he turned it over. There were only black lines, nothing else. Not a sign, not a letter. Just a mysterious riddle hidden within a barcode.

He gritted his teeth and shook his head.

What are you trying to tell us with this, you fucking son of a bitch? he thought.

At that moment, the boss came in to look at the paper.

"When will we have the autopsy results?" he asked.

"We dropped everything else we were doing and got on with it immediately. I think we'll have it by the end of this afternoon," said Alba, visibly thrilled at what she had in front of her.

"And when will we know whose corpse it's?" asked Alex.

"This afternoon, I'll give you my opinion. It'll be a deduction of the color of the skin, the cuts, and the section. We'll have the DNA confirmation in twenty-four hours."

"I think we should ask for the body to be identified through the fingerprints," said Alex. "Can you get it done, boss? You could ask the judge."

As he spoke, Alex noticed that the forensic scientist was watching him in a subtle, feline way. She seemed to like him, but he hadn't realized it until then. Up to that moment, his senses had been clouded by a filter called Mary.

"I'll take care of that," agreed the boss.

"How soon can we have it?"

"If I ask for it to be a priority, I believe that in twenty-four hours, we'll have it."

"Wait," said Alba. "There's something I want to tell you. Something that's caught my attention." The two policemen turned in unison. "Something is bothering me, but I can't figure out what it is. The skin on this body is almost perfect. If we look at all the bodies, we have a crushing incongruity. The body has a strong decomposition of both skin and internal tissues. However, the condition of the head and limbs shows little sign of decay, as if only a few days had passed," she said. "I'm sure the autopsy will tell us more."

Alex nodded.

"Thank you for your time, Alba. I look forward to reading your report as soon as possible," he said, removing his mask, not realizing what he was doing. The smell of blood and rot flooded his nostrils.

He quickly put his arm in front of his face and left the room, gasping to get fresh air back in his lungs. He was about to take off the overalls when his phone rang.

He took off his gloves and answered.

"Cortes."

"Alex, it's Karla. I sent some officers to the DHL shop to investigate, and guess what?"

"I don't know," he said between coughs.

"It's one of the few shops that don't have surveillance cameras. No one remembers anything weird. Our guy paid in cash, and there are no traces. I checked the name he signed the document with, and it's false. We've collected the delivery man's and the employees' prints, but Mario says everything is clean. All the prints on the box are from the people we have checked."

"I knew it. This guy isn't an improviser. He's a schemer."

There was silence.

"Are you still there, Alex?"

"Yes. Anything else?"

"There is some good news. We have a clue in the box. It

looks like a good one."

"Great, we also have a clue. A piece of paper between the dead man's teeth with some sort of riddle on it."

"He's playing with us."

"Exactly. Listen, we're leaving Sabadell now and will be in Barcelona shortly. We need to prepare ourselves because this won't be the last parcel we get.

30

Alex returned to the police station.

Being driven by a chauffeur pleased him, even if it was sporadic.

The patrol car entered Travessera de les Corts. Parked as far as the eye could see were vans belonging to some of the biggest national and international TV channels.

"Have you ever seen anything like this?" asked Alex to Rexach.

"Yes, once. Years ago, there was a case with the same intense media coverage," answered the Lieutenant. "We were following the trail of a murderer. A clue led us to believe that a girl's body could be in the Sau swamp. The press found out. It looked like a journalism college camp. They stalked us for a week. It was absolute chaos."

The army of journalists was waiting for any signs of movement inside and outside the station.

"Not even the rain stops them. They're relentless."

"It's a juicy case. If you were a journalist, would you be just like them?"

"I sure would. I'd be here for as long as I needed to be,"

said the chief as the car entered the garage, camera flashes blinding them through the windows. "I just hope nobody leaks sensitive information in our case."

"Did you manage to find anything?" mused Alex.

"You mean the girl's murderer?"

"No, the body."

"It wasn't in the swamp. It was in her house, under a concrete slab," he concluded, climbing out of the vehicle.

Alex entered the office. When Karla saw him, she motioned for him to join her in the meeting room.

They both entered.

"Please tell me you found something else," he said without preamble.

"Roberto has made a mistake."

Alex was surprised.

"What do you mean?"

"I think that in his haste, he forgot to remove a small manufacturer's mark from the cardboard box."

"Go on."

"I thought about the following things; when you tried to remove the cardboard box from the outer one, they were so tight it was almost impossible. So I thought that the manufacturer of both boxes could be the same. I found out that this manufacturer always prints a small mark. I guess it was covered with the tape, which is why we didn't spot it at first."

"And did you call the manufacturer?"

"It's a box for shipments of refrigerated products. Or rather, it's designed for refrigerated orders placed in online stores."

"Interesting."

30

"I have spoken to the manufacturer. They only sell to wholesalers. He has four main customers and sells through his website. He will provide us with all the lists of his sales for the boxes."

"Excellent, it may be a good lead to follow."

"What about yours?"

Alex pulled out his cell phone and showed her what they'd found between the dead man's teeth.

"What's this?"

"It looks like a bar code," he said.

"Wait," said Karla, pulling out her phone. "I have an app that can help us. When I go to the supermarket, I scan all the bar codes. This app tells me if food has gluten in them, if it's healthy, and so on."

Karla scanned the code, and the application searched for a match.

"No. It doesn't match any regular products."

"I didn't think it would be that easy," sighed Alex, putting his phone on the table.

Then he turned to the board where they had collated all the clues.

"This has just begun, Karla. It's just begun," he repeated disconsolately and clasped his hands behind his head.

There were a few moments of silence.

"Wait, I've got an idea," she said, taking out her cell phone again. "Alan, hi, it's Karla Ramirez from the investigation unit. Can you come to the meeting room next to the boss's immediately? Thanks."

"Immediately?" asked Alex.

"Yes, otherwise, it'll take him half an hour," Karla replied.

"Who is he?"

"Alan, the forensic IT guy. He's a genius, you'll see."

Within minutes there was a soft, almost timid knock at the door.

"Come in, Alan."

The door opened slowly. As soon as it was half open, a head popped around it.

"Is this the right room?" said Alan, looking relieved when he spotted Karla.

A cap covered his hair, and his rectangular glasses appeared held together with tape. He wasn't in uniform and was wearing a long-sleeved checked shirt.

"Come in, please, Alan."

With the speed of a sloth, he entered.

"Before we start, you can't say a word to anyone about anything you see here. This case has been declared legally confidential by the court."

The man had already scanned the board and nodded.

"Come and sit down," said Karla. She showed him the photo of the barcode. "This was left for us by a serial killer."

"The one with the van?" he said, looking at the board over his glasses and wrinkling his nose.

Karla looked at Alex, who shrugged.

"Yes."

"We think it contains a message, but we have no idea how to decipher it."

Alan grunted.

"Barcodes are a sequence of bars of different thicknesses that follow a pattern and an algorithm, and these bars represent a specific number. Let me look up something on your cell phone," said Alan to Karla, "We don't know the number, but we can find out."

He opened an internet search engine, downloaded an application and scanned the code.

"Here it is! This barcode represents the number 18.09.06.05.20.21," he said, handing the phone back to Karla and adjusting his glasses.

He stood up to leave, but Alex held out his hand.

"Not so fast, Alan. What does this number mean?"

"I don't know. I have no idea."

"But wait, we need your help. Imagine if all the corpses have one of these numbers on them. What should we do?"

Alan glanced at Karla.

"I don't know. When you have them all, we'll see," said Alan.

"Yeah, but what if it's a message from the killer? What I mean is, if we could get ahead of him, we could catch him before he decides to send us any more body parts."

"When you get the second one, we'll talk again," replied the computer scientist.

"I don't understand," Alex replied.

"It's simple. When you only have one coordinate of a map, you can't understand anything, right? But when you have more than one, even if it's only two, we can intuit the movement, the direction. I don't mean it's a direction or a map. If it's a riddle that the killer is giving us, we must wait to understand the pattern. Until then, we don't know anything. Can I go now?"

"Yes, thanks, buddy."

Alan left without another word.

"He's a little weird, but he's so smart," said Karla once the door closed.

They had a number, but it wasn't enough. The game had

begun, and the two policemen had no idea what the rules were. They only had one number, which probably wouldn't be the only one.

His phone vibrated on the table. Alex picked it up, frowning as he saw the caller's name. He looked at the clock; it was almost night.

"Excuse me, Karla, I have to get this," he said, leaving the room.

The policewoman went over the clues. She wrote down the number Alan had given her on the blackboard and made a note of pending issues for the next day.

When she finished, Alex returned.

"Your girlfriend?

"My mother," he said, staring at the floor.

"What happened with Mary?"

"It's none of your business."

The woman raised her hands.

"I see that you're still on the defensive."

"Life is a swing; sometimes you're up, sometimes you're down," said Alex pausing in the doorway. "I need to clear my head. See you tomorrow," he said and slammed the door shut.

The windows rattled, and Karla tutted, grateful she wouldn't have to put up with the sergeant much longer before he left for his new position in Tarragona.

31

Alex needed to go for a run.

When he got home, he changed his clothes and went along the promenade to release some dopamine. He didn't want to be tempted to call any of his ex's willing to reminisce about old times. Nor did he feel like going to a bar for too much alcohol that he would regret the following day or crawling into bed to mourn Mary's absence.

He turned up the music in his earbuds and ran faster.

The image of the severed head wouldn't leave him, just as the putrid smell had stayed with him.

"Why did they send that package to me? Why me?"

He remembered the label on the box. His name. Then he remembered one more detail. One that had slipped his mind.

Sergeant Cortes.

Sergeant, not corporal!

The promotion was still so recent.

He ran to Maremágnum, passing in front of a store with a television screen broadcasting the news about the kidnapped child and the press conference.

Then it dawned on him. Whoever had sent the package to him must have followed the kidnapped kid's story. Maybe he'd been picked because of that. His new rank, Sergeant, had been assigned to him after that case.

Karla informed him that the package had been held at the DHL store from Monday to Wednesday. Therefore, it must have been prepared over the weekend. On Sunday, the killer had chosen him.

But why him?

He took out his phone and sent a message. He wanted to see *her*; he needed to talk and feel affection. She was the only person who could understand him and his situation, or at least that was what he hoped.

Ana was many things to Alex, but more than anything, she was a good friend.

32

He took a quick shower.

He jumped in the car and headed to the other side of Barcelona. Something told him it would be worth the drive. He took the Ronda Litoral and continued to his exit. The sound of the rain lulled him, and he pressed the Spotify audio to play one of his favorite songs, *Secret Garden* by Bruce Springsteen. Just what he needed.

He parked and climbed the four floors, taking the steps two at a time.

"Don't ring the doorbell. Text me," he remembered her telling him.

Alex did as instructed.

He waited at the door, brushing back his wet hair. The door opened, and Ana leaned against it, inspecting him.

"You look awful," she said bluntly.

He sighed.

"Can I come in?"

"Go through to the living room. I'll be back in a minute," she said, closing the front door and disappearing into her bedroom.

Alex followed her with his eyes and went into the living room, looking at her impressive collection of books.

The house smelled of freshly made food and baby cologne. Despite her challenging but successful career, Ana had also achieved everything she had longed for in the personal sphere. A partner, a beautiful son and a place to call home in her adoptive city, Barcelona.

Books filled the room. But the most beautiful shelf was the one with her name printed on the spines. Three years younger than him, yet she'd already published four books in her specialization. The latest one had just been published.

"Ana Cortes: The Criminal Mind and its Environment."

Alex picked it up and leafed through it.

On the first page was a dedication where she mentioned her family and the families torn apart by serial killers.

He was proud of his sister. It was four hundred pages of work, effort and many sacrifices.

He'd just put it back on the shelf when Ana returned.

"Have you eaten anything today?"

"No, but it doesn't matter."

"It does matter! Have you seen yourself?"

Alex glanced at his reflection in the mirror on the wall.

"Why? What's wrong with me?"

"Come on, let's see if I can find something for you."

"Every day, you remind me more of Mom." He followed her into the kitchen, "Is he asleep?"

"Yes, not long ago."

She opened the refrigerator, took out a plastic container and put it in the microwave.

"What happened this time with Mary?"

32

"How do you know about Mary?"

His sister turned and looked at him with narrowed eyes.

"Whenever you show up here so late, it's because of your love life! Don't you see the pattern?"

He laughed.

"It's over."

"You said the same with the one you had before. What was her name?"

"Agustina."

"Agustina, yes! When are you going to settle down?"

"This time, it's different. She's gone back to the USA, returned her keys and left."

Ana left the refrigerator door open and turned around with her eyes wide open.

"Really?"

He nodded, somewhat embarrassed.

She took out some bread and put it in the toaster.

"Mom's going to be so upset," she said. "You know how much she takes our relationships and partners to heart. Did she at least call Mom to say goodbye?"

"I doubt it very much. She just got her stuff and left."

Ana leaned on the counter to wait for the microwave to finish.

Alex looked admiringly at her. She was wearing high-waisted pants, a style he didn't like. They looked old-fashioned to him, even though they were all the rage again. She wore them with a white blouse that gave her authority. Two open buttons hid her bra but accentuated her curves. Her beautiful curly brunette hair was pulled up in a scrunchie. The curls were a family trademark from their father, that said, *"these children are mine"*.

"Alex, I'm sorry, but you should have seen it coming for months! I guess you were blinded by infatuation."

He let out a sigh. Another lost battle. He heard a mewing sound from the bedroom, probably his nephew, asleep in his crib.

"Where's Alberto?"

"He's working. He had a long meeting today. By the way, congratulations on saving the president's son. At least work is going well for you," she said, putting some chicken with roasted peppers on one plate and some bread on another.

"Thanks," he said, picking up his fork. "I just really needed to talk tonight."

"What you should be doing is eating, not talking."

"What's this?" he said, grabbing her hand and pointing to her new ring. "Is it new?"

"You're the first to see it. We were planning to announce it on Sunday."

"You're getting married?" He looked at the engagement ring, a solitaire diamond in a white gold band.

"Alberto gave it to me last weekend."

"Jeez, what a rock! Business must be going well for him!"

"Yes, he's pleased. What about your job?"

"Work isn't going as well as you imagine. That's partly why I've come round," he said, frowning as he poked the chicken with his fork. "I've asked for a transfer."

"What for?"

"I want to go back to Tarragona. The Corps has accepted my request, so I'm leaving in a few weeks."

"Really? When did you make this decision?"

"I wanted to go with Mary, but she preferred New York to Tarragona," he said with a short laugh.

His sister grimaced.

"Man, I don't blame her for that."

"But Ana, Tarragona is our home, not this big city, so unfriendly…"

"Unfriendly for you because you haven't found *your* Barcelona yet."

"Look at this madman, for example. Do you know what he just did?"

"What are you talking about now?"

"The van guy."

The woman raised her eyebrows, and instantly her interest in the conversation increased.

"What's going on? Can you talk about it?"

"I can trust you, right? There's a confidentiality ruling in place, so you know how it is."

The woman made a gesture as if zipping her mouth shut.

Alex explained everything that had happened: the van full of corpses, the macabre package and all the incongruities of the case.

"Oh, man. What I'd give to be involved in a case like that."

"C'mon, Ana. This guy is a psycho. The further away from this, the better."

"But he's the most prolific serial killer in the city's history. It'll mark a before and after in your station and throughout Catalunya. And you want to leave?" she cried, "You're crazy!"

Alex scratched his head.

"What do you think?"

The woman chewed her lip and looked thoughtful.

"When I was studying in Massachusetts, one of the classes was about the *modus operandi of* serial killers. These guys look normal, just like anyone else. They're not the typical weirdos you can spot from a mile away. No! What makes them different is that they're calculating, meticulous, and detail-oriented. When investigators thought they'd found a clue or a thread to pull, it was only because the killer had *decided* to leave them a clue. They're usually people of great intelligence, who lack humor and with little or no empathy," said Ana as Alex ate. "When the investigators caught them, they seemed like regular people. But there were two types. The ones who killed for fun and had so many corpses piling up that they had to get rid of them however they could. The second type comes up with a plan and executes it to a T. The latter are the most difficult because they're harder to catch. If the police eventually catch them, it's usually many years later or because the killer wants to be caught."

Ana paused for a moment to think.

"I don't think you're going to catch this guy anytime soon, and I don't doubt that he has more surprises in store," she said, folding her arms. "Get ready because they're coming."

Alex was finishing the chicken. It was so delicious that he cleaned his plate with the bread.

"I don't care, Ana. I'm going to Tarragona in a week, so they'll have to manage without me."

She took his empty plate and put it into the dishwasher.

"Mom called me yesterday. Are you coming on Sunday?"

Alex scratched his head.

"She only just told me today. Can I go with you?"

"Of course. I'll message you to confirm the time."

Alex's phone vibrated in his back pocket. For an instant, he hoped it was Mary. But when he looked at the screen, it was Karla.

"Cortes here."

32

"Alex, we've found a fingerprint. Let's go and get the son of a bitch!"

33

Alex felt the same fear he'd felt when he'd opened the box.

No other investigation had affected him quite like this one. The memory of the severed heads and the expressions on their faces was tormenting him. What had those eyes seen? He wished he could put duty aside and do what he always used to do when he was a kid: crawl under the comforter and wait for the ghosts to go away.

"All right, wait for me. I'll be at headquarters in twenty minutes," he told Karla.

He hung up and looked at his sister.

"We have something. I've got to go."

"Good luck, little brother."

"Thank you for the chicken. It hit the spot."

She walked him to the door, and they hugged.

"Take care," said Ana before closing the door.

As soon as it closed, he heard the key turn three times.

Alex ran down the stairs, looking at the clock. He was feeling much better. It wasn't because of the chicken or the warmth of his sister's home: it was the simple fact of talking to a loved one, a friend and a sister who also acted like a mother when necessary.

33

He sped toward the police station. Traffic was almost nonexistent at that time of night.

He rolled down the window and turned the music up so loud that he couldn't hear the engine. He turned down the volume when he left Avinguda Diagonal and entered Travessera de les Corts, parking the car right outside the entrance. There was no sign of the press and guessed that even they needed a break sometimes. He went down to the garage in the basement, where everyone was already waiting. The Lieutenant and Karla were wearing bulletproof vests. There was also an assault team with an SUV, two vans and several camouflaged cars.

"Okay, everyone's here," said the boss when he saw Alex arrive. "Come on, let's go."

They all got into their cars and quickly left the station. The convoy was headed by a patrol car leading the way with blues lights but no sirens.

Karla was driving, the Lieutenant was in the passenger seat, and Alex was in the back.

"We've got him, Alex," said the chief, turning around. "We've identified him."

"Where was the print?" asked Alex.

"In the van. The son of a bitch had wiped it squeaky clean, but the team found a print on the fuse box. The guy changed a component without gloves. We've caught him. We'll be at his house in an hour."

Alex listened in surprise.

"What's his name?"

"Pere Franco. Look at the file in this folder," said the boss handing it to him.

Alex picked it up and began to flick through it. On the flap on the inside was a photograph of the individual. It was a man with heavy stubble and dark, disturbing eyes.

"If I saw him on the street, I'd cross the street," said the sergeant. "What does he do for a living?"

"As far as we know, he's a meat dealer. He has a lamb farm and exports to France. Apparently, he's self-employed and up to date with social security and taxes. He's had a few fines but nothing worth mentioning."

Alex looked at the file while the car traveled along the highway toward Girona. A few years ago, the man had been convicted of theft and swindling. All the signs pointed to him being their man.

After reading the documents, Alex stared out the window. His sister's words went around his mind on a loop.

He looked at his phone; still no word from Mary. He logged into the instant messaging app and saw that she was online.

He tampered down the urge to message her.

"We're almost there," said the chief.

The cars entered the road that led to the house. The building was on the outskirts, at the foot of the Gabarres, the mountains surrounding Girona.

A helicopter arrived at the scene, suddenly illuminating the building as the procession of cars and vans arrived.

The beams of lights from the cars made a strange, almost funereal dance on the dusty road.

The farm consisted of several buildings: a barn, a house and a building in the middle, flat and gray.

When the vans stopped, a swarm of tactical officers spread throughout the complex.

One used a battering ram on the front door, which smashed open effortlessly. They entered in twos.

33

"I'm going in," said Alex, drawing his weapon and going in last.

The chief stood outside with radio in hand, and Karla followed Alex.

Alex followed the officers' trail as the doors slammed and officers shouted *'Clear'*.

Once they'd checked the first floor, they went upstairs. When the first two officers were on the second floor, a message on the radio froze them in their tracks.

"He's escaped out the back door."

Half of the officers stopped and turned around. Alex and Karla found themselves leading the team and left through the back door.

"He's running through the woods."

Once they were outside, they received another message from the helicopter.

When they reached the rear of the house where the forest began, the vehicle's beam of light indicated the location of the fleeing fugitive. As they ran toward him, Alex put his gun. Without it, he could run faster than the others.

After several minutes of sprinting, he began to catch up with the man.

"Stop! Police!" he shouted.

But the fugitive ignored him and carried on running. Alex was almost within touching distance when the man disappeared from view. They were at the top of a steep slope, and the man was putting more distance between them.

He turned around and saw Karla panting to keep up, followed by more officers with lights on their helmets

They were too slow; he would have to go on alone.

He threw himself down the slope.

Trying to increase his speed was difficult, but he was almost on top of the man. He suddenly noticed that the suspect was running barefoot. He must be really desperate, thought Alex, gritting his teeth.

"Stop! Damn it! Stop!" Alex shouted, throwing himself on top of him in a desperate rugby tackle. They fell together into the bushes, and Alex didn't loosen his grip despite the blows raining down on his head.

"Got you, you fucking bastard," he shouted.

A few seconds later, Karla appeared, the lights from the helicopter illuminating her. She pointed her gun at the man without taking her eyes off his face.

"We've got him," crackled the radio.

34

On the other side of the two-way mirror, the cameras were recording. Alex's head was bandaged, covering the scratches caused by the fall. The suspect wore handcuffs, and his eyes darted around the room like a caged animal.

He was older than he'd looked in the photos. He had a dark complexion, but his hair was longer. A long, thick white beard covered the bottom half of his face.

"I want to go in and talk to him," said Alex to the boss.

The chief waved his hand, allowing him to pass.

"I want to be there, too," said Karla.

Alex nodded at her.

"Okay, but give me some time alone with him, and then he's all yours."

She shook her head and pursed her lips but complied without protest.

Alex nodded, swallowed the last sip of coffee, took another from the machine and walked into the interrogation room.

He rested the file on the table next to the two-way mirror and sat back in his chair, looking out the window. He knew who was on the other side and that they were recording. The man must have known it too. Alex turned to look at the suspect and stared at him.

The detainee said nothing.

They held each other's gaze. Alex didn't plan to lower it, even though he was wary of the man. Showing fear was a weakness.

After a minute, the man lowered his eyes.

"What's your name?"

"Fuck you."

"I don't think that's your name," he said without taking his eyes off him. "Try again."

The man showed no signs of cooperating.

Alex slammed his hand down on the metal table, and the man looked startled.

They looked at each other contemptuously.

"Why do you want to know?" he spat.

"For the record. To know if you're the person we think you are."

The man didn't answer.

"Look, I'm telling you, you're in the shit, not me."

He still didn't react.

"Your house is being turned upside down right at this very second by forensics. If you have even one thing out of place, a stain that doesn't belong there, or an invoice you haven't paid tax for, they will find it.

The man licked his lip but didn't speak.

"Why don't you tell me why you did it?"

Despite the air conditioning, the man began to sweat. His right leg jiggled nervously.

"Do you want us to stay here all night?" asked Alex, folding his arms and pushing away from the table. "I'm in no hurry."

34

"I want to make a call. It's within my rights."

"Sorry, buddy. You don't have any rights, and if you do, I don't give a fuck. You're going to stay here as long as I say. Do you hear me?"

The man swallowed loudly, and Alex saw him tremble.

Alex took a sip from the cup. He hadn't slept for ages, but unlike the other man, he had his ally, coffee.

"Look, it's straightforward," he said. He put down the glass and wiped a drop of the black liquid from his mouth. "You have two choices. The first one is that we stay here for as many days as you need to tell me the truth. But you'll stay in that chair while I go out to eat, sleep, and come back in, fresh as a daisy, with nothing to lose. You will only eat and drink when I say you can. Trust me; you will talk," he said, standing with his arms crossed, looking in disdain at the man.

The other man banged his handcuffed hands on the table, shaking uncontrollably.

"Damn it! I didn't want to do it, but he talked me into it!"

35

The early morning had suddenly taken an interesting turn.

Alex uncrossed his arms and approached the suspect, frowning; he couldn't believe what he was hearing.

The boss and Karla listened to the conversation on the other side of the glass without missing a single detail.

"You got it, Alex. Squeeze him like a lemon."

"Nah, it's too easy, boss," Karla replied.

"Ramirez, don't be such a pessimist. It's him; he just said it was."

Karla added nothing more. She remained seated, waiting to see how the scene in front of them would pan out.

"Tomas convinced me to do it. I didn't want to," said the detainee between sobs. "But no. Fuck, man! I didn't think we would have so many problems. I have a family to feed, you know?"

"Who's Tomas?"

The man looked around.

"If I snitch, he'll make me pay."

"If you don't help me, you'll pay for it anyway."

"What a load of shit, man. I didn't expect this."

"Nobody expects it until it happens. Come on, tell me who Tomas is and what he made you do."

"It's the farmer next door. I buy the lambs from him."

Alex was surprised.

"What else?"

"He offered me a deal."

"What kind of deal?"

"He had some goats that weren't registered, you know, not legal."

"No, I don't know, tell me."

"Tomas has a farm that public health doesn't know about. He has a lot of unregistered cattle. You know, they're cheaper. Damn it!"

"So?"

"We sell them in France and make a lot of money."

"France?"

"Yes, they pay a lot in France, and we don't legally declare the money."

Alex scratched his beard and looked through the glass.

"Now I understand the new van. It's a Mercedes Vito, right? Registered six months ago, brand new, bought with cash," said Alex, grimacing as he looked at the tax report. "Not bad."

"Fuck. Yes," said the man, running his hands through his hair.

On the other side of the glass, Karla cleared her throat and glanced sideways at the Lieutenant.

"What did I tell you?"

"This guy's not our man, damn it!" the Lieutenant shouted, sweeping a glass of water off the table onto the floor. He opened the door and stomped out, leaving Karla alone.

She got up, closed the door and stayed to see what Alex was doing on the other side.

"So, you don't pay taxes on those lambs, right?"

"I'm sorry, man," he said tearfully.

Alex looked at the file and looked up.

"And your old van, what make was it?"

The man looked at him and thought.

"An Opel Vivaro."

"Why didn't you trade it in when you bought the Mercedes?"

"Because I put it up for sale, and a guy called me the next day. I sold it for more than the Mercedes dealership valued it at."

"And this guy… did he contact you?" said Alex, surprised.

"Yeah, man. A real weirdo. What's this all about?"

"Do you remember his face?"

"I don't know. It was about six months ago. Besides, the freak never took off his glasses."

"Wait, wait, let's go back to the day he came to see you. What happened?"

The man looked at the table and raised his hands.

"I don't know, the usual. He came, he liked it, we did the paperwork, and he paid me."

"How did he pay you?"

"The van wasn't expensive because it had high mileage, and when he saw it, he told me he'd pay more if I accepted cash in hand. What was I supposed to do? I needed the money fast to buy another one. I couldn't have two vans."

"When did he call you? Did he call you from a cell phone? Do you have his number?"

"He always had his caller ID blocked. I never called him."

"He didn't give you a phone number to text him?"

"No."

"Did you have a contract?"

The man nodded.

"Where is it?" asked Alex.

The man pondered for a moment.

"In the office. I think it's in the second drawer in the desk."

Alex sent a message to Karla from his phone.

On the other side of the glass, Karla opened it.

"Do you remember which pen you used to sign the contract?"

"I can't remember, just a random pen." Then he corrected himself. "No! Wait, he had a pen, and I used that. I think it had a company logo on the side."

"Can you remember the name?"

"No."

"Think hard. Anything you remember could be relevant."

"I think it was blue and orange."

"What else do you remember?"

"It was cold, and he was wearing gloves but didn't take them off."

"The voice? What was his voice like?"

"I don't know, very deep. And the glasses were like aviator glasses, dark."

Alex kept taking notes.

"What else, what else do you remember about him?"

"Now that you mention it, I did wonder why he needed an isothermal van. He was quite classy. Polite, calm. I made a couple of jokes, but the guy didn't even crack a smile. I wasn't bothered. I was just happy to have gotten such a good deal.

He took it and left."

Alex pondered on the man's words. He scratched his head and sighed.

"We need you to work with our artist to sketch an impression."

"Okay, but what happened to my van?" asked the man, his face changing as the realization dawned. "Don't fuck with me, man. The killer's van is mine? I can't believe it. Wait til I get to the bar and tell my friends about this! I'm going to be the fucking boss!"

Alex stood up suddenly, and his chair clattered back onto the floor.

"You know that we found dead people in that vehicle? And you want to brag that it was your car? What if your sister or daughter had been in there? Or you? Would you be talking like this?"

Clenching his jaw, Alex glared at the man.

"I'm sorry," the man said, his cheeks flushing.

"You'd better keep this quiet. If you go around leaking sensitive information, you'll be breaking the law, and we can re-arrest you. You could get several years in jail if you let any comments slip out."

"All right, man, I won't say a thing. Can I go now?"

"Not yet. Some of my colleagues need to speak to you, and then we'll see."

Alex picked up his papers and gulped back the last sip of coffee.

He approached the door. He was about to leave but then stopped.

"Hang on, if this guy left with your van… how did he get to your house?"

36

Barcelona.
Thursday.

Alex left the interrogation room.

Karla was waiting for him. On the other side of the glass, he could see the man leaning on the table in a desperate attempt to rest despite the lights and the discomfort of the metal chair.

Alex said nothing until he put the folder on his desk and poured a glass of water from the carafe.

"What do you think?" she asked.

"We think we're moving forward, but in reality, we're just going in circles."

"I think it's a good step, even if it doesn't seem like it right now."

"But don't you see? That guy doesn't know anything. He's a fucking dead end. Why the hell can't you see it, Karla?" he shouted, pushing the folder to the floor.

The woman looked at him out of the corner of her eye without speaking.

"You're tired. Why don't you go and rest for a while?"

"Tired…what the fuck?"

"Hey, chill out," she said, cutting him off. "We're on the same side. I want to catch Roberto just as much as you do, okay?"

Alex didn't answer. He ran his hands over his forehead and sat down while Karla picked up the folder and its contents from the floor.

"I'm sorry. You're right. I am tired."

"We're all starting to feel the pressure, but it's not an excuse to yell at each other." He gave her a tight smile. "Did you do what I asked?"

"Yes."

"And?"

"I've got it."

"Why didn't you tell me?" he shouted again.

"I don't give a damn if you're my boss. I won't tolerate you yelling at me."

Alex stood up and took another glass of water. He took a deep breath and stretched his back. Then he closed his eyes, rolled his neck from side to side, and when he opened them again, he saw Karla frowning at him with her arms crossed.

"Have you finished your little show?"

"Come on, please. Show me what you got," said Alex in a completely different tone.

Karla walked over and rested her phone on the table, pointing at a photo.

"An officer on scene has just sent me this. It was right where he told you it was."

"What name was it?"

"The same as the one who sent the package."

"Bastard."

"He's planned everything well. When I was listening to you, I wondered why he wanted to pay in cash and took the contract with him. He promised to send it to the traffic authorities, and the seller was fine with that. But the killer didn't do anything. He never filed any documents and used the van pretending he was the previous owner."

"Well, yes. Even if the car needed an inspection, he could have said he was an employee of the original owner," commented Alex. "We have to find out how he made his way to pick up the car."

"Maybe by bus. But no one will remember something that happened six months ago, and there probably won't be any CCTV available now."

Alex pressed his hand to his mouth.

"We need to ask Alan about the barcode number."

"I'll ask him as soon as he arrives," she said, glancing at the clock.

"Why don't we go and get something to eat? The coffee shop opens in fifteen minutes. I need to talk to you about something."

Alex nodded. He looked one last time at the man sitting with his head in his hands and followed her.

The two officers waited a few minutes outside the closed coffee shop until it opened at six.

The aroma of freshly baked croissants was even more comforting than the cozy ceiling lights.

They picked up some pastries and coffee and went to sit at the back. The shop was still empty; they were the first customers.

"Do you remember when we used to come here together all the time?" Karla asked, stirring sugar into her coffee.

"I can't believe you're still thinking about that. You're getting married in a few months, and you come up with this."

The woman clenched her jaw.

"We can't change the past, but we can't forget it either," she replied.

"What did you want to tell me? You said that you'd discovered something."

Karla sighed.

"I've reviewed the purchases on the company website that makes the boxes."

Alex nodded as he ate his *ensaimada*.

"I've screened all the purchases of only four, five or six units."

"And?"

"There are tons!"

"Just from Barcelona?"

"No. There's only one company and one private buyer from here," she said, shrugging. "I'll send two officers to check them out this morning."

Alex let out a grunt.

"What else have we got?"

"The corpse's fingerprints. We'll know more this morning."

"We need to find out who the victim was," said Alex. He took a sip of his latte and continued, "Have your guys been able to find any clues about the route the van took?"

"We have some CCTV to check."

"Is it usual to keep the recordings for more than a month?"

"In this case, yes. The cameras belong to a company that

stores compressed recordings in the cloud for at least over a year."

"So, where do the clues lead us?"

"To an extraordinary place that I'd like to show you."

37

Alex wondered if his sister was right after all.

Perhaps all the clues they'd found were only crumbs scattered intentionally by the killer.

How could he know?

The only possible answer was to systematically investigate the clues they'd found until now. Statistically, one could be a mistake or an oversight.

No one could commit a perfect homicide. At least, that was what Ana Cortes always claimed during TV and radio interviews. Since her brother had found the most mediatic kidnapped child in Spanish history, she'd been inundated with invitations to give her expert opinion.

The Cortes name had become a burden, a responsibility.

If he could, Alex would have preferred to remain invisible, so he could keep investigating without being recognized everywhere he went. It didn't bother Ana, though; she knew how to comfortably surf the media wave her brother's fame generated.

Alex was in the passenger seat, sitting next to Karla. The

undercover car was stuck in traffic on what was an ordinary Thursday for most people. On the radio, a national morning talk show debated what the media had to say about the serial killer.

Alex thought he knew what to expect but was surprised when the radio host did a call-in for members of the public to ask questions. The first was from a woman.

"Hello, Juanma," she said.

"What's your name, and where are you calling from?" the host asked.

"My name's Montse and I'm from Barcelona."

"Hello, Montse from Barcelona. What do you think about all this?"

"Juanma, I listen to you every day. Today was the first time I've ever dared to call you."

"Thank you, Montse! How are you? Tell us your opinion on the news."

"You're lucky you live in Madrid. Here in Barcelona, everyone is afraid. Living in a city with a serial killer on the streets is terrifying. I think the police are incompetent. They're not doing or saying anything. The national police should take over the investigation or even get the army out on the streets so we feel safe again."

"Montse, don't you think that's an over-exaggeration?"

"No, absolutely not! We're afraid to take the subway and walk around the city at night. We're afraid to go places alone. We're terrified, and we can't go on like this."

"Why do you speak in plural?"

"Because all my friends and I think the same. We walk our children to school in pairs, and my friends' kids, who go to university, always go in groups so that no one has to be alone.

College students have stopped going out at night or partying. We're just praying for this to end soon, Juanma."

The host sighed audibly and, after a beat, said,

"Well, thank you, Montse. We've heard the testimony of a listener from Barcelona. Now we'll hear more from our guests right after this commercial break!"

Alex looked at his partner.

"This sucks. It was the damn judge who ordered a blackout on the information we can share. But the public thinks we're not doing anything," he said, annoyed.

"It's a marketing principle: if it's not communicated, it doesn't exist."

"Since when did you become a marketing expert?"

"Never said I was, but my mother thinks the same as that woman, and so do her friends. They live miles away, but they're still afraid."

"Anyway, where are we going?"

"We're almost there."

After several kilometers of traffic jams, she parked in a street parallel to Diagonal.

The first light of day peeked out from behind the skyscrapers, making them sparkle and casting shadows between them.

Alex looked around. It was a university area full of expensive apartments. Garden sprinklers enhanced the aroma of freshly mowed lawns.

"What are we doing here?"

"Look," said Karla. "This is the area. Over there is where we got some of the CCTV."

The woman pointed to a house with a camera pointing to the main road.

"Looks like the house belongs to a millionaire. Are they from Barcelona?"

"Russian," she said, showing him some photos. They were images from the surveillance camera.

"I can't see much," he said.

"Look at this one," she said, passing him the next one.

He peered closely at it. The upper right corner was enlarged and showed a car wash.

"This is our van, but we lose trace after this."

"But wait a minute. I remember that day, and it was raining. What's the guy doing, washing a car in the rain?"

The girl shrugged.

"Maybe he was removing dust or something else. Mud, blood marks. I have no idea."

"No, there was no blood on the bodywork. Mario's report clearly stated that."

"I've read it too, but he was washing it for a reason."

Alex looked at the site and turned around.

"Let's go and check the place out."

The two policemen drove to the site and parked up.

"My guys are looking at the before and after recordings. All possible leads and pathways."

"You're doing an excellent job, Karla."

Alex started to walk without checking if she was following him.

The car wash was part of a gas station. There was an automatic car wash and a row of four boxes with a hose for self-service. The one in the photograph was the last one on the right. In the photo, the make of the van was visible as a man sprayed a pressure hose on its bodywork.

Alex walked around, scanning the whole place. He checked the box from the photograph, inch by inch. He checked the hosepipe, but the prints would be long gone by now—too much time had passed. Same with the coin; the guy had probably been wearing gloves, making identification almost impossible.

He searched for all cameras, but they all had screens covering the periphery view.

"What are you thinking?" asked Karla.

Alex turned around in surprise. He'd forgotten about her. "Sorry, what?"

"What do you think?" she repeated.

"I don't know. I'm weighing up all the possibilities," said the sergeant without looking at her. "If the van came in that way, stopped here to wash off Christ knows what, and then continued on to our station. We need to know what he had to clean. And above all – why here? I mean, why not somewhere else, further from the station? If he came from a quieter place with less risk of standing out, why didn't he wash the car full of bodies there? Or even the day before? What's clear is that our man did it intentionally. Roberto hasn't left anything to chance, Karla. If he stopped here, it was for a reason; we have to find out what that reason was."

"I agree with you, but what the hell are we looking for?" she said, stopping to look at him. "What are you doing, Alex?"

The sergeant crouched in the center of the car wash. He squinted at the slits where the dirty water pooled.

"I know it's crazy, but we have to try everything. Tell our science guys to check the sewer below this box. Who knows, maybe we'll find something."

37

"Are you kidding? You really want that checked?"

"Call the Lieutenant. If judicial permission is needed, let him call Her Honor and get it," he said, looking at the camera from where the photo he was holding came from. "Karla, the whole damn city is watching us, and we have to catch this son of a bitch. We can't leave any stone unturned. By the way, don't forget the filter in the central sewage treatment plant."

As soon as the policeman finished speaking, he turned to Karla and put his hand on her shoulder.

"Your team is doing an outstanding job. Really," he repeated with a smile.

She looked down at the ground and thanked him, returning the smile. Alex started walking toward the car, leaving her behind. As he turned around, he thought he saw her cheeks flush, but he couldn't tell for sure because she had her head down, staring at her phone.

"Shall we go?" he said, waiting for her to open the car.

Karla took a deep breath, fumbled in her pocket for the key, and the doors clicked open.

As Alex settled into his seat, his phone pinged with a text. He took it out and unlocked the screen.

"Come back to headquarters. We've identified the first man."

Karla got into the car after him. She waited a few seconds before inserting the key into the slot. Alex thought she was about to tell him something and felt uncomfortable as he observed her strange behavior. He looked straight ahead, waiting for the woman to say something.

"Should we go?" asked Alex cautiously, trying to change the subject so she wouldn't say something she might regret later.

"Yes," she replied, sighing as she started the car.

Alex didn't say anything else during the rest of the trip, knowing that sometimes silence speaks more than a long conversation.

38

The judge had authorized the identification of the first body.

For officers and forensics, that's all they were; a number or a body.

But the body in question was someone who had died—or, rather, someone *whose life had been taken away* by a ruthless killer.

Roberto had left nothing to chance. And it couldn't be by chance that he had sent the remains of the first corpse in a package addressed to the newly-promoted sergeant.

Roberto was astute and wouldn't have felt remorse for his victim. He'd used him to draw attention to something the police didn't yet know. He couldn't have shouted it out any louder if he'd tried.

The radio told Alex it was eight o'clock. They were only a few blocks from the station when there was a special announcement on the radio.

"A source has just confirmed that the van contained five cadavers."

Alex and Karla looked at each other, stunned.

"I'll be damned! How the hell did they find that out?" yelled Alex, punching the dashboard and almost triggering the airbag. "If I catch the guy who leaked that information, I'll hang him up by his balls."

"Wait, listen," said Karla, turning up the volume on the radio.

"We have been told that some media outlets have received insider information from the killer. He has left a code, a riddle, an enigma. We have checked the newspapers and can confirm that this code is front-page news. The code comprises around ten or twelve vertical parallel lines of different thicknesses, similar to a bar code without numbers. The killer has thrown down his gauntlet. The message says that each body will have a riddle to decipher, and he calls himself the Cryptogram Killer. *We'll hear more from our guests on this special news bulletin right after we take a short commercial break.*

"Fuck! The public will hang us out to dry," said Alex as they entered Travessera.

The car stopped at a red light as an ever-growing swarm of journalists surrounded their vehicle, trying to get a photo or a statement from Sergeant Cortes. Karla put her foot on the gas and drove toward the parking lot, leaving a trail of disappointed photographers in her wake.

"This is crazy," said Alex as the door closed.

The entire investigation team was seated in the meeting room.

"We've been waiting for you before we get started," said the Lieutenant.

"Have you seen the madness outside? We just heard the latest on the radio, and they know every goddamn detail. How the hell have they got this information? Alex said, taking a seat. He glared around the room. "Have we managed to get a copy of his email to the press yet?"

"Maria has already asked them to send us the email, and I've told Alan from IT to try and trace the IP address. Journos are blowing up our phone lines begging for more information."

"He's bringing us to our knees. We're more concerned about the journalists than the investigation," said Alex.

"Maybe we should have a small press conference to reassure the public," suggested Karla.

Rexach, who was coordinating the case, said nothing.

"Right, let's get on with the briefing," said the boss. "Our colleagues have been working against the clock and have just confirmed the identity of the first body. The victim's name is Miguel Rodriguez. Each of you has a copy of the photo in the folder on your chairs. Please open it."

The thirty officers gathered in the room all opened their folders. The chief handed one to Alex and Karla. They both opened it.

The man in the photo was young and slim, with dark hair and brown eyes.

"Miguel Rodriguez, twenty-two years old. According to the tax office, he was working in a small supermarket. Originally from Cáceres, we know he'd lived in Barcelona for several years. In the initial report, you can see his address, which is the only one he appears to have had," concluded the Lieutenant and then looked at Alex, who had stood up and was pacing.

"All right, we need to find out everything about this guy.

Who he is, where he's from, where he works and if he has any other jobs that he doesn't declare. His roommates. If he smokes, what brand he smokes. What he does in his spare time or if he has a girlfriend or a boyfriend. How often he goes to the toilet. We need to know everything," said Alex. "We need to find out his last steps and, most importantly, how he met Roberto. That last one is our priority."

He fell silent, looking at the team.

"Find out what Miguel did in the last days of his life and where and when he crossed paths with our killer," he concluded, pointing to the top of the whiteboard, where the name Roberto was written with the composite sketch below.

"Any questions?" asked Karla.

No one in the room spoke.

"Who's following the search for the box that arrived by DHL?" asked Alex.

A couple of officers raised their hands.

"How is it going?"

"There's no trace of Roberto," said one of the two officers pointing to the board. "The shop has no cameras, and no one remembers him. It's a very busy place. The surrounding stores don't have cameras either. The trail has vanished. We've checked public transport cameras, but we got nothing."

Alex looked at them, narrowing his eyes.

"Maybe we're looking for someone who comes in and out of town when he actually lives in the center. Maybe we should narrow the search area. He also went to a car wash on a rainy day. Why did he need to wash it?" said Alex, throwing the question out to everyone. Why did he have to wash it? The Luminol didn't reveal any blood stains on the bodywork; even if there had been, they wouldn't have come off with a hose.

Why did he wash it before parking it?" he wondered, almost to himself.

"Maybe he was cleaning off some mud? Perhaps the guy has a house outside the city and wanted to remove any trace of his location," said an officer.

"Well, it's a possibility, I guess. But something doesn't add up, and I'm not sure what it is. I think we're missing something. We need to think about it," concluded Alex, standing at the window with his hands stuffed in his pockets.

The sky was clear that morning; the bad weather had given the city a temporary break.

"Karla?"

She raised her eyebrows.

"How's the search going in the other delivery agencies? Any more packages?"

"We're checking them one by one, but it's taking a while because there are thousands," said one of her team.

"Okay, keep investigating," Karla confirmed and looked at Alex again.

"Good job. We need to move on. Karla, assign the officers who will be investigating the first victim."

She complied and assigned two pairs of officers to dig into the life of Miguel. Then they adjourned, and just Alex, Karla and the boss remained.

"I need to talk to you both," said the Lieutenant once they were alone. "It's clear we've got a mole in the team."

39

Everything gets complicated when sensitive information leaks out. It spreads like a tsunami, and when it gets into the wrong hands, it can mess up the whole investigation. It takes less time for a secret to spread than one thinks.

And secrets are the fodder of fools. They spread them as easily as you can pluck a petal off a daisy. And once money enters the equation, a secret is no longer water but gunpowder: the speed of propagation accelerates even more.

"We have a problem," said the Lieutenant. "We don't know where the information came from. The judge called me and asked me how the information could have gotten out. She didn't pull any punches and warned me to find out who the mole is."

"Yes, but some of the information was leaked by Roberto himself," said Karla, defending her team.

"In his e-mail, there was no information about the five bodies. It only mentioned the riddle."

Alex was silent, his jaw clenched.

"This damn case is supposed to be confidential. Who the

hell is risking the whole investigation?"

"I was wondering why the family haven't reported him missing," said Alex, "Don't you think that's strange?"

"Maybe they filed a missing person report in Cáceres, which, to be fair, is a long way from here," Karla replied.

"Yeah, we need to contact the local police," answered the Lieutenant.

"I'll take care of it," she replied.

"Who will inform the family?" asked Alex.

"Karla, call Cáceres to ask them to send someone to break the news, and while you're on to them, ask them if he's been reported missing," instructed the Lieutenant.

She nodded, and Alex tutted. The boss gave him a dirty look.

"You know what that means?" said Alex to the boss. "It will be all over the news in less than twelve hours."

"Anything else?" concluded the boss, ignoring Alex. "Keep your eyes open because I still think we have a mole."

"Boss, given the siege of journalists outside and the fact that I'll be staying to help you with this, is it okay if I park my car in the underground parking lot from now on?"

"Do you really want to stay?"

"Just a few days. So, yes or no?"

The boss nodded, and Alex left.

Once at his desk, he went through the messages on his phone. When he saw one from Mary, his heart began to thump. It started with an icy cold greeting that didn't sound like her. Alex didn't want to open it. He threw the cell phone across his desk and went to get a coffee.

"Aren't you overdoing it with the coffee?" asked Karla.

He didn't answer; the morning was turning to shit.

"Have you assigned anyone to check out the supermarket yet?" he asked Karla.

"Yes, two officers. Why?"

"I want to go myself."

She stared at him, her eyebrows raised.

"Can I come with you?"

"No, no worries. I know you've got a lot of work to do here. I'll keep you in the loop."

Alex returned to his desk. He searched for an online Catalan newspaper and clicked. The headlines screamed, *The Cryptogram Killer*. Roberto already had a public name: clearly, he wanted to be remembered. The article mentioned the riddle inside the parcel and the five bodies. He shook his head in frustration and closed the browser.

His email box was overflowing with emails from work colleagues wishing him all the best on his transfer. But then one caught his eye, with the subject line;

Did you like the package?

His blood turned to ice, and as his finger hovered over the mail, he noticed his hand was trembling. Maybe it was a hoax?

He opened the email, and his chest tightened.

It wasn't a mistake.

It was him.

It was from Roberto.

40

Alex scanned the screen.

He felt like he was falling, unsure how to react to the e-mail. He felt like the killer's plaything. And he felt the danger, too. What did this crazy bastard want from him?

He'd already opened the message, and it crossed his mind that he shouldn't have.

But he couldn't turn back.

He picked up the phone.

"Mario? No questions; just send Alan here right away."

"I can't, Alex. He's in the middle of examining a rapist's cell phone."

"It'll be ten minutes tops. It's urgent."

"What's wrong?"

"I can't tell you. Will you send him, please?"

Within a few minutes, Alan mooched into the room and sat at Alex's computer, watched by a concerned Alex and Karla.

"It's no problem that you opened it," he said, reassuring

Alex that he hadn't messed up.

"Can you find out where he sent it from?"

"That's what I'm working on."

He opened a program with green numbers on a black background, with code only a programmer could understand.

"It was sent from an encrypted email via a Swiss server. But before that, it was bounced by several DNSs worldwide."

"Explain it to me like you would a three-year-old."

Alan turned around and blinked.

"Ah, ok! The guy has used several firewalls, and we can't locate him. Switzerland won't tell us who owns an encrypted email account. It's like having an anonymous Swiss bank account, and they won't tell us who's the owner."

"Wait. I'll call the judge, and we'll send them an Interpol warrant. And then they'll have to damn well tell us!" said Alex with a cockiness he didn't feel.

"That's not how these things work, I'm afraid, Sir. Firstly, a Spanish judge can't do anything in Switzerland. Secondly, even if they wanted to, they couldn't tell us anything because it's anonymous. And with the game of bouncing around on various servers, it's impossible to find out who sent it."

"Are you telling me this guy just sent me an email, and we can't trace him?"

Alan turned and nodded.

"If you want to know, it's the same mail the newspapers received. I can't help you," he said, closing his laptop. As energetically as he came, he got up to leave.

"Is that it?"

Alan gave them a grin that looked more like a smirk and left without another word.

As soon as he disappeared through the door, Alex exploded.

40

"These IT guys are freaking weird," he growled.
Karla sat down and read the email:

"Did you like the package?
　It won't be the last.
　Get ready for another riddle.
　The girl went crazy when she saw it!"

"Another one is coming," said Alex, gritting his teeth as he looked out the window. "I wonder when."

41

Alex managed to escape using a typical magician's trick: capture the attention with the left hand and perform the trick with the right.

The same car came out of the parking lot with Karla at the wheel and another officer beside her. They sped off, and as soon as they stopped at the intersection, the journalists realized it wasn't Alex in the passenger seat.

He'd already left through the side door.

He crossed the city in his Mini.

The address he'd entered in the GPS took him to La Mina, a troubled neighborhood where some days /not even the police dared to enter. The car didn't go unnoticed, attracting small gangs of young people who swarmed the streets and did everything except go to school.

Alex parked on the street, praying nothing would happen to his new car.

He fumbled in the jacket to feel his weapon and check it wasn't visible.

He grabbed his phone and climbed out of the car.

41

The streets were filled with violence and tension, an uneasy atmosphere that unsettled Alex.

People looked at him as if he'd just landed from Mars. He took a deep breath and locked the vehicle.

He looked up and checked for cameras around him. Poverty was all around him, and he felt a moment's pity for those forced to live here. None of the grim-looking shops looked to have CCTV, and most were covered in graffiti

He followed the directions on his phone. Before turning and leaving the main road, he saw a tram stop, but again, he couldn't see any surveillance cameras, either on the canopy or on the poles. It felt like a ghost town in a Western.

He walked down some narrow streets and crossed the main road, constantly scanning for possible details and clues.

He arrived at his destination, a dirty, dilapidated supermarket with posters in various languages covering the windows. The dirt and grime accumulated outside on the sidewalk made one wonder about the hygiene of the premises.

He put his cell phone away and went inside.

As he walked through the door, the stench of fish hit him, and he pressed his fingers to his nose as he glanced around the store. He'd never been in such a dump and was surprised to see how busy it was.

He approached the counter and pulled the lapel of his jacket aside just enough for the man to see the badge.

"Police? What's going on?" said the man, his eyes flicking from side to side.

"My name's Sergeant Cortes. We're investigating the disappearance of your employee, Miguel Rodriguez."

"Miguel?" he asked with a frown a second before he

narrowed his eyes. "That scumbag scoundrel!"

"Scoundrel? Why do you say that?"

"Why? Because he left me in the shit. He hasn't been near the place for around a month! He's fired," he said and continued in a different tone. "Was he illegal?"

Alex ran his hand over his face. He looked around and noticed a girl listening nearby.

"What's your name?" he asked the supermarket owner.

"Yasir."

"I'm going to be straight with you, Mr. Yasir. Miguel is dead. I can't tell you anything else now, but I need all the information you can give me. The last day he came to work, his cell phone number, and so on."

The owner told Alex everything he knew, and Alex left him his business card in case he remembered anything else.

He took one last look around and left the store.

"Excuse me…"

Alex turned around and saw the girl who had been eavesdropping.

She was wearing a vest with the supermarket's name on it. When Alex saw tears welling in her eyes, something inside him twisted.

"I overheard you saying that Miguel is…" she said, unable to finish the sentence.

"Yes, did you know him?" he asked gently.

The girl nodded.

"How did you meet him?"

"We worked together here," she said between sobs. "What happened to him?"

"I'm afraid I can't tell you," said Alex, taking her elbow and guiding her to a bench to sit down.

"Did you notice any strange behavior in the last few days before he disappeared?"

"No... well, yes. He was looking for a job because he wanted to leave this place. He sent out dozens of CVs every day, and he'd been to a few employment agencies. Things were hard for him. He'd come from Cáceres to find a better life in Barcelona, but this job wasn't what he wanted, and he was desperate to leave," she said, sniffing.

Alex nodded.

"Do you know which agencies he went to?"

"No, he was a quiet guy, more so at work. He didn't want Yasir to know he was looking for another job."

"The owner gave me this phone number," said Alex, showing it to her. "Can you confirm that it's Miguel's?"

The girl checked her phone and confirmed it was.

"When was the last time you saw him?"

"Must have been about five weeks ago. I remember because we'd just celebrated his birthday at my house."

"And then?"

"Well... the earth swallowed him up. He stopped answering my calls and only answered by text. But he seemed really weird, saying he was fine but nothing else. It didn't sound like him."

"What do you mean?"

"Look."

The girl opened a messaging app and showed him their conversation.

"That's interesting," said Alex, looking at the screen.

From nowhere, an idea flashed through his mind. Something that might break the rules of Roberto's game.

"Text him now."

"Now? But he's dead!"

"I know. Send it anyway."

The girl didn't understand, but she did what Alex asked.

"Hi Miguel, are you there?" she typed on the screen and pressed send.

A second later, a tick appeared, confirming it had been delivered and the phone was still on.

"Do you expect him to answer or what?"

"Let's wait a minute."

They both stared at the screen, mesmerized.

After a few minutes, the ticks turned blue. *Message read.* The girl gasped, and Alex felt a rush of adrenalin. They looked at each other. The girl's eyes filled with tears again. She stood hugging her arms tightly around her and looked terrified.

Alex frowned.

Then the last thing he had expected happened. Under the name "Miguel" appeared the word "*Typing...*"

Alex inhaled sharply through his nose, trying to stay calm.

"Hi, Carmen. Yes, I'm here," read the reply.

With a gasp of horror, the girl dropped the phone, and it crashed to the ground.

"Shit," said Alex, picking it up and checking that it wasn't damaged. Luckily, the girl's pink silicone case had protected it.

He kept hold of the phone.

'Miguel' was still *online.* Alex swallowed noisily, plucked up his courage and pressed the call icon.

Slowly, fearfully, he lifted the device to his ear.

41

On the other side, he could hear it ring.

A bead of cold sweat broke out on his forehead and trickled into his eye.

He heard a click, and someone answered.

"Hey... cop," whispered a deep, rasping voice.

42

Alex froze to the spot, the hairs on his neck prickling.

There was a few seconds of silence.

"Has the cat got your tongue, Sergeant Cortes?"

"Who the fuck are you, son of a bitch?"

The other man gave a loud sigh.

"Relax, this is merely the beginning. We'll have plenty of chances to get to know each other better, don't worry."

"Why don't you reveal yourself and quit playing stupid games?"

"I'm sorry, Officer Cortes. I'm afraid I have to leave you now."

"I'm going to catch you, and when I do, you'll be in jail longer than you can ever imagine."

"I'm glad you told me; I hear you're no longer moving to Tarragona. Perfect!"

After a startled pause, Alex spoke.

"How do you know about Tarragona?"

"I know a lot more than you think. Goodbye, Alex. We'll see each other soon. Hopefully."

"Wait, you fucking bastard. When I get hold of you, I will kill you with my bare hands…"

"I very much doubt it, Sergeant Cortes, but keep up the good work. You're doing great. Bye-bye..."

And there was a click as the caller hung up.

"Hey! HEY!"

Alex looked at the phone.

He called the number back, but they didn't pick up.

He typed 'call me back', but the message didn't go through.

The phone had been turned off.

The bustle and chaos at the station was unprecedented.

Public opinion, public peace and the corps' reputation were at stake.

Alex entered the building with Carmen, Miguel's co-worker.

Karla and Alan were waiting for them in the meeting room.

Alan immediately pulled up the message history from the girl's phone and looked to see if it was possible to trace the call.

Meanwhile, Alex explained the conversation he'd had with Roberto.

He was still upset, and his hands were visibly shaking. While two officers took the girl's statement in another office, Alex explained what had happened to Karla.

"I can't believe it," she said. "You're shaking like a leaf, Alex."

"I know. I think I'm still in shock."

"Yes, too much coffee and stress. What was his voice like?"

"Deep, calm, measured words. How did he know my name? How did he know I'd call him?"

"He knows more than we think. He's one step ahead of us."

Alex closed his eyes and inhaled slowly, letting out a long

breath.

"Feeling better?" she asked, touching his face.

"Yes, thank you," he said, shocked at the intimacy of the gesture and moved just enough for her to pull her hand away from his face. "What do we know about the victim's parents?"

"That's what I wanted to talk to you about. The Guardia Civil was there first thing this morning. The parents have been divorced for ten years. The mother was inconsolable; she had no idea. They had to call an ambulance and take her to the hospital for shock. The younger sister said that Miguel hadn't called or answered their calls and the messages he'd sent were oddly detached."

"What about the father?"

"The father... The officer's exact words were: *"The father seemed completely indifferent to the news,"* she said with a grimace of disgust. "Seems the guy didn't care a bit."

Alex's hand had almost stopped shaking.

"What do you think?" he asked.

"The family is in Cáceres. Roberto is answering the bare minimum; he won't answer calls and sends text messages instead."

"Roberto keeps the victim's phone," said Alex, standing up and glancing at Karla. "And he responds to messages as if he was Miguel himself."

"If a parent doesn't hear back from their child, they worry, right?"

"Yes, but if you're from a low-income family, jumping on a plane or train to check up on your child isn't easy. What can you do?"

"Pray," said Karla.

"He's been pretending to be Miguel all along so as not

to arouse suspicion. And even if the family had suspected anything, Miguel is long gone," said Alex, his mind whirring with questions. "I've had an idea. Come with me!"

Alex jogged down the hallway, and everybody looked up as he burst into the room, followed by Karla.

They entered the room where Alan was working on Carmen's cell phone.

"Alan ....," said Alex, unfazed by the computer genius. Can you locate the last triangulation of the cell phone?"

"Is this your big idea?"

"No, actually, it's not," he said stiffly, irritated by the condescending response.

"I've already done it. I have a friend who works in the same company as the victim, and he's already told me. It's downtown Barcelona, around Plaza Catalunya. I'm expecting a mail from him any time now about the latest activity. Anything else?" he asked, peering at him over his glasses.

Alex raised an eyebrow.

"Listen, if I put my phone on airplane mode and turn on the home Wi-Fi, can you find me? Can you triangulate me?"

Alan thought for a moment.

"No, because the phone doesn't emit any signal. You could try the "Find my phone" option, but if we don't know which type of device it is, there's very little we can do."

"I think he keeps the phone somewhere that's only connected to the house Wi-Fi."

Alex exchanged a glance with Karla, and they left. After updating his notebook with new clues and hypotheses, he went downstairs to buy a couple of sandwiches from the vending machine and ate them in the dining room. He closed his eyes and napped for a half-hour to catch up on sleep, afraid he wouldn't make it through the night. He was almost running on empty.

The afternoon passed quickly, updating reports and monitoring what was happening in the press.

The sun disappeared behind Montjuic.

Alex stood up; he was flagging. He approached the window and saw that the reporters had thinned out. Traffic was back on the roads, and customers were sitting outside on the coffee shop terrace opposite the station.

His phone rang.

When the call ended ten minutes later, he went to Karla's desk.

"Are you leaving?" she asked.

Alex looked at his watch.

"Yes, and you should go, too. It's been a long day."

She nodded.

Just as Alex was about to walk through the door, he turned. "By the way, Alba called me and told me she's got something interesting for us."

"Alba?" said Karla sounding like a jealous cat. "So it's not Dr. Guevara anymore; it's... *Alba*."

"I'm not even going to reply to that," he replied. "Go home to your fiancé. This is pushing us to the limit, but it hasn't even started yet. We need to rest so we're clear-headed tomorrow," he said before walking out the door.

He got into his car, which he'd parked in the basement, and came out onto the street, dodging the reporters and wondering what Alba had to tell him.

43

Once again, Alex was stuck in the slow evening rush-hour traffic.

"Jesus Christ," he thought, drumming his fingers impatiently on the steering wheel.

The traffic on the Ronda de Dalt had swallowed him up, but there was no other way to reach the Mossos headquarters. He could have requested a helicopter, but they would have laughed at him.

He turned on the radio and tuned in to his favorite rock station, feeling his mood lifting. He opened the soft top and then checked his phone. He'd received a message from Carmen, Miguel's friend, who had arrived home and wanted to thank him for his help. He wondered why she was thanking him when she was the one that had helped them.

By the time he came off the Ronda, the traffic flowed smoothly, and he arrived at headquarters earlier than expected.

He identified himself at the entrance, and the gates to the visitors' parking lot opened.

The place was almost empty; working hours for most officers were over.

The coroner was in her office waiting for him at the morgue. He tapped lightly on the door.

"It's open," she called out.

She was sitting at her desk, and when he entered, she turned to look up at him.

"I came as soon as I could."

She smiled at him.

There was something different about her.

"Thanks for coming, Alex."

"What was so urgent that you couldn't tell me over the phone?" he asked, noticing her striking red lipstick.

"I'd like to show you something," she said, getting up.

She went to the refrigerated area and pulled out one of the freezer drawers.

"Look what I found," she said, beckoning him over. When Alex didn't move, she glanced at him. "Can you come here? I can't take it there."

He approached her cautiously.

As he approached her, he saw her eyes appraising him, and he suddenly felt self-conscious—the t-shirt under his leather jacket was one size too small. He knew it didn't hide what was underneath.

Alba flushed and cleared her throat.

"Come here," she said. "Come a little closer."

On the table were the remains of Miguel. Although he'd already seen them, the image of the head resting on the stainless-steel table made his stomach turn.

"What have you found?"

The woman took out a report and showed him.

"We found dirt under the fingernails."

"And?"

"I've been checking the chemical composition, and the result was interesting," she said, unfolding another table to rest the report on.

"The minerals and molecular composition of the dirt are found in the seabed."

Alex frowned.

"I have it here. Look," she said, pointing at the report.

"Miguel was in the sea?"

"No, I believe he was in the mountains," she said, her tongue flickering over her lips.

Alex flicked through the report and didn't notice that she had moved to his side until he felt her breath near his ear.

"There are some areas of the Pyrenees that, despite being in high mountains, have the same properties as those that are present when the tide goes out," she said softly. "Dirt can tell us many things, you know?"

Her proximity startled him, and when he turned around, her scarlet lips almost touched his. He gazed into her beautiful deep-set eyes and felt himself falling under her spell. Her long, mascaraed lashes trembled as she maintained eye contact.

Alex swallowed hard.

Her nonverbal communication left no room for confusion. And she was a beautiful woman, despite her age.

Her lips were getting closer, and he felt his pulse quicken. He saw a flash of red under her blouse, the same shade as her lipstick.

Maybe it was time he got over Mary?

There was no denying that Alba was sexy as hell. He felt

himself becoming aroused, and when Alba brushed up against him, he felt a surge of desire.

"I think we should probably get out of here," he croaked, looking around the sterile room.

He stepped away, but Alba raised her leg onto the table, blocking him.

She smiled lazily at him

"We're completely alone. Everyone has left for the day," she said, trailing her long nails along his jaw.

The woman pressed her lips on Alex's, staining them crimson.

Their kisses became more heated. Alba grabbed the back of his head and pulled him close. Alex responded with equal passion as his excitement grew.

She lowered her leg from the examination table and ran her hand over his groin.

"Mmm," she murmured, rubbing him through his jeans.

"Wait," said Alex, pulling her aside. "Not here. Let's go to your place."

"To my place? Are you crazy?" she said, again seeking his lips. "My husband will be there! What are you talking about?" She continued stroking him and began to fumble with his zip, but Alex hesitated. Not only was Alba married, but she was also a colleague. It was wrong.

Gently, he removed himself from her grasp and stepped back.

"I can't," said Alex. "I'm sorry," and walked toward the door.

"Do you know how much planning it took to get us to this moment? You and I, alone in the whole building," she spat angrily. "You have no fucking idea."

43

"Please send me the report of the *subungual scraping* by e-mail. Thanks," he said without turning around.

"You've just thrown away an opportunity you'll *never* have again."

"If you want my honest opinion, Dr. Guevara," he said from the doorway, "you should focus on the five murdered bodies in your lab instead of thinking about fucking me. One of them could have been your child."

He disappeared down the same hallway he'd entered only minutes earlier without another glance at her.

He sat in his car, feeling torn.

Part of him thought he'd been an idiot: she'd offered it to him on a plate. They were both adults, and it wouldn't have hurt anyone

But the other half was proud that he'd resisted her advances, done the right thing.

He took a deep breath and raked his fingers through his curls before heading home.

Even though it was late, Alex needed to get rid of his pent-up emotions, so he went for a run. The rock music in his headphones set the rhythm of his strides.

He arrived home after a five-mile sprint, exhausted.

It wasn't exactly a substitute for sex, but it was the next best thing.

He ate the previous day's leftovers for dinner and fell asleep after reading the same page of his book several times.

The alarm clock sounded early.

He got up to turn off his phone on the other side of the room and stood in front of the bedroom window in his underwear.

The sea was as gray as the sky, and it looked like the rain wouldn't let up anytime soon.

He left his house as he did every morning. The news on the radio was becoming increasingly distressing, stirring the public's fear day after day.

He arrived at the station before the packs of journalists had arrived, parked in the basement and grabbed a coffee as he passed the machine.

Sipping his drink, he looked out the window, longing for a time when he could have breakfast with Mario in the coffee shop without having to dodge the media.

Traffic was increasing by the minute, and a small truck that pulled up into the space reserved for patrol cars caught Alex's attention.

It was a white and blue truck: *FedEx*.

Alex watched, his eyes narrowed.

The delivery man entered the station and disappeared from view.

Alex kept his eyes trained on the street, and when he saw the delivery guy, he let out a breath that he hadn't realized he'd been holding.

But the delivery man reappeared within a minute, dragging a package out of the van. He held it with one hand while he closed the door with the other.

Alex froze.

"Shit," he muttered. "The second package."

44

Duality.

Alex was numb as he ran down the stairs as fast as he could. Two at a time.

When he reached the first floor, one of his colleagues was talking to the delivery man, and another was calling Alex. He jumped over the security scanner and landed directly in front of the FedEx guy.

The man's eyes widened, and he took a step backward. "What the —?"

"Don't you read the newspapers?" Alex snapped.

The delivery man shrugged.

"The… the newspapers… Why?"

Alex ignored him and looked closely at the package, which had the same dimensions and shape as the previous one. The seal that closed it was a different color, but the rest was the same. The company label was also similar to the first one: a made-up sender and addressed to Sergeant Alex Cortes of the Travessera de les Corts police station.

Without thinking, Alex was just about to touch it but snatched his hand back as if he'd been burned.

He heard a commotion coming from the other side of the automatic glass door. When he turned around, he saw an army of journalists trying to barge in to get a shot of the scene.

"I want those doors cleared. NOW!" shouted Alex pointing to the media.

He looked at the delivery man and then glanced at another colleague.

"Take this man inside, get him fingerprinted and take a statement."

The man put his hands up and shook his head.

"No, no, no, I have a route to follow. I'll get fired if I'm late!"

Alex scratched his chin, staring at the package.

"Your boss should have called us earlier, not just handed this over. For Christ's sake!" he muttered, pulling out his phone and jabbing the screen. "Karla, we have a problem."

Within minutes, a corps van with sirens blaring and a patrol car were on their way to Sabadell. This time, they opted to transport the parcel intact to the central facilities and open it there.

Officers followed the sergeant's orders and took a statement from the dazed delivery driver. Meanwhile, out on the street, journalists called in copy and photos to the newsdesk, much to the delight of their editors.

The coroner was in charge of opening this early Christmas present. When the box was in front of her on the table, she carefully proceeded to open it. Everyone watched with bated breath.

The coroner was in charge of opening this early Christmas present.

She tore off the label and attached it to a sheet of paper. Then she did the same with the seal to later test for Roberto's fingerprints or DNA particles

She opened the side flaps, giving a running commentary about what she was doing to the cameras documenting everything.

Once opened, her assistant cut the sides with a sharp cutter and put the cardboard on another table.

When they had the porexpan box in front of them, the doctor looked at Alex, who nodded from the other side of the glass. He saw a trace of arrogance and ill feeling cross her face and averted his gaze for a second.

When he looked back, she'd opened the box and was carefully lifting out its contents. There was a tense silence as the bag appeared, and then a hushed ripple of excitement spread through the room. It was what they had been expecting.

A vacuum bag with the missing parts of the second corpse was visible.

One head, two hands and two feet.

Alex ran his hand over his face and pressed his fingers to his lips.

Jesus Christ. What the hell was going on?

The severed parts were a woman's.

The doctor proceeded to trim the sides of the bag, and just like last time, as soon as she pierced it, the vacuum was lost, and the bag swelled with a loud hiss.

She placed the head on the table, separating it from the bag while the assistant held the rest of the contents for her; the long blond hair was tangled.

Dr. Guevara gently peeled back the plastic and removed it from her face. Pinkish fluid clung to it as if it were amniotic liquid.

Then she pulled up her eyelids: the victim's pupils were a light, icy blue.

Her skin was pale, Nordic.

Once everything was on the table, the doctor gave them the signal to enter and take a closer look. There was something that wasn't visible from the viewing chamber.

45

Alex and Karla put on their masks and entered the laboratory.

Despite the protection, the smell of blood and death filled their lungs. When they glanced at each other, the expressions on their faces bore testament that no amount of time in that job was enough to get used to the smell of death; and the closer they came, the more oppressive it became.

"Look at this. I think we can get more information here," said Alba as she turned one of the hands over. There was no jewelry, only the chipped remains of a cheap manicure.

There was dirt under the nails.

"I bet it's the same thing as last time," she said, turning to Alex.

"Don't bet. Analyze it," he snapped sharply. She flushed and turned back to the table. By Alex's side, Karla shifted and glanced at him, clearly puzzled by his rudeness.

"Anything else?" Alex asked, ignoring both of them.

The doctor put the hand to one side and continued with the other body parts.

"The first thing I notice is this," she said, her voice much cooler. "For some reason, the killer has left this on the foot."

The feet were petite with a high bridge. One ankle still had a thin red cotton ankle bracelet attached.

"Well, find out why. That's what you're supposed to do," he replied, equally coolly. "Anything else?"

The doctor shook her head.

"No, nothing else. You can leave now. We have a lot of work to do here," she said, not even glancing at him.

He turned and walked out the door without another word.

"What the hell's wrong with you?" said Karla before getting into the patrol car where no one could overhear them. "You jumped when she asked you over last night, but now you can't even look at each other?"

"It's none of your business, okay?"

"What are you two up to?" Karla insisted.

Alex frowned, his eyes narrowing coldly.

"I don't need to explain my personal affairs to you. Just do your job," he said through gritted teeth. "Do you understand? Your focus should be on catching this killer, not my personal life." he climbed in the car and slammed the door shut.

Karla watched him, shocked at his vitriol, and as she got in the car, she rolled her eyes. Something was going on, but she knew he always kept his cards close to his chest and pushed down his emotions. Maybe that was why he was such a good cop.

Alex received a message from the Lieutenant as they were leaving the Sabadell facility.

"I need to talk to you urgently. Come to my office."

Alex turned off the screen and punched the door. The drive

back to the station was tense.

46

Yelling reverberated through the whole office.

The Lieutenant was livid, and Alex was glad he would be leaving soon. He wouldn't have to endure his boss's temper much longer.

"I agreed to stay and help, and now the asshole is treating me like I'm the one sending the damn parcels," he thought.

It took him back to the days when his father would yell at him when he got bad grades at school: now, he felt like an invisible pressure was crushing him, and he shrunk down in his chair, annoyed yet humiliated.

"Do you know who called me this morning?" shouted Alfonso Rexach, the Lieutenant. Alex froze.

"The Minister of Internal Affairs, from Madrid! And do you know what he told me? That maybe this case is too much for the Mossos d'Esquadra. He even asked if we wanted him to send us a goddamn super-inspector. Son of a bitch! Do you want them to take the case away from us or send us a fucking *babysitter* from the capital? Is that what you want, Alex?"

Alex kept quiet, feeling some of the pressure his boss was

under. But unlike Alex, Rexach was caught in the crossfire between his superiors and the press. None of them had been taught how to handle that. Taking things out on others was par for the course, and Alex understood this.

The Lieutenant stopped yelling and stared out the window, his anger spent. Alex felt bruised emotionally, like his boss's personal punch bag.

"What else do you want me to do?" he asked Rexach, who turned around, looking defeated.

"More. I want you to do more. We've got to catch this bastard."

"Alfonso, listen to me," said Alex, trying to keep his temper in check. "We can't do any more than we're already doing."

"NO! You're not doing enough," the boss shouted again.

Alex stood up.

"I'm not staying here to listen to your bullshit any more," he said, holding up his hand to silence Rexach. "If you have nothing more to say to me, I'll be in my office, working and coordinating this case," he said calmly and left the room. The boss was still shouting as Alex closed the door on him.

Once outside, he closed his eyes and took a deep breath as he went to the room where Karla and her team worked.

He raised his hands and asked for everyone's attention.

"Guys, you're doing a great job, and I know we've all been working long hours almost without a break, but as you all probably heard, I just had a bollocking from upstairs," said Alex at the top of his lungs. "I know how easy it's for me to stand here and ask you to go the extra mile: trust me, not long ago, I was where you guys are. But I need to ask you to dig deep and try and do more. If we want to catch Roberto, we need to outsmart him; if we go that extra mile, I know we can do it. Maybe more imagination to predict his next steps; do whatever you can. We have to pluck something out of the air, or this case could be the last one in our careers."

He waited for a second, looking around at all the officers. He felt slightly guilty for ambushing them without warning, but there was no time for formalities. It was the first time he'd ever done something like this.

"Any questions?" he said and waited, but no one spoke. "Good. Who's in charge of talking to the shipping companies?"

An officer raised his hand.

"Okay. We know the killer's *modus operandi* is to send us packages. We have to get ahead of him. Write a standard e-mail and send it to all the transport agencies in this nation, whether they're in Girona, Barcelona or Timbuktu. To all of them. Is that clear? Any company that even touches an envelope, a box or a pallet. We're so and so looking for this… contact us here… Understood?"

The man nodded in agreement.

"Okay. It won't be long before we find out the girl's identity in the second package, and you know what to do. Who manages the media?"

Everyone looked around the room, and no one raised their hand.

"Karla?"

"No. We don't have anyone for that," she said, her cheeks reddening.

"I could appoint someone randomly, but that wouldn't be fair. Any volunteers to send a press release to the media?"

At the back of the room, a girl timidly raised her hand.

"Cool, what's your name?"

"Clara."

"Perfect, Clara. Can you write a press release stating that we're holding a press conference about the Cryptogram Killer at six p.m. this evening and send it to all TV stations, radios, newspapers, and blogs? Everyone you can think of."

"Have you cleared that with the boss, Alex?" asked Karla.

"Fuck him. He wants results, so we'll give him results. We'll talk to the judge to advise us on how much we can say to reassure the public. We're an efficient team, working our balls off to solve this case. And we have to say it aloud. Everything that isn't spoken doesn't exist. And, ladies and gentlemen, we have a bumpy road ahead of us and can't afford to take our foot off the accelerator. If someone isn't willing to give it their all, there are other departments in the station. No hard feelings, but if you're not up for the ride, this isn't the place for you."

Alex paused, looking at the whole team with raised eyebrows as if daring them to admit they weren't up for the job.

"Nobody? Ok, let's get to work. If you need anything, call Karla or me," he said and clapped his hands.

He then looked at Karla.

"We're leaving. Follow me," he said.

"Where are we going?" asked Karla, hurrying to keep up with him.

"Somewhere we should have visited long before now."

47

They entered the port, following the GPS instructions and parked in front of a warehouse. The facade was white and blue with the name of the courier company that had delivered the package that morning.

They entered the premises.

"Good morning. What can I do for you?" asked the receptionist.

"Police, Sergeant Cortes and Corporal Ramirez," said Alex, pulling back his leather jacket to show her his badge. "We're here to talk to the person in charge."

"Can I ask the reason for your visit?"

"Jeez, is she dumb or what?" thought Alex.

"Police business. Are you going to call him, or do we have to wait all day?" he said in an authoritative tone.

The woman looked shocked at first, but when she picked up her phone, her nostril flared slightly.

Two minutes later, she led them to an office.

The logistics floor was visible through the glass walls and was so big that he couldn't see where it ended. Trucks picked up packages, long shipping belts sorted them, and pallet jacks moved cargo back and forth: frenetic parcel traffic. Alex and

Karla gawked at the display.

"I don't know if it's a good idea to take out the Kalashnikov right away, Alex," whispered Karla.

The office door opened before he could respond.

"Good morning. How can I help you?" said a tall, lanky man, looking up from his cluttered desk.

"We need information about a package you delivered this morning."

The man burst out laughing.

"We deliver hundreds of thousands of packages every day," he said without inviting them to sit.

"At 8:00 a.m. this morning, one of your guys delivered a package to the Travessera police station," said Alex, pausing for a second. "Do you understand now?"

The man stood up and closed the door, studying Alex.

"I know you. You're the one that saved the Barça president's boy," he said and fell silent. "Shit, don't tell me *that* package was one of ours," he said, running his hand through his hair.

Alex nodded.

"Well done," said Alex dryly.

The man's face twisted in disgust.

"Jesus Christ," he said in horror. "We'll have to get everything sanitized, especially the van."

"That won't be necessary. There's absolutely no risk to your employees or the general public; believe me, you'd be the first to know. We're here for two different issues. The first one is, why didn't you separate it before delivering it?

"Separate it? We have millions of packages a week. How could we do that?"

"What my colleague means is that you're the expert. Maybe, with a computer program..." said Karla, trying to soften her partner's bluntness.

"Maybe yes. I mean, it might be possible, but we haven't had any instructions to do so, just some confusing phone calls from one of your lot. Who could ever have imagined something like this would happen?" he said, a dazed expression on his face.

"The second thing we need to know is if we can check your CCTV to see who delivered it?" said Alex.

"Sure thing," said the man, crossing the room and sitting at his computer.

He swiped his magnetic card through a slot and unlocked the device. After a few tense minutes, he glanced up and pointed to the screen.

"I've got the truck's license plate, the name of the employee who delivered it and the location. It was, indeed, at eight o'clock today. And," he said, rubbing his chin and squinting at the screen, "it was delivered to our Raval branch a week ago with express orders to deliver it today."

"So you're telling me you've had it here on your premises for almost a week?"

"Now you understand my disgust. I'm going to disinfect the whole damn place, even if you don't think it's necessary," he said grimly.

"Can you see if you have any other parcels with the same instructions?"

"With the same delivery address?"

Alex nodded, and the man stared at the screen.

"As of today, no," he said, looking at them again. "Anything else?"

"Do you have CCTV in all the branches?"

"No, none of our collection and delivery points has a

recording system. It's not necessary," said the man and shrugged.

Alex approached him and held out his hand.

"Thanks for your help."

The manager looked at the policeman's hand but didn't shake it.

Alex put it back into his pocket and left the room, followed by Karla.

Once in the car, Alex checked his phone and then spoke to Karla.

"Send two officers to the parcel company's pickup point and see if they can get anything."

Karla pulled out her phone and began searching through her contacts, but before she had put the call through, he added,

"By the way, we've identified the girl in the second package."

48

The two officers headed back to the station.

Karla preferred to take the wheel because Alex's driving triggered her car sickness.

He looked out the window, deep in thought.

She glanced at him several times before asking,

"What are you thinking about?" she asked.

Alex looked at her and then turned his gaze back to the sea and the port.

"I was thinking about cruises. They always go to such exotic destinations. I'd like to go on one."

"Have you been away lately?"

"You mean apart from our trip?"

She smiled mischievously instead of replying.

"No," he said. "I prefer to keep the memory of ours. It was our little impulsive splurge."

"I have fond memories of that time, too," she said, smiling without taking her eyes off the road. "We were always reading, can you remember?"

"We could have stayed at home because in the end, all we

did was read and…" Alex cleared his throat and continued, "Well, you know. You were there too."

"Do you still read as much as you used to?" she asked, changing the subject.

"No, much less than before. You?"

"As much as I can. Now I'm reading an excellent book by Poveda. Eccentric, but I like it."

"What's the book called?" he asked, his interest piqued.

"*Laura Coves*, a murder mystery… no, hang on… *Who killed Laura Coves?* Yes, that's it."

Alex nodded.

"What about you?" she asked him.

"Me? Maxime Garanger, *Blood of Roses*."

"Oh yes, a huge phenomenon… and self-published! Is it good?"

"His success is well-deserved."

"Can I borrow it? I'll lend you the Poveda book in exchange, just like in the old days," Karla said, grinning.

"Yeah, of course you can. You can take it on your honeymoon," he replied, glancing sideways at her.

His words broke the magic of the moment, and Karla frowned.

Alex went back to looking out the window. He could no longer see the ships, only buildings and gray warehouses.

Patricia Morales.

That was how the corner's report about the second body began. Before she was murdered and dismembered, she had been a beautiful girl.

The girl in the ID photo looked like a runway model. Blue

eyes that held dreams, a past. When he saw the photo, Alex punched his fist on his desk, drawing curious stares from the rest of the team.

"It's a travesty that someone so young has died at the hand of a ruthless killer like Roberto. Damn it!" said Alex angrily. "You can't lose your life when you're twenty-three years old because of the homicidal whim of a psycho."

"Calm down," Karla said, shaking the paper cup she had just taken from the machine. "You should drink less of this."

Alex looked at her and took the coffee from her hands, chugging it down in one gulp. Then he crumpled the cup and threw it away.

"Discussion over."

He continued reading the document.

Patricia was originally from a village near Zaragoza and was an orphan. A family from Teruel adopted her, and she left home when she was eighteen. Her last known job was as a waitress in a club.

"Look at this—w*aitress in a nightclub*," said Alex to his companion. "It's downtown near Plaza de España."

He grabbed the folder, darted into the meeting room, and stood looking at the map pinned to the board, waiting for Karla to enter.

"And look," he said, pointing to the map. "It's all in the center of Barcelona. The Raval, where Roberto leaves the second package. El Paralelo, the first one. La Mina, where Miguel worked. Plaza Catalunya, Patricia's job. All within the same radius."

"It's true. Everything has a certain coherence."

"But what did all the victims have in common with

Roberto?" said Alex, holding up two fingers. "Miguel and Patricia. They must have something in common, and it's something connected to this area," he concluded, drawing a circle around it. "The answer is here. When we discover what the link is, we'll catch Roberto."

"There's one thing that isn't in this circle," she said. Alex turned around. "The report of the dirt under the nails found the soil was from the Pyrenees."

"Yes. You're right. The Pyrenees. What's your connection there, Roberto…?"

"What if we call our colleagues there and ask them to be on alert?"

"Good idea, Karla. Just in case," said Alex, looking satisfied, "Will you take care of it?"

She lifted her shoulders, resigned.

"While you're at it, you can also contact the Teruel police to go break the news to Patricia's parents and find out any pertinent info," said Alex.

"Okay. What are you going to do in the meantime?"

Alex looked at his watch and sighed.

"I have to call the judge and convince her about the press conference."

"But it's already programmed."

"Yeah, that's why I'm worried. It's already programmed, but she doesn't know yet."

49

First ring.
Silence.
Second ring.
He regretted having organized that press conference out of anger.
In situations like this, Alex always remembered his sister's words:
"When emotion goes up, intelligence goes down."

Third ring.
He felt like hanging up, but the damage was already done, and it was too late to back out.

There was a metallic noise.
Alex bit his lip.
"Hello?" came a tinny voice.
"Good morning, Your Honor," he said, clearing his throat.
The judge was silent for a second as if trying to place who it was.
"Sergeant Cortes?" she asked, not hiding the surprise in her

voice.

Alex let out a breath: it was the first time he'd spoken to a judge on the phone without getting the green light from a superior.

"Sergeant? How can I help you? I hope it's good news."

Alex remained silent: no matter how hard he tried, no words came out.

"Sergeant, I don't have all day. Are you still there?"

"Yes, Your Honor. Yes and no."

"Yes and no, what?"

"Yes, I'm still here, but no, it's not good news. As you know, a second package arrived, and more are coming. We need to stop this macabre game, and I need to ask you something. I'm afraid I must disagree with you about the media and public blackout."

"Which part of my ban on leaking information on such an important case do you disagree with, Sergeant Cortes?" she asked, clearly affronted by his admission.

"I understand that it's a serious case, but the public is afraid and distrustful because they don't have any information. All they know is what they see and read in the press, which, as you know, isn't always accurate.

"Sergeant Cortes, what exactly do you want from me?"

"We have to let the public know what's going on."

"Absolutely not."

"And use the media to help us."

"Have you lost your mind?" she asked shrilly.

"No, Your Honor. We have to inform them, or the hysteria will spread. They need to know about the five dismembered bodies in the van and that a madman is sending gruesome packages."

"And what good will that do?"

"Hopefully, the killer will feel more vulnerable. We'll call on the population to be our eyes and ears. Our sentinels. Roberto will feel—"

"Who's Roberto?" she interrupted.

Alex swallowed, but the judge continued.

"Do you know something that I don't, Sergeant Cortes?"

"No, Your Honor, of course not. It's the name we've given him," Alex said in a placating tone, "a code name to identify the murderer."

There was a short silence. "Sergent Cortes, contacting me directly is highly unethical and unacceptable. I will overlook it this time, but I will not permit you to talk to the press. I must go now because I'm due in court soon."

"I've called a press conference," Alex blurted out, closing his eyes as if dodging a blow.

"What? Are you out of your mind? Cancel it immediately, or I'll charge you for contempt of court."

"Please, Your Honor. You have no idea what's happening at street level. We risk our lives every single day. Our families never know if or when a colleague will ring the doorbell and tell them we won't be coming home ever again. Any day we could be shot or attacked. And if you understood me and truly supported the corps, you'd help us and grant permission for a press conference instead of hiding in your ivory tower and traveling in your armored car."

He paused, breathless, realizing that he'd completely overstepped the mark.

"Are you finished, Sergeant?" said the judge with barely disguised contempt. "This is the last time you will call me. Ever. This call will have consequences: you have crossed a

49

boundary here."

There was a click, and the phone went dead.

Alex looked at the screen, and his heart sank.

She'd hung up on him. Things weren't looking good.

50

Alex had never been so insecure about a case in all his career and was afraid he'd lose the investigation. Calling the judge had been a stupid move. And insulting her wouldn't have helped.

Lieutenant Rexach had taken out his anger on Alex, pushing him to make that call. The whole situation had gone to shit. But it wasn't all his fault.

He sat down at his desk and clicked on his overflowing inbox.

Karla had been watching him but didn't say a word. She could only guess how the call with the judge had gone.

"Cortes!" yelled the Lieutenant, coming out of his office and storming down the corridor. "Cortes! Where the hell are you?"

Alex felt the blood draining from his face and stood up.

"Cortes, are you out of your goddamn mind calling the judge directly?" he roared as his words bounced off the walls.

There was an uneasy hush as everyone stopped what they were doing to watch the show.

"What the fuck did you say to her? Do you want me to get

fired for not knowing how to run an investigation or control my team?"

"I'm sorry, Alfonso, I won't do it again," replied Alex quietly.

"Damn right, you won't! What on earth did you think you were playing at? If you think I'll agree to this, you must be insane."

"Sir?"

"A press conference? A bloody press conference? Have you lost your mind?"

"People are scared and need reassurance."

The Lieutenant shook his head and exhaled heavily.

"Have you brought a clean shirt, at least?"

"Shirt?"

The Lieutenant tutted and glared at Alex.

"The judge has thought it over, and while she doesn't condone your idea, she's told me that if it backfires, you will be the one to face the consequences," he said, jabbing his finger at Alex. "And she won't transfer you to Tarragona; she'll fire your ass. No games from now on, and keep me informed about everything. And get changed because you look like you're in a damn rock group," he said, turning around.

As soon as he disappeared down the aisle, the room exploded with applause for Alex.

The sky looked like another storm was coming.

The forecast had confirmed it, but the weather was steady for the time being

Alex hadn't thought to bring a shirt, so he went from room to room, asking if someone could lend him one. He applied his badge and tucked it into his jeans.

A table had been set up outside the station entrance door. The whole street was crowded with cameras and microphones identifying all major national and international news channels.

A mob of journalists awaited the appearance of the man who had called the press conference.

Television cameras and photographers were ready to broadcast the information live worldwide. Camera operators had waterproofed their television cameras, fearing the impending storm.

It was past six o'clock.

Finally, the doors opened.

Alex came out first, followed by Karla and next to her, the Lieutenant. On the other side, more than ten million people watched it in real-time. Among them, probably the judge and Roberto.

Alex came out with a script in his hand. He looked around and recognized Rafa, the coffee shop manager among the attendees.

"My name is Alex Cortes, and I'm the sergeant overseeing this investigation. Five mutilated bodies were found in a van right in front of this station.

He swallowed and looked at his notes.

"We've decided to break the silence today to reassure the public about what's happening. We're investigating tirelessly. We have several leads which are promising. The bodies we've identified up to now are young people. We are appealing to the public: if you know anyone aged between twenty and thirty years old who has disappeared within the past four to six weeks or has radically changed their way of communicating with friends or family, please inform us. We have a confidential phone line and promise to take every call seriously."

He looked at his piece of paper again. With every gesture he made, an explosion of cameras almost blinded him.

"Two days ago, we received a small package containing body parts in cardboard boxes addressed to me. We need twelve million eyes. Two for each member of the public so the murderer feels cornered. We need your help to bring this person to justice. But, by the same token, if you see something, do nothing. Inform us immediately."

He looked again at the paper and then up at the sky.

"In conclusion, I'd like to offer my condolences to the victims and their families. As for the person who has carried out this heinous act on young, innocent people, I know you are watching us. Rest assured that I *will* come after you until I catch you," said Alex, staring into the nearest camera.

"That's all. We don't have time for any questions. The aim of this press conference was simply to reassure the public. The whole team of the Mossos d'Esquadra and the rest of the corps will continue working to restore order to this beautiful city. Thank you, and good afternoon."

The journalists started shouting questions when he stood up, and flashbulbs went off. When he walked through the door, the first drops of rain began to fall.

"Well done, Alex," said the Lieutenant. "You did a good job."

Karla grabbed him by one shoulder, forcing him to turn around.

"What does that mean, what you just said?" she said in a tone Alex couldn't decipher. "Are you staying, then?"

"You were the one who said you wanted me to leave? Have you changed your mind in less than a week?" he asked, his mouth turning up at the corners.

Karla tutted at him.

As the three of them started to walk up the stairs, a colleague came running down.

"Alex, we got a call!"

Alex paused.

"And?"

"A refrigerated courier company called. They say they have something for us."

51

Alex and Karla looked at each other.

"What do you mean they have something for us?"
"They said that, after receiving our e-mail, they checked their shipping and found one addressed to the police station. For you," said the officer. "It was scheduled for delivery in a few days."
"Okay, thanks," said Alex to the officer. "Keep me informed if there's anything else."
He turned around and looked over at Karla.
"Are you coming?" he asked her.
"What do you think?" she replied.
He smiled at her, and they walked together toward the underground garage.

They left amidst the rain, which was once again lashing down. Once more, a convoy of Mossos van and a patrol car with lights and sirens headed for the transport agency.

It was the first time in a long time that Alex had felt so

energetic and alive: the protagonist of the story and not the prey. It was the first time they'd managed to be one step ahead of Roberto, which was a good sign. The e-mail that had been sent to the shipping agencies, together with the press conference, was beginning to take effect. His prediction had been correct: people perform better under pressure. If he squeezed them, they worked harder than when he allowed them to do as they pleased.

Ultimately, he had no choice but to be grateful for the Lieutenant's scolding.

It had stung, but he had to admit it had helped him.

"What's the name of the agency?" asked Alex.

"Chronus Frius," said Karla, looking at the info they'd received.

"How long will it take to get there?"

"About twenty minutes. It's in Zona Franca."

When they arrived, Alex and Karla, followed by backup, entered the building. They were taken to the warehouse and introduced to the manager.

"We knew right away when you sent the mail this morning," he told them.

"Where are you taking us?" asked Alex.

"We have a refrigerated chamber to keep expired food for health and safety reasons."

The facility was huge, so much so that staff moved around inside on electric scooters.

The industrial complex was about thirty feet high, like a three-story building. They passed between aisles of shelves that could fit four rows of stacked pallets. Pallet jacks crossed at breakneck speed, driving around the warehouse as if dancing to the beat of an opera.

They arrived at an enormous door, and the manager stopped.
"Here we are."
He grabbed a cord hanging from the ceiling and pulled. A siren sounded, and the door began to open automatically.
The space was dark, but when the door opened fully, the lights flickered on.

The space was diaphanous and empty. In the center, like the Holy Grail itself, was a stainless-steel table with a box on top.
They approached it cautiously, and Alex recognized it immediately. The dimensions, the seal, and the label left no room for doubt. It was the third package.
Alex touched it, and even through his gloves, it was icy cold.
"We'll take it with us," said Alex, and ordered an officer to load it into the police car.

The manager accompanied them back to the exit. As they walked, Alex asked him:
"How long has it been here?"
"A week. We had explicit orders to deliver it on Monday."
Alex nodded: it followed the pattern of two days between one parcel and the next.
"How did the client pay?"
"Cash. And, by the way, he was very polite."
Alex stopped and looked at him in disbelief.
"Did you see him?"
"I didn't, but our secretary did. She was the one who dealt

with him."

52

Alex shuddered.

He didn't have time to articulate his question because this information hit him like lightning.

"What?"

"Yes, the secretary almost fainted when we told her. She had a panic attack. You know, it's not very pleasant to be told that you've been talking to a serial killer."

"Could she describe the man to our artist?"

"I'm not sure it would be wise to ask her because she's had a terrible shock. However, I have something better," the manager said and resumed walking. "Follow me."

They followed the manager to his office, a small space cluttered with papers and thick with dust. Alex was surprised by the mess, given the man's orderly appearance.

The manager sat down at the computer and opened a program.

"As soon as we found out and knew you were on your way,

I asked myself, what else can I do? How can I help them?" He opened another window on his browser. "So, here you are."

He turned the screen toward them, where they saw a video of a man arriving on foot and carrying something. The man stopped, and someone opened the door from inside. From what they could see, Roberto's face was friendly and courteous, with nothing to suggest that he could be a serial killer.

"Any videos from the inside?"

"We don't have surveillance cameras inside the offices for customer and employee privacy. We have them in the cold storage rooms and the warehouse, but there's nothing interesting there."

Alex ran his hand through his hair and looked at Karla, disappointed. The external recordings didn't give them more than they already had. The sketch they had was a carbon copy of the man on the screen: a man in dark clothing with short brown hair and a pair of aviator-style sunglasses. Nothing new.

"But there's something else," said the manager. "I was thinking that if this guy shows up with a bulky box in Zona Franca, where did he come from?"

Alex and Karla turned to look at each other.

"I mean, you don't just show up out of nowhere, and he didn't arrive here in a car because we could identify the vehicle or the license plate. So I asked the security checkpoint for some recordings of the entrance at that hour. And… bingo!"

As he spoke, he opened an email with a link to another

recording.

The camera covering the entrance showed trucks and cars entering and leaving the site. The manager speeded up the recording, and after a minute, a bus appeared. Several people who looked like workers got off. Among them was Roberto. He took his macabre parcel, entered the transport agency, and the bus continued on its route.

"We need these images," said Alex, excited. "By bus? And then, on the way back, what does he do?"

"Same thing. He waits, motionless, for the next bus. You'll see it on the cameras."

The others were silent.

Alex let out a cynical laugh.

"He's jerking us around. I bet he even glanced at the camera because he knew we'd be looking at the images. But he's wearing glasses, so we can't see him," Alex said and paused. "But the question is, why a bus?"

"There's no subway here. It's a half-mile walk. The other option is the train a mile away."

"No, no. There's something else, for sure: this guy is extremely calculating. There must be something else."

"Alex, I think it's obvious. He couldn't come in the van because the cameras would have identified it," said Karla.

"No," Alex replied, looking around. "Karla, the van was parked in front of the station a week ago."

Karla smacked her forehead.

"But he couldn't come with his private car either because we would have tracked the license plates with the help of the traffic authorities."

"A bus leaves no trace," said the manager.

"I beg your pardon?"

"If you take a train or a streetcar, they have cameras everywhere, even over the ticket machines. But if you go by bus, you buy your ticket from the driver in cash, and there are no cameras inside the vehicle or in the bus shelters. If there's no trace, there's no crime."

Alex looked at him, following his reasoning.

"Excuse me. What's your name?"

"Antonio," he replied, standing up and holding out his hand.

"Take this," said Alex, handing him a business card, "If you want to change jobs, we need brains and logic like yours in the police. Think about it!"

The man flushed.

"Thank you, but I'm fine at Chronus," he said, slipping the card into his pocket. "But you never know."

"My email address is on the card. Could you send us the recordings?"

Karla and Alex got into the car and put on the sirens and lights. They went straight to the Sabadell headquarters to open the third package: the second of the day.

Being one step ahead of the killer was like a drug. *Now we're ahead of the piece of shit*, thought

Alex.

He had no idea how wrong he was.

53

They arrived in Sabadell once again.

When the doctor opened the porexpan box, she realized this one was different.

Removing the lid, she bent down to look inside. The stench coming from the plastic package made her flinch. The mask and camphor had failed to counteract the olfactory impact.

Dr. Guevara turned on the exhaust fans, conscious that there was something different about this package.

She picked it up with both hands and placed it on the table.

The bag had the same grim contents as the others, but the wrapping hadn't retained the vacuum.

She cut away the plastic and pulled out the head of a young Hispanic man.

His hands were severely calloused, with half-eaten fingernails.

Alex and Karla followed her every move from the viewing gallery.

The doctor opened the man's jaw to remove the third clue.

Unfolding it, she revealed another sequence of bars, identical to the previous two. She passed it to her assistant to take pictures.

The doctor then took a soft cloth and gently wiped the victim's face. Finally, she opened his eyes.

Two minutes later, she left the examination room.

"It's different from the other packages," she said, furrowing her brows.

"What do you mean?" asked Karla.

"The bag was open, having been already perforated. It's the first time it's happened, and I don't understand why."

"What don't you understand?" Karla insisted.

"A vacuum bag so thick doesn't break easily at all."

"Perhaps it was because of being transported?"

Alba shook her head.

"I don't think so. There was no metal in the box, let alone a sharp object."

"So what do you think?"

"I don't know. It's the first time a package has come to us with a potential error, or at least something we can interpret as such."

"Are you saying this is an oversight by Roberto?"

The doctor didn't answer.

"There's something else. The stench from the body parts is very interesting," said Alba, crossing her arms. "The corpse I have in the fridge has one level of decomposition, but the limbs have another. Completely different."

"I don't understand."

"Body and limbs should have the same decomposition level, but they're in two completely different phases, even though they're from the same body."

"Well, that's because the van was in the sun and the rest in cold storage for a week, right?"

"Yes and no. Let me explain. If that were so, the same would be true for the other victims. In this case, the body looks like it's been dead for around one month, while the hands and head appear to have been dead for only a couple of days. There's something not right here."

"Doctor, it's already very late. We're going back to headquarters. Could you send all the information you get as soon as possible?"

The doctor didn't even say goodbye. She turned around and pushed the swinging doors that led to her ice kingdom.

The day was coming to an end. A black Friday, despite the good feelings that Alex had had earlier. He watched the lights of cars and shops pass by—everyone was getting ready for the weekend. Images of the bodies in the morgue flashed through his mind—for them, it didn't matter anymore whether it was Monday or Friday.

It was hard for him to accept that there was a serial killer on the streets, yet he couldn't catch him.

Roberto was playing with him and with the public. What did he want to prove? That he was smarter than the police?

So many questions were whirring through Alex's mind.

The weekend would bring him closer to where Roberto wanted him to be. That much was sure.

Now Mary was gone, there was no point in returning home early. He would rather sleep at the station and study the clues they had so far; or rather, the crumbs that Roberto was leaving for him.

54

Barcelona.
Saturday.

On Saturday morning, Alex woke up stiff and disheveled at his desk.

He hadn't fallen asleep on the job since training at the academy.

He opened his eyes. The light of a new day was streaming through the window.

"Wake up, sleepyhead."

He lifted his head and saw Karla with a paper bag and coffee to go.

She'd brought him breakfast.

"I fell asleep here."

As he sat up, something fell from his shoulders.

"Yes, I saw you. I put your jacket around your shoulders so you wouldn't be cold," she explained. "Did you sleep well?" she asked, pulling a chair up to the desk.

"It's been years since I fell asleep like this," he said, stretching.

Then he looked at the watch.

"Shit."

"What's wrong?"

"It's my mother's birthday today."

"And that's bad?"

"I have to go to Tarragona for lunch. She's expecting the whole family," he said, wincing as his neck cracked.

"Yeah? Well, don't even think about going to Tarragona alone," said the Lieutenant, who had just entered the office.

"Don't worry, Boss, I'll catch a ride with my brother and sister."

"You don't get it, Alex. You're too exposed in this case. I understand you want to go, but two secret officers will accompany you. Until this is over, you'll be escorted everywhere."

"C'mon, Boss," Alex said, shaking his head.

"No. You'll go with a bodyguard. Everything's already been arranged. I don't want any excuses," concluded the lieutenant sitting heavily in a chair.

Alex scrunched up his face.

"Do we know anything about Patricia yet?"

"Yes. Her parents hadn't heard anything from her for a while. Her colleagues didn't find it strange because it wasn't the first time she'd disappeared for weeks. Apparently, not turning up for work was a regular thing; due to boyfriends, drugs and festivals. She was a piece of work, according to her boss."

"Jeez, Roberto knows how to pick them," said the boss, watching Alex polish off his breakfast. "And the riddles?"

"Packages two and three also had a bar code."

The Lieutenant ran his hand over his face.

"Anyway, keep me informed and, above all," he said, pointing at Alex, "don't even think of leaving Barcelona without a bodyguard."

With a nod, Alex snorted as the Lieutenant stood up and disappeared down the hallway.

"Wow, now you're famous, you get to travel with a bodyguard," sniggered Karla. "What more could you ask?"

"To leave here and relocate to Tarragona."

"But you can go. The Boss just told you."

"No, I mean forever," said Alex, looking out the window.

Karla tried to hide her look of disapproval, but not before Alex had noticed. She clearly hadn't liked his last comment but kept eating her croissant as if nothing had happened.

55

Ana, Marc and Alex.

The prodigal children return for their mother's birthday party.

Life had led all three of them away from home.

Ana, a psychologist and a writer, had a practice in Barcelona.

Marc, his younger brother, was nonbinary and had left Tarragona to escape the small-town gossip.

They were separated by miles, but their family bonds were unbreakable.

"Are they going to follow us all day?" asked Ana, jerking her head toward the window.

Alex turned around. The secret police car was trailing a few yards behind them.

"Don't worry. They won't join us for lunch," he grinned.

"You're already famous. Mom will be happy," said Alberto, his brother-in-law, who was driving.

"My mother will be happy because we're coming and even happier when she sees the rock Ana is wearing on her finger."

Alberto took his future wife's hand and kissed it.

"Wow, Ana, you didn't tell me anything!" said Marc. "It's beautiful!"

"It was a surprise, but you know Alex can't keep a secret," said Ana, slapping him.

"Alberto, things are going well for you, eh," said Alex, stroking the soft leather seats of the luxurious SUV.

"I can't complain. We bought it in case our family grows in the future," he said without taking his eyes off the road.

Alex smiled.

"Another one?" he said, glancing down at his nephew, who was fast asleep. "I wish you all the best, you deserve it, and you make a good couple," he said, looking at Ana. "And most importantly, Dad likes Alberto, which is unheard of."

The three siblings burst out laughing.

"Marc and I used to have so much fun when he chased away all the boyfriends Ana brought home."

They both laughed again.

"Hey, you never told me you were so popular in Tarragona," said Alberto to his future wife.

"Well, let's say I've never lied to you, but I haven't told you the whole truth either," she said coquettishly. "But it wasn't only in Tarragona; it was during college, too," she laughed.

"Look at my little Ana, such a dark horse."

"Don't worry, Alberto, you got the upper hand in the end," said Alex. "Otherwise, we wouldn't be here."

"She's the way she is because of all the pranks we played on her as kids. You owe us," Alex said, shooting Ana a fond look.

Between laughter and memories, the miles passed quickly, and they soon arrived at their parent's house.

55

When a grown-up child goes back home, it's always a party.

It was their mother's seventieth birthday. The table was festively decorated, with the best cutlery and their grandmother's china. Half a dozen gifts waited impatiently to be opened on a side table.

The celebration was at their grandparent's house. Since their grandmother had died and their grandfather had moved to a care home, the parents enjoyed weekends at the country house in a picturesque village in Priorat, the land of wine and rest.

Sitting at the table, they began to pick at the appetizers. Only their father was missing—he was still in the garden, cooking the main course.

"I'm disgusted that Mary just upped and left. I hope she never comes back," said their mother, glancing pointedly at Alex.

"Don't worry, Mother, I doubt we'll ever see her again. She'll never come back from New York."

"Ana, please tell your brother to eat more," she said, squeezing Alex's cheeks. "Look how thin he is!"

"Mom, please stop telling him what to do. He's old enough to do whatever he wants!"

"I'm sorry, but I think you're the most sensitive of my three children, and I can't be everywhere. I can't be in Barcelona *and* here caring for your father."

"What are you talking about? Taking care of who?" said their father, appearing through the door with an enormous paella.

Everyone applauded his famous wood-fired rice with lobster.

They passed out the plates and began to eat.

"Mmmm, Dad, I've sure missed your cooking," said Marc.

"Thank you. They don't know what good food is in Barcelona, not like we do."

The three of them laughed.

"Alex, sweetheart. Look at the dark circles under your eyes. You look like a panda. Are you sleeping enough? Is it because Mary left you?" his mother fussed, heaping his plate with paella.

"Mom, please stop! Do you want to check if I'm wearing a vest, too? I'm not five anymore!"

"Yes, make fun of me, but when I made you wear one, you never got sick," said his mother smugly. "Look at you now. You're like a ghost. Nothing like the strong boy you used to be."

"Dad, this paella is exquisite. Bravo," said Alex to his father, trying to change the subject.

"What are you on about, Mom? Alex was always sick. He was a total wimp," said Ana.

"I just did it to skip school!" laughed Alex. "By the way, I've asked for a transfer to the Tarragona station."

"Really?" asked the mother, her eyes shining. "So, are you coming back home to live with us?"

"No, I'll look for an apartment in the center of Tarragona."

"Don't be ridiculous! Come back home, your room is still empty, and it's where you belong! You'll save money and keep me company," she said, beaming at him.

"Okay, Mom, we'll see," he said, turning to his younger brother and whispering in his ear. "Oh man, sometimes I forget what Mom is like."

The two brothers laughed.

"Anyway, Ana, you've been hiding your left hand all morning. When were you thinking of telling us?" said their mother.

Alberto choked on his glass of beer and started coughing.

"The truth is that we wanted to save it for dessert, but since you asked…" said Ana, gazing at Alberto.

She held out her hand and showed off her sparkling diamond ring.

"Alberto has proposed."

"And? I hope you bit his hand off," asked their mother, reaching for her daughter's hand to see the ring better.

"Of course I did! We want to get married in November."

The family stood up and applauded the couple, patting Alberto on the back and hugging Ana.

When everyone had returned to their seat, Ana remained standing.

"There's one more thing…"

"No…!" cried her mother, flushing in delight.

"Yes, we're expecting our second baby," she said while Alberto caressed her belly.

When they'd finished eating and opened the presents, their parents, Alberto and Marc, took their coffee into the garden to enjoy the pleasant May sun. Ana and Alex stayed inside.

"How are you?" she said, "and tell me the truth."

"Tired and worried."

"I see you. I know you even better than Mom does."

"This guy is too smart for us. He's outstanding, the best I've ever seen."

"I've been following the news, and the press is only adding to the drama, saying such stupid things about the killer, about the police… about you."

"I don't care what they say about me; I only care about

245

catching him. But I'm scared that we won't or that we'll only find him when he wants us to."

"What if he never wants you to?"

Alex raised an eyebrow.

"Has he made any mistakes?" she asked.

"A couple, but not significant."

"I've been investigating similar cases," she said. "These guys think they're arm wrestling with the police. Just like you and I can have a game of cards, for serial killers, the whole thing is like a game."

"Which isn't very encouraging."

"You have to keep your eyes wide open. I guess being in the spotlight isn't helping."

"Not at all."

"I'm glad they gave you a bodyguard."

Alex flapped his hand.

"Bullshit, that piece of shit won't do anything to me."

"By the way, I enjoyed the press conference. I was so proud of you," she said and hugged him. "You'll see, this will end. You'll get to the truth, and the city will return to normal. You know, all of us believe in you, even if we don't tell you often enough."

Ana rested her head on Alex's shoulder.

"All authority carries a responsibility with it, but I'm not sure I'm ready for it," he stated.

"You can put your head in the sand, Alex, and walk away, but if we want to grow and move forward, we have to face the obstacles thrown in our path. No one asks if you're prepared to face cancer, the death of a loved one, or an accident. Life doesn't ask you because you'd say no. None of us chooses responsibility. But we're stronger than we think and tougher than fear would have us believe."

Ana reached over and stroked his cheek.

"It's all a question of attitude. And you're doing it excellently because that's how the Cortes do it! We always defy the odds."

"Gee, thanks Mom," grinned Alex.

Ana punched him lightly on the arm.

"I already have one kid and another on the way. I don't need another big kid, thanks!" she said, smiling.

"Now you're gonna have two," he said, rubbing her belly. "You're such a great mom."

She nodded, and they embraced again.

As they returned to the small birthday party, Alex added:

"And you're not a bad psychologist either."

"Psychiatrist, Alex, psychiatrist. How many times do I have to tell you?"

56

Barcelona.
Monday.

Rock music was blaring in his earbuds.

One foot after the other. On and on.

Alex dodged the early morning tourists. It was only six o'clock in the morning, but the seafront was already full of joggers, cyclists and hangover partygoers returning home.

Alex got rid of his bodyguard and went running alone. He needed it.

Spending Saturday with his family had been a balm for his soul, but Sunday had been spent in the office, buried in papers and research. He still felt they were moving around in circles, following the trail of breadcrumbs Roberto had laid for them. He could be watching him right now.

Anyone could be Roberto. The man behind him in the supermarket queue, at the gas station, or the one he greeted on the stairs of his apartment building. Thoughts like this tormented him and wondered if he'd recognize him.

56

He showered and went to the police station. A new day awaited him.

Karla was already there. They had the usual morning meeting with the team, but there was little to add. Things felt stagnant. Alex could see it in everyone's eyes: they were all tired and feeling down.

Following Roberto's pattern, they received the package with the third corpse on Monday. He'd been identified as a Peruvian male called Mauricio David Lopez. A common name and a regular guy: no family, no girlfriend, no traces left behind.

Roberto was good at selecting his victims, and Alex grudgingly admired him.

Mauricio had lived in the city and worked on a construction site downtown. How could he have met Roberto? However, trusting Roberto had cost him the most valuable thing he had: his life.

The riddles were proving difficult for the team and seemed illogical.

Alan had been working on the investigation, despite being initially underwhelmed. But it soon became a challenge, a puzzle he had vowed to solve. It became his new Rubik's cube, and he was doggedly determined to find the solution.

Alex thought about the van continually. The smell of putrefaction was still strong in his nostrils; the memory of the stench fed his curiosity to solve the enigma and catch the most wanted man in the country.

He was checking his email when a voice interrupted him.

"We may have something."

Alex looked up. It was Karla, with Alan standing beside her.

"What is it?" he asked.

"You explain it to him," said Karla to Alan.

"We know that Miguel was looking for another job because the position at the supermarket in La Mina wasn't what he wanted. Patricia intended to leave the nightclub and become a beautician. We know this because her adoptive mother told the Guardia Civil during the interrogation."

Alex nodded.

"And we talked to Mauricio's roommate. Guess what he wanted to do?"

"I don't know," said Alex.

"He wanted to leave his job because he was sick of it. This could connect all the victims."

"Interesting. We have three people who wanted to change jobs. It's a good start."

"Yes, but that's not all. Go on!" said Karla, nudging Alan.

Alan continued.

"We don't know about Patricia because we have no information about her, but we have two coincidences regarding Miguel and Mauricio. Both wanted to change jobs and had been actively searching and sending out resumes to agencies. And both had used the same agency," he said, looking smug.

"Which one?" asked Alex.

"Work Job Institute. It's a temp agency. You know, they match workers and employers for short and long-term positions. Like an external personnel selection."

"How interesting. And do we know where it is?"

"It's in Portal del Angel. Both victims visited the same one."

"Bingo!"

56

"Well, it may be nothing, just a coincidence," said Karla.

"Well, we won't know until we find out more," said Alex, getting up from the desk. "Shall we go take a look? It's the only lead we have."

57

Within thirty minutes, Alex and Karla had arrived at the temp agency unannounced.

The place was bright, with boldly colored furniture featuring the brand's corporate image. The company had several offices all over Spain. An illuminated sign with their blue and orange logo was hanging on the wall behind the reception desk.

A young girl greeted them with a wide smile. A dozen tables were dotted around with employees and clients in conversation.

"Good morning. How can I help you?" asked the receptionist.

"Morning. We are officers Ramirez and Cortes from the criminal investigation department," said Alex. "We'd like to speak with the manager."

"I'm afraid he's currently on vacation. Maybe I can help you?"

Alex and Karla looked at each other.

"How long has he been on vacation?"

"Well, it must have been…" she said, checking her screen.

"About ten days. He'll be back this Thursday."

"Do you have a photo of him?"

"Are you looking for anything in particular?"

"We need it for an investigation."

"Erm, I'm not sure I have one to hand," said the receptionist, looking flustered. "Shall I call the assistant manager?"

"Yes, that would be great."

The receptionist punched in a number, and in under a minute, a man approached them.

"Good morning, officers," he said. "How can we help you?"

The man reminded Alex of a banker: he was sporting a 90's looking short-sleeved shirt, cropped hair and a perfectly shaved beard.

"We'd like to ask you some questions about a case we're investigating. Do you have somewhere quiet we can talk?"

"Of course, follow me."

They entered an interview room and sat at a table opposite the assistant manager.

"Excuse me, what did you say your name was?"

"Nestor, I hadn't introduced myself."

"So, Nestor, we're investigating the disappearance of two men who, according to sources, both came to this agency looking for a job."

The man nodded. He looked pleasant and collaborative, although his eyes were dark and expressionless.

"Please be assured that Work Job Institute will fully cooperate with the authorities. If you tell me their names, I'll bring you any files we have," he said crisply.

Alex told him the full names of Miguel and Mauricio, and the manager left the room. After several minutes he returned carrying a couple of folders and accompanied by the receptionist.

She left the room when she'd told them everything she knew without adding anything the officers didn't already know.

"Do you mind if we take both files with us?" asked Alex.

"Of course, take them with you. Unfortunately, I don't think we'll need them anymore."

"Thanks very much," said Karla. "We still need to speak to your manager."

"He's on vacation."

"Was it a planned vacation?" Alex asked.

"I don't know; employees ask for their vacation whenever they want. Our company is very flexible in this respect."

"And do you know where he went?"

The man's smile didn't falter.

"I have no idea. He doesn't tell us about his private life, but you can ask him yourself," said Nestor.

"How can I contact him?"

"I can give you his phone number."

"Perfect, thank you. The name?"

"Nestor Luna."

"No, I mean your boss's."

"Ah! Sorry! Tomas Fernandez," he said, writing the number down on a piece of paper.

"You don't need to look it up? "Karla asked, "Do you know it by heart?"

The man looked at them and laughed.

"I have a good memory," he said, putting his pen in his shirt pocket.

"Thank you very much, Mr. Luna," said Alex, standing up and offering his hand for him to shake.

The man stood up, looked at Alex's outstretched hand for a

second, and then shook it.

When they were back on the street, Alex and Karla went and stood on the opposite side. Alex watched the man talking to the receptionist, making her laugh before he returned to his workstation. He didn't give the officers a second glance.

"Do you fancy a coffee?" asked Karla to Alex.

"Yes, that's a good idea."

They walked a few yards up the street toward Plaza Catalunya until they found a coffee shop. They ordered their drinks and sat down at a table.

Alex began to leaf through the folders of the two victims, which were simple computer-transcribed interviews and the original copy of their resumes.

Seeing photos of the men pre-death shocked Alex, and he tried to bat away the memory of the two severed heads resting on a cold stainless-steel table in the morgue. Despite his best efforts, he found it difficult to dislodge it from his mind.

"What do you think?" Karla asked.

"First, tell me what you thought of that guy?"

"I didn't like him at all."

Alex grunted.

"What about you?"

"Me neither," he answered.

"Do you think...?" she said and paused.

"Go on."

"Do you think he could be Roberto?" she whispered, glancing around.

"Too easy," replied Alex. "But..."

"Yes?" she said, surprised.

"What if it's the manager?"

She frowned.

"Could be, I guess."

"It could be a coincidence, but it's odd that he's on vacation these particular weeks, right?

"True."

"And another thing – What if this Nestor has been selecting the victims for Roberto? They could be in it together."

The woman pursed her lips and then took a sip of coffee, cursing as it burned her tongue.

"What does your intuition tell you about this guy? How would you react if he asked you out on a date?" Alex asked.

"No way would I go. I found him slimy, calculating, a creep, although that doesn't necessarily point to him being a serial killer."

She glanced out of the window.

"What did you notice when he shook your hand?" she asked.

"It was damp, sweaty, but I didn't notice anything in particular," he replied, following her gaze to the agency down the street.

Then he took a sip of his coffee and also burned his tongue. He glared at the waiter behind the bar.

"What's going on with this coffee? It's boiling!" Alex called out, tutting.

Before the man could respond, Alex's phone vibrated. He took it out and replied.

"Hey, Alberto, can I call you later? What? My sister? Are you sure? Why didn't you call me earlier? Damn it," he said and got up. "I'll be right there."

58

Alberto felt like the world was crumbling around him.

He'd met Ana at college. They'd been introduced by mutual friends, and after several attempts, the most popular girl in the psychiatry faculty had agreed to go out with him.

He'd recently been appointed as CEO of a German company. This promotion meant more money, better family health insurance, a company car and other perks. He was a loving partner to Ana and a good father, or at least he had been up to that point.

Sirens blaring, Alex crossed the city with his bodyguard, weaving in and out of the slow-moving traffic.

He raced up the stairs to his sister's apartment and banged on the door. When Alberto opened the door, Alex took a step back. He'd never seen his brother-in-law looking so terrible. His eyes were red and swollen from crying, and his white shirt was sweat-stained and crumpled.

They embraced, and then Alberto ushered him inside.

"What the hell is going on?"

Alberto began but was struggling for breath and began

hyperventilating.

Alex had often seen this reaction in his job and led Alberto to sit on the couch.

"Breathe deeply, Alberto. It's okay," he said, trying to calm him down.

He picked up a magazine and fanned it in front of his face.

Alberto's face regained color as the minutes passed, and his breathing slowed.

"Alberto, please try and tell me what's happened."

"Yesterday, I went to work, as usual. In the afternoon, I had to prepare for an important meeting later today."

"Ok," nodded Alex, trying to curb his impatience.

"It took longer than expected, so I worked in the office until late."

"Are you screwing your secretary?"

The man looked at him with wide eyes, shocked at the aberration Alex had just asked him.

"Of course not! What the fuck? We're in the middle of an important acquisition, and I had to prepare for the meeting."

Alex let out a grunt.

"Okay, go on."

"I came home late."

"What time?"

"Late…"

"No, late isn't a time. What time was it? Think, Alberto."

"I don't know, I guess around eleven."

"Okay, and then what happened?"

"I called her around seven o'clock to tell her that I wouldn't make it back for dinner and not to wait for me, and told her to give the baby a kiss from me."

Alex stiffened.

"Where is he?"

"He's sleeping in his bedroom. He's fine."

Alex sighed and said:

"Okay, go on."

"When I got home, she wasn't here. The baby was screaming in his cot. I called her name, but she didn't answer. So I looked everywhere and still couldn't find her. I thought it was a prank or something, I don't even know what I thought, but I was sure she would come back. The door hadn't been forced, but there was no sign of her. I just don't get it, Alex!"

"Why the hell didn't you call me before now?"

"I don't know. I guess I kept expecting her to turn up."

"Jeez, Alberto! You should have called me right away, damn it! I can't believe you haven't done anything since last night!"

Alberto opened his mouth and tried to speak, raising both hands.

"I don't know. I couldn't think of anything else. I took the kid, drove him to Ana's best friend's house, and then went to work. I thought she'd come back. Fuck…" He burst into tears, covering his face with both hands, and Alex regretted yelling at him.

After a while, when Alberto had regained his composure, he suddenly turned to Alex.

"Then, this morning, I realized something…."

Alex frowned.

"What?"

"I don't know, maybe it's silly, but I found it strange."

"What are you talking about?"

"I don't know, maybe it's not important, you tell me," he said, handing him a folded piece of paper. "This was stuck on the mirror, over the sink."

Alex took it and unfolded it slowly, dreading what he would find.

"No!" he bellowed, the blood draining from his face.

Startled by Alex's roar, his nephew woke up and began to cry.

On the piece of paper were the unmistakable lines of a bar code.

59

It was like a bolt of lightning had split Alex in two.

He was paralyzed, overcome by a wave of helplessness, a feeling which soon turned to white-hot rage.

A tropical storm called Roberto was no longer a public problem; it had come crashing into Alex's world like a tsunami. It had just become personal.

He crumpled the paper in his hand and covered his face. Until he'd seen the bar code, he had never imagined such a thing could happen to him. To his family.

He looked around his sister's house, now stripped of its most important thing. Tears blurred his vision, and his thoughts were jumbled.

When he had managed to collect himself, he took a sharp intake of breath.

"The phone, Alberto, where's the phone?"

"What phone, Alex?" said Alberto looking around.

"Ana's cell phone, where is it?"

"I haven't seen it."

"You must have called her?"

"Yes, I did, but it's turned off."

Alex started rummaging through the house, then stopped. He pulled out his phone and called his sister.

The answering machine immediately went off. He recalled what had happened with Miguel's phone and logged onto a texting app, trying to steady his trembling hands. He sent a message, and two gray ticks appeared immediately. *Delivered.*

"I can't believe it."

Then his sister's phone showed someone was online, and the ticks turned blue.

Alex's stomach clenched as he pressed the call icon.

It rang, but no one answered.

After a few rings, he hung up.

"Son of a bitch," muttered Alex.

When he ended the call, he received a voice note. It hadn't been recorded with Ana's phone, only forwarded. It was forty seconds long.

He pressed play.

"Hello, Sergeant. What you did in Chronus Frius wasn't nice; you changed the course of the game and the order of events. You're too impatient, my friend. That's why I decided to change the plan and take your sister. Nothing personal, of course; just business. Let's say I took her as collateral. I want to offer you a deal. You don't change my master plan, and I don't do anything to her. What do you think? Well, you don't need to answer me, the truth is that it's already decided. If you make me change my plans again, I don't need to tell you who will join all our friends in the Morgue, do I? Ciao, Sergeant."

Alex stared at his screen and saw the online status disappear from Ana's cell phone and, with it, the chance of seeing his sister again.

An hour later, forensics were searching the apartment for clues.

Alberto took the baby to his mother's house, and the apartment was sealed.

The lieutenant arrived with Karla, and reporters began to besiege the entrance to Ana's apartment building.

"Have you checked on the temp agency guy?" Alex asked Karla.

"Yes. He stayed at the office and then walked home a couple of blocks downtown," she replied.

"It's his boss. We need to search his apartment; I'm sure it's him who has my sister's cell phone."

"Alex, go home and rest. You can't accuse a man without proof. Tomorrow you'll see things differently. Go home; we're here to take care of things. You're too close to the case now, and it's too personal. Another parcel might arrive on Wednesday, and we'll need you to be well-rested."

Alex ignored her.

"What does Alan say? Has he checked the last triangulations on my sister's phone?"

"Yes, but they come from here. It's like it never left the apartment."

"But it's not here," said Alex, slumping onto the couch and holding his head in his hands.

"Go home," said Rexach. "That's an order."

"Did Alan manage to crack the code?" he insisted, his eyes pinned on Rexach's.

"Alex! I told you to go home."

Alex fell silent, putting his hand over his mouth to stop himself from saying something he might regret.

"We'll handle things now; the boss is right. Do you want me to go with you?"

"No, Ramirez, let the bodyguard take him. I need you here," said the Lieutenant.

Alex nodded and left without saying goodbye. He walked back to his car, dragging his feet like a wounded animal, and each step he took felt like an eternity.

The chief looked at the bodyguards and jerked his head toward a retreating Alex. They nodded.

"This isn't easy for him, boss," Karla said after Alex had left.

"I know, but he's an officer of the law before he's a brother," he replied. "He has to maintain a certain conduct, a certain discipline, and go by the ethical code of the force; he can't do as he pleases. I hope this doesn't tip him over the edge."

Alex arrived home escorted like a witness but felt like a prisoner. He rummaged through the cupboards, which contained several bottles of wine he'd bought with Mary. But he kept looking until he found an expensive bottle of vintage Bourbon, which they'd been saving for a special occasion.

This wasn't a special occasion, but he needed to drink enough to knock himself out; otherwise, he was in for a long sleepless night.

The more he drank, the more lucidly he thought he saw things.

He passed out, hugging the bottle, until the early morning rays of sunlight penetrated his eyelids, making sleep impossible

His head was pounding, and he had no memory of the previous night.

The hangover was monumental, and he couldn't recall ever suffering one of this magnitude.

Tuesday had begun.

Only when he stretched his stiff back and yawned widely did he remember why he'd been drinking Bourbon: Roberto, the Barcelona serial killer, had kidnapped his sister.

60

Barcelona.
Tuesday.

His head felt like it was about to explode.

Aspirin wasn't enough; he needed something strong enough to knock out a racehorse. He went to the pharmacy and asked for the most powerful painkiller they sold. He could only remember a comparable hangover the day he'd graduated from his police training when he'd mixed different types of alcohol and smoked cigars. Although he's been considerably younger then, the consequences had been similar.

He went into the coffee shop. He needed another dose of coffee before going to the station and taking his pills. He called Karla, who told him to stay where he was, and she'd come down.

Sitting opposite him, she raised her eyebrows and grimaced

when she saw the state of him.

"What happened to you?" she asked.

He'd shown up with wet hair and a three-day beard. The dark circles under his eyes and his grayish pallor made him look ill.

"Don't ask."

She moved closer and sniffed.

"Have you been drinking?" she asked, frowning at him. "Is that how you're dealing with Ana's disappearance?"

Alex sipped his coffee.

"Give me a break, please. Today is shit, my head is pounding, and I don't need you lecturing me, too," he said, holding his forehead while he rested his elbow on the table.

She kept talking, but Alex wasn't receptive, and his thoughts were muddled, pain and mental fog vying for space.

He glanced over Karla's shoulder, and something caught his attention.

She followed his gaze and then looked at him quizzically.

Rafa was talking to a young man who had placed a large parcel on the counter. Something didn't fit. It looked familiar but out of place. Alex and Karla looked closer, and both gasped at the same time: there was no doubt that this was one of Roberto's packages. Rafa spotted Alex jumping out of his seat and trying to grab the man's wrist, but the man slapped Rafa's hand away and fled toward the door.

Alex and Karla raced after him and saw him disappear around the corner.

"Get after him", he yelled at his bodyguards, who'd been smoking outside as they waited for Alex. "Let's go!"

The two undercover officers and Alex began chasing after

the man.

Karla went back inside and carefully stowed the package in the kitchen. She called someone from her team to take care of it and then joined the chase.

The man turned left onto Carrer del Berguedà, pushing people out of the way. Shouts of anger and bewildered pedestrians made it difficult for the officers to keep up with him.

The young man ran faster than the police and was half a block ahead.

Alex's temples throbbed, increasing the pressure and the pain in his head. But he needed to catch Roberto's messenger.

The two officers following him were tall and strong but not as fast or agile. Alex realized they were losing him.

When the man reached the end of the street, he turned right onto Carrer del Montnegre, running across the road without looking. A cacophony of horns blared, and chaos ensued.

The man was still half a block ahead, and Alex dug deep, putting all his training to the test. He couldn't let the man escape; he could be their only link to Roberto.

They passed by Plaza de Les Corts, a small park with a winding path through the middle. A flock of pigeons were startled and fluttered up in the air, but the man ran through them, undeterred and turned left onto Calle Numancia. The man was getting further ahead, and the distance between them had widened almost a block. Despite the hangover, Alex had a vague idea of where the man was heading.

Suddenly the man disappeared to the right. Now Alex understood, and he entered a supermarket, hot on the man's heels

Four.

He entered through the checkout, swerving shopping carts.

Three.

He crossed the grocery section, past bananas and lettuces, going as fast as he could and scanning the other side of the supermarket toward the glass doors.

Two.

He passed through the perfume department. He needed to make one last push. His sneakers slipped on the tiled floor, but he stabilized.

One.

Alex's heart was racing. All the noises around him faded, and he only heard the sound of his heart bursting painfully out of his chest. But it wasn't enough. He needed to go faster. He kept his eye on the exit to the shop and saw the man about to leave. In desperation, Alex jumped over a closed checkout and collided with a customer.

Zero.

In a desperate attempt to grab the man, Alex launched himself at the doors, praying that he hadn't missed the opportunity to stop this slippery son of a bitch.

The man was approaching the exit. When he saw Alex colliding with the customer, he slowed down, but just as he stepped through the door, Alex grabbed him from behind and rugby-tackled him to the ground.

They crashed against a blue dumpster and landed on a pile

of old cardboard boxes.

A few seconds later, Alex's two bodyguards arrived. The man was trapped, pinned to the ground with guns trained on him.

61

The race had been worth it.

The unexpected sprint had left Alex soaked in sweat, but at least his headache had disappeared.

He was drinking his third coffee of the day.

Roberto's courier was handcuffed and furious in the interrogation room.

It had taken three people to get him into the police van. Being captured had definitely not been part of his or Roberto's plan.

While Alex questioned him, Karla took the fourth package to Sabadell for the macabre routine that was becoming depressingly familiar.

"What's your name?" he asked.

The man bit his lip and turned to the two-way mirror.

"Are you recording me?" he said. "I've seen it in the movies."

Alex nodded.

"We have to, for your safety."

"Then I want to talk to a lawyer."

"This isn't like in the movies. It's real life. Do you know what was in the box you left in the coffee shop?"

The boy didn't look at him and shrugged.

"Look at me," demanded Alex, his voice hardening.

The boy gave him a sidelong glance.

"Do you know what was in the box?"

"No, man, I don't know," he said. "I don't give a damn, okay? I only did it for the money."

"Well, I'll tell you what was in the package: human limbs and someone's decapitated head. You're a courier of death. Aiding and abetting a murderer. Do you realize that? Ten to thirty years in prison. If you don't cooperate, we'll consider charging you with homicide. Understand?"

The man's jaw dropped.

"You're shitting me, man! Is this the guy with the van?" he said, eyes wide and incredulous.

"I don't think you fully understand your situation. You're in deep shit, you know?"

Alex took a breath and took a sip of coffee.

"Let's try again. What's your name?"

"Fernando," he said, looking away from the glass.

"Very well, Fernando, listen to me. I know you had nothing to do with it, but I want to know what happened exactly."

The boy began to shake his head.

"He told me he'd kill me if I talked."

"I assure you it won't happen because if you help me catch him, you and everyone else will be safe."

Fernando snorted. Then he ran his hands over his head and face.

"He told me it was imperative not to get caught. He said the cops were too dumb to catch me."

"Well, it seems he was wrong," said Alex. Come on, start at the beginning. Explain everything to me, and you'll soon be home, yeah?"

"A few weeks ago, a guy stopped me in my neighborhood. He was driving a white van. He told me he had an easy little job and offered me a wad of cash in exchange for dropping off a parcel." Fernando shrugged. "He's not the first nutcase I meet in my neighborhood."

"Carry on."

* * *

Karla returned from Sabadell with some news.

She ran up the stairs, her long brunette hair swaying in time with her steps. She was pretty, with delicate features, although her appearance didn't completely camouflage the sharp temper she'd developed during her police training.

When she entered the room, Alex was working at his computer.

"Hey, Alex. I've got the photos of the contents from the fourth package. There's a surprise inside. Come with me," she said.

The two of them went to the meeting room.

"What's happened?"

"There was something else in this package."

"A message?"

"Worse…"

"Why so much secrecy? Just spit it out," said Alex folding his arms.

"There was the usual: the head, hands and feet. The victim

was male. But there was something else," said Karla.

She took out some photos and showed him the last one.

"There was one extra hand."

"What do you mean, an extra hand?" said Alex. A shiver ran down his spine.

She passed him the photo.

When Alex looked at it, he collapsed into the chair, his mouth open, his eyes wide with shock.

Karla crouched beside him and placed her hand on his back, waiting for his reaction.

A sob escaped him, and he began to cry with howls of anger and hatred.

His free hand closed into a fist.

"Do you recognize it, Alex?" she asked gently, "Do you think it's... hers?"

Alex recognized the color of the nail polish, but it was the ring that got him. It was unmistakably the one Alberto had given Ana for their engagement.

It was his sister's hand.

Alex couldn't speak. He nodded his head, and tears poured down his cheeks.

Karla rested her hand on his knee, but it didn't feel enough. She got up and wrapped him in her arms, feeling the love she still had for him come flooding back, a love that had survived despite the passing of time.

"We'll catch him, Alex. Never doubt that."

Alex couldn't speak. He was afraid of his anger.

After several soaked handkerchiefs, he managed to speak.

"I need to tell my parents and Alberto."

"Wait for a while. We don't know anything for sure."

"What do you mean we don't know anything for sure?" he said, pointing to the photo.

"Listen to me, Alex, that's just a hand. Your sister may still be alive. This photo doesn't prove anything."

"He'll send us more parts like he did with the others."

"We don't know that, Alex. You're jumping to conclusions."

He looked out of the window.

"I have a hunch that's what he'll do."

"Listen to me; let's not predict events. You're not a fortune teller. You're only a cop," she said, a soft smile playing on her lips as she tried to reassure him. "We have to keep investigating."

Alex nodded, staring into Karla's eyes, losing himself in her captivating hazel irises. They held each other's gaze for an instant, but he pulled away.

"Did you check what Nestor did yesterday?"

"He stayed home all night," replied Karla, clearing her throat. "I don't think it's him, Alex. It's too easy."

"I know, you've already told me," he said dryly.

"What have you been able to get out of the kid?"

"He's a slum boy from La Mina. He's not important. But Roberto contacted him weeks ago and convinced him to make the delivery in exchange for a few hundred euros. He gave him the parcel yesterday with instructions on when and where to deliver it."

"Yesterday?"

"Yes, he said that Roberto arrived by bus and then simply disappeared."

"Do you think the kid was counting on us catching him?"

"I don't think so because he's fast, very fast. That's probably why Roberto chose him."

"What else did you get from him?"

"A description of Roberto which is the same as the one we already have. They're doing the identikit, but it's a waste of time. We need more than that to catch the son of a bitch," he said, banging the palm of his hand on the table.

Karla was startled.

"Sometimes your outbursts scare me, Alex."

"I'm sorry, but I don't know how to handle all this."

"You're doing the best you can, like any good brother," she said.

The door opened, and an officer entered.

"Sorry to interrupt, bosses, but I needed to talk to you."

"This isn't a good time," she said.

"I wouldn't have bothered you unless I thought it was important," said the officer, closing the door. "I'll come back later."

"No," Alex called after him. "What is it?"

Karla stood up.

"I think we have something. Since the press conference, we've had several calls from members of the public complaining about annoying neighbors and bad smells. Some claim to have seen the murderer, and others claim they've received strange packages."

"Officer," said Alex impatiently, gesturing for the officer to get to the point.

"Let me finish, Sir. I just got a call from a lady who says that there's a putrid smell coming from her neighbor's house, and they don't know what to do. We've had a bunch of false alarms all over the city, but—"

"But what?" barked Karla.

"We've had various calls from the same apartment block."

61

"Where?" Alex and Karla asked in unison.

62

Bellvitge.

A quiet neighborhood that had no idea what was about to hit it.

It was a mainly working-class area, full of hard-working families and retirees. Stores, cinemas, supermarkets. A neighborhood with common, everyday problems and people from all walks of life.

Without warning, three patrol cars and two riot vans pulled up in a quiet street. Behind them, Karla, Alex and the bodyguards followed in two camouflaged vehicles.

Sirens and flashing lights shattered the peace. Lights came on in the surrounding apartments, and people came out onto their balconies to see what was happening,

The police followed the directions they'd received and reached a door on the second floor of a run-down apartment building: *door B.* According to a neighbor, a rank smell had been coming from the apartment for days.

When they reached the landing, the lady who had called the police came out, still wearing her dressing gown.

"Do you know how long we've had to put up with this?"

she said.

"Go back inside, ma'am!" said an officer, his face hidden under a balaclava, training his machine gun up toward the ceiling.

The woman's eyes widened, and she obeyed.

Alex came rushing up the stairs and immediately noticed the smell. As soon as they reached the landing, he exchanged a glance with Karla. She shook her head, grimacing in disgust.

Someone had placed a cushion along the bottom of the door to prevent the odor from escaping.

An officer kicked it aside and rang the doorbell.

There was no sound from inside.

"Police, open the door!" he yelled, hammering on the door.

There was no response.

He then signaled his colleagues, who began battering down the door with an enforcer to gain entry.

The wood splintered, and the cops piled in the apartment. In less than a minute, the whole place had been cleared. There was no one in the apartment.

The team leader came back out onto the landing.

"Sergeant, come take a look at this," he said to Alex, who had been pacing the hallway.

Karla and Alex followed him inside. The further inside they went, the worst the stench got.

Officers searched the property, going in and out of all the rooms, opening cupboards and drawers. Finally, Karla and Alex reached the end of the corridor, and the team leader opened the bathroom door.

Alex peered in and recoiled in horror, coughing and gagging, desperately trying not to vomit.

He rushed out with his hand covering his mouth and nose.

***

Meanwhile, downstairs, the Mossos d'Esquadra security forces, joined by local police, began to seal off the area.

The officers followed the usual protocol while dealing with curious residents demanding to know what was happening.

A man carrying a bag full of something that looked like a bunch of cans approached the entrance to the block. When he saw police officers all over the building, he stopped suddenly, glancing around nervously. Then he turned around and quickly walked away.

An officer noticed and immediately put a call out on the radio for someone to follow the man.

There was a shout, and several officers began chasing him. When he realized that was happening, he dropped his bag and ran, disappearing down the steps into the subway.

***

Karla entered the bathroom after Alex, seemingly undeterred by the sickening scene. She pulled the sleeve of her leather jacket in front of her face, helping the modest job the mask was doing.

A body lay in the bathtub, partially protruding from the liquid it was immersed in. The area that wasn't underwater appeared to have shriveled up. The greenish liquid, full of

62

fermentation bubbles and greasy welts on the surface, allowed Karla a faint glimpse of the bare skeleton underneath. Sparse, white hair covered the skull.

Karla opened the window to try and get rid of the unbearable smell. Her radio crackled, and she answered.

"We've got him."

Karla turned to Alex, standing in the doorway, his face still pale, and raised her eyebrows.

63

The man was shaking from head to toe, beads of sweat tricking down his face, and he squirmed uncomfortably in the chair.

His sweatshirt was filthy, and his jeans were torn and faded. He wore cheap supermarket sneakers.

His hair was cropped, greasy and flat to his head.

He'd been there for nearly an hour when the door opened. It was Karla's turn.

She sat down, placed a folder on the table and slowly opened it, revealing the photo of the human remains in the bathtub.

The man saw it and turned away.

"Carmen Garcia," she said quietly.

The man swallowed and clenched his fists.

"Why?" Karla asked.

"N-no, I didn't kill her!"

The woman nodded without saying anything.

"I swear to you, I didn't kill her!"

"Did someone pay you to do it? For revenge?"

"No," he cried, looking terrified.

"So?"

"I didn't do it... I swear."

"I don't believe you."

"Please believe me! I'm not a murderer."

Karla turned over the photo of the woman over and pushed it toward the man.

"No? Are you sure? Because right now, all the evidence is pointing to you."

The man didn't answer.

"Enrique Diaz Garcia. You've never committed a crime before, or at least caught until now," she said solemnly. "You killed your grandmother and put her in a bathtub filled with hydrochloric acid. You wanted to dissolve her body in acid and thought nobody would notice anything. Stick the bones in the trash, and it would be over," she concluded with a shrug.

"No, it wasn't like that."

"Then tell me exactly what happened, Enrique, and make it snappy because I'm extremely busy."

"Okay," he said, taking a shuddering breath. "I'll tell you everything. I lost my job months ago. I couldn't afford to feed my family and didn't know what to do. All we had to live on was my grandma's pension. But she died alone at home one night. I swear she was dead when we found her," he said, crying with his hand on his heart. "We couldn't make ends meet…"

"So you thought you could hide her death?" Karla asked in disgust.

"We just wanted to keep getting her pension, and I didn't think it would harm anyone. I did it for my family," he said, covering his face with his hands and sobbing loudly.

Karla watched him and then looked at the two-way mirror. She exhaled loudly and closed her eyes.

"Are you sure, Enrique? Nobody asked you to kill your

grandmother?"

"I swear, Officer," he said with his hand on his heart again. "I swear on my kids' lives. I swear…"

A few minutes later, Karla left the interrogation room and entered the dimly lit room next door.

"What do you think?" she asked the others.

"He's just a messed-up creep," said the lieutenant, "who misguidedly tried to take advantage of his dead granny."

"He's certainly not Roberto," confirmed Alex. "We've just caught a desperate man, damn it!"

"Calm down, Alex. We have to keep our wits about us and remain professional," the lieutenant scolded.

"Professional? If we'd been *professional*, my sister wouldn't be…" shouted Alex, pointing to the side of the room, "who knows fucking where… probably dead! So don't start with the motivational speeches now!"

"Please, Alex."

"Are you seriously asking me to calm down? How the hell am I supposed to calm down, for fuck's sake?"

"Alex! I've got orders from the chief inspector to take you off the case. Do you understand me?" the lieutenant shouted.

Alex looked at the boss, his eyes glinting dangerously.

"He's asked me to remove you from this case because your personal involvement is clouding your judgement."

"What about you? Is that what you think, too?" asked Alex.

Rexach looked at Alex, his expression unreadable as he turned to Karla.

"Ramirez, you're officially taking command of this investigation."

"What? Are you seriously taking me off the case? Jesus

Christ! "Alex spat, walking away from the lieutenant. "Wait a minute!" he snarled, turning back to Rexach and jabbing his finger at the boss.

"If I remember correctly, you asked me, NO! You *begged* me not to go to Tarragona. So I fucking stayed to help you. And now you're getting rid of me?"

"Don't make this harder than it already is," Rexach said, grabbing Alex by the arm. "Listen to me. I said, "officially" Alex, *officially*."

They stared at each other.

"We want you to stay, but you're too close to the case. Please don't make me feel bad. It's for your own good," said the lieutenant.

"Listen to me, boss. It's him. Roberto is Nestor. We have to bring him in and get the truth out of him," he said, trying to reign in the hysteria that was threatening to overwhelm. "It's him, I know it, damn it! How many more times have I got to tell you?"

"It can't be him, Alex," Karla said firmly, standing between Alex and Rexach and holding out her hands as if to appease them. "He was under surveillance yesterday, and nothing was out of the ordinary. Just home-work-home."

Alex broke away and sat down, holding his head in his hands.

"Look at you, Alex, you're losing it. Go home and rest," said the boss more softly now. "When you're like this, you make things more difficult for the team.

"The boss is right," Karla nodded. "Go home, and I'll keep you posted."

Alex raised his eyebrows and stood up.

"Okay, I'm leaving," he said, walking toward the door. "I'll see you tomorrow."

"I'll *call* you tomorrow... if there's any news."

Alex's hand was on the doorknob when Karla's words sank in. He turned and faced her.

"Okay. Understood."

And then he left.

"Boss, are you sure you've made the right decision? I don't think we can do this without Alex," protested Karla.

The lieutenant stared at her for a moment before walking to the door. "You've got this, Corporal. Keep up the good work," he said, opening the door. He jerked his head toward the two-way mirror. "Now go take care of that idiot."

Enrique Diaz Garcia, the grandson of the woman in the bathtub, was still crying with his head on the table when Karla returned to the room.

"What's going to happen to me," he moaned piteously, raking his hand through his greasy hair.

On the other side of the building, Alex gathered his things and went upstairs, followed by his bodyguard.

He knocked on a door.

"Can I come in?" he asked, putting his head around the door.

"Yes, come in, Sergeant," said Alan, "I was about to call you. I've had a breakthrough with the cryptograms."

64

Measured.

Or, rather, at his own speed. Alan appeared to be a sloth on the outside, but, in reality, he was as quick as a whippet

Most people didn't like him. In his childhood, he'd probably been a bespectacled nerd who was in the school chess club.

"Pull up a chair, Sergeant."

Alex entered the depressing windowless room. Shelves full of cables, various shapes and colors, lined the walls alongside random computer equipment. The smell of mold and mildew tickled his nostrils.

Alan's computer revealed an Excel spreadsheet full of codes and numbers.

"Look at this. These are the codes from the messages the killer sent us," Alan said, moving the mouse pointer. "I've tried the Morse code, but it didn't work. I knew that would be too easy. I tried the Caesar system but got nothing, either. Then I changed some letters, recombined the alphabet, and switched one letter forward and one letter backwards."

"Hang on; I'm not following…"

"Well, it will probably be impossible to interpret it until we have the fifth barcode," he said, glancing sideways at Alex.

"Hmmm, I don't think we'll have to wait long until it arrives," said Alex grimly. "The work you're doing is great, but you have to predict what he wants to tell us before he does. We need to be one step ahead of him without waiting until he sends the whole message. Do you understand?"

Alan turned slightly in his chair and turned to face Alex.

"It's impossible to predict without having all the information available. I think there are two scenarios. Either the killer will give us a translation key at the end, or he's based his messages on known cryptograms: then it would just be a matter of playing with them and combining them to understand which system it is. Do you know what I mean?"

"I suppose I should understand, but…"

Alan turned back to his computer.

"Have you had any luck with my sister's phone?" asked Alex.

"Not a lot. It's not given any more signs of life. It's still saying that it's at her address."

Alex nodded his head.

"What about the message I found at her house?"

Alan doubled clicked on a file. "Here it is. Same format, same system, but there's something different about it."

His words caught Alex's attention.

"What do you mean?"

"The paper isn't laminated," said Alan, taking out the photos from the morgue. "The ones we found on the heads were laminated. I guess so they wouldn't get wet in the bag, and we could see the message. But the one you found in her house, apart from being wrinkled," said Alan looking pointedly at Alex, "wasn't laminated. It was just a piece of plain white printed paper."

"And? What does that suggest?"

"That it wasn't planned. From what I've read, the killer is calculating. Everything he does is part of a plan. But this seems to have been done spontaneously. So I thought I'd put this bar code at the end, like a different message."

"Well spotted," he said and waited for Alan to continue. "Anything else?"

"No, not for now."

Alex sighed and went to the door.

"I'm leaving. If you find anything else, text me, I'm going home."

"That's a wise decision."

But as Alex took the stairs to the underground car park, he was reluctant to go home. He drove the car to the end of the street and turned in the opposite direction to home. Although he'd had strict instructions to stay well away, Alex didn't care.

He needed to see the person he believed was Roberto.

65

The sergeant's car moved slowly along Avenida Diagonal. The traffic stopped and started, giving him time to reconsider his plan, and he contemplated giving in and going home. But his instinct won.

There were three traffic lights until he reached Paseo de Gracia, and he was stuck behind a mini-bus and an Uber. He checked in his rearview mirror and pressed the "sport" button before he could change his mind. The engine revved, unleashing a small orchestra under the hood, and when the traffic light turned amber, Alex squeezed the clutch, went up a gear and pressed the pedal hard. He passed the vehicles in front, weaving in and out, jumping a red light. He shifted gears, sped up again, and was through the next red light in the blink of an eye.

The bodyguard in the car trailing him had disappeared from the rearview mirror of his Mini, swallowed up by traffic.

He turned right and sped down Passeig de Gracia, passing Casa Mila with its queues of tourists photographing the facade. A clap of thunder rumbled in the overcast sky, casting shadows on the four historical buildings affectionately called

The Apple of Discord.

He drove around Plaza Catalunya and left the car in an underground car park.

As he left the parking, he glanced up and down the street for the undercover police car, but there was no sign of it.

He walked down Portal del Angel and entered a coffee shop a few yards away from the employment agency where Nestor Luna worked. He ordered a coffee and waited, losing himself in his thoughts. The waiter placed his coffee on the counter, and Alex shook himself. He needed to think less and act more.

He snapped some photos while he drank his coffee and then settled back into the cushioned chair and his eyes closed. The sound of his own snoring woke him up.

Two blonde women at the next table glanced at him in disdain: he looked down at his crumpled clothes and realized he was a shadow of the handsome policeman he'd once been. He sat up in his seat and looked at his watch. He'd been asleep for a couple of hours.

A bunch of missed calls and message notifications filled his phone screen. He was about to unlock it when someone sat down opposite him.

"You're so predictable," huffed Karla.

"What are you doing here?"

"No, what are *you* doing here? You should be at home."

"How did you find me?"

"Because I know how your mind works. I got a call from the bodyguard saying that he'd lost you. You weren't at home, and I guessed you could only be in one place," said Karla. "And here you are. What the hell are you doing here?"

Alex shrugged. "What can I say?"

"You're obsessed."

"Does Rexach know?"

"Do you think you'd still be here if he knew?"

"Any news about my sister?"

"I could be investigating her case instead of babysitting you if you'd gone straight home," she said wearily. "Lucia Zapatero Perez."

"Who's that?"

"Woman number four. We just found out."

"What else do you know about her?"

"Twenty-six years old, from southern Andalusia, born into a well-respected but low-income family in a small village. Came to Barcelona when she was twenty and had several boyfriends, some worse than others. Many jobs, and guess what…"

Alex shook his head.

"Was she a friend of Nestor's?"

Karla looked at him and folded her arms impatiently.

"No! She worked as a waitress in a trendy *tapas* bar for tourists on Paseo de Gracia."

"And don't tell me – she wanted to get a new job," concluded Alex.

Karla reached across the table and took Alex's hand. He was surprised but didn't draw his hand away.

"Do us both a favor, Alex. Go home and go to sleep. I feel we're getting close to the end, and when that time comes, I need you to be on top form. I don't want this version of you."

She paused to see his reaction, wondering if she'd gone too far.

Alex stared at her, captivated by her hair trailing down in loose waves. Thank God they were in a public place, or he might have been tempted to do or say something he probably would have regretted later. He felt weak in body and spirit. Karla was right. He nodded and looked up: just outside, at the door of the coffee shop, he saw his bodyguard approaching.

"I think you're right. I'm going home," he said and stood up, slowly pulling his hand away from Karla's.

He didn't say goodbye or look back. When he passed the bodyguard, he smirked.

"How's the traffic on Avenida Diagonal?"

Alex parked the car at home and went straight to bed. He was so tired that he even resisted the magnetic lure of the bourbon bottle. Having it in the house was dangerous, and he needed to get rid of it. He was too tired to undress, so he lay face down, fully clothed, on the bed and fell asleep immediately.

He stayed in the warm arms of Morpheus for a long time and was woken by his cell phone vibrating on the gray hardwood floor.

He woke up, startled, and when he opened his eyes, he looked at the clock: it was four o'clock. But it was too light be the early hours. He stretched and moved his neck from left to right, sore from spending so long in the same position. Through the window, the sky was overcast, and clouds dominated the horizon. He'd slept for almost twenty-four hours straight.

He picked up the phone and unlocked the screen.

The last message was Karla's.

"Jalilah Tahiri. *The fifth package has been delivered. I'll wait for you at the station. The enigma is almost solved. And there's something else.*"

66

The anvil of justice.

No matter what a judge ruled, the public formed its own opinions—usually based on biased information, with the political influence of one media outlet or another.

Barcelona was under pressure from the media, who were doing an excellent job of stirring fear and mistrust.

The papers were full of sensationalist headlines written to sell more copies.

Radio stations broadcast programs with talk show hosts who had become criminologists overnight.

Television programs sowed the seed of panic, and people were terrified even to leave their houses and remained at home, glued to the lies on TV.

The police force was under pressure from all angles. It wasn't the first time they'd found themselves in this situation, although this case was decisive.

Alex arrived at the police station and went straight to Karla's department.

"Finally. I thought the earth had swallowed you up," she said. "But it's nice to see you like this."

"What do you mean? Like what?"

"Well..." she said, pointing at him. "Shaved, showered... you know."

"I need to look decent when she comes for me."

"Who? You mean Mary?" asked Karla, with a flicker of disappointment in her eyes.

"I meant *Death*. You never know when your last day will be," said Alex, completely serious.

"Jesus, Alex," she said, rolling her eyes. "Come on. We've got some important stuff to deal with. While you were hibernating, the last package arrived. It's already with your friend."

"My friend?"

"Coroner Guevara."

Alex felt his cheeks grow hot and narrowed his eyes at Karla.

"The guy was born in Morocco, twenty-one years old. He'd been in Spain for a few months. The report from the tax department says that he did several small jobs. The last one was as a childminder in a community center. And guess what!"

"The center in near Plaza Catalunya."

She nodded and cocked her eyebrow.

"And you know the worst part?"

"Surprise me!"

"You'll like this. Nestor has disappeared."

"What do you mean he's disappeared?" asked Alex with surprise. "I thought we were trailing him?"

"We were, but he didn't leave the house this morning to go

to work."

"See, I told you from the beginning! Damn it! I use simple words, I vocalize well, and despite that, people *never* freaking listen to me!"

"Wait, I haven't told you the worst yet. He used a small door to leave at the back of the building, and the officers didn't notice. We made the mistake of introducing ourselves during our visit to the temp agency."

"Of course, and he knew we'd follow him from then on."

"And now?" he said, flicking through the folder on the last corpse. "What's the next step?"

"I've passed Nestor's photograph on to all police stations, airports, etc. If he makes a wrong move, we'll catch him. Now, we don't know for sure that Nestor is Roberto. He might only be an accomplice."

Alex sat up and rubbed his chin.

Think. Think. Think, he thought.

Suddenly, he picked up the phone and dialed a number.

"Alan, Morning. It's Alex Cortes."

"Good morning," Alan replied, and there was silence. "You must mean *afternoon!*"

"Whatever. Have you got all the codes to the riddle now?"

"Yes. I've been working on it since I got the sixth one."

"And?"

"Nothing yet. I still think the guy has given us a combination of encryptions. I'm trying Fibonacci with the Caesar system, but it doesn't make sense at the moment."

"Ok, I'll let you get on with it. Bye," Alex said and hung up.

He looked at Karla.

"Our main priority is locating Nestor."

"Just because he's disappeared doesn't make him guilty."

"Come on, Karla! Sneaking out through the back door makes him a suspect," said Alex, standing up. "We need to get a warrant from the judge."

"I've already spoken to Rexach. We won't get it until we have some evidence against him. Right now, we don't have anything concrete, just suspicions."

Alex punched the table. He winced and rubbed his hand, feeling like a jerk.

"Fuck!"

Karla rested her hand on his shoulder.

"I get your frustration, but our hands are tied," she said. "The lieutenant is right. He doesn't want us to make a mistake that we'd have to explain to the judge. He's worried that she'll think we're incompetent, and the department will be left red-faced."

Alex frowned.

"Wait… red!"

"Alex, Rexach is right—"

"No. Wait… red… orange… blue! The colors. I've got it!" he said excitedly.

"I beg your pardon?" said Karla looking puzzled.

Alex stood up and kissed her on the forehead.

"You're a genius, Karla," he said, walking to the door.

"A genius? I didn't say anything. What are you talking about? Where are you going?"

Alex didn't answer, so Karla followed him to the meeting room. He began to scan all the papers pinned on the board.

"What are you looking for?" she asked but again got no answer.

Alex seemed to have been possessed by his new idea as he carefully studied the reports and photos of the van. He began searching for a folder on the table until he found what he was looking for and rifled through the files.

"Here it is. The colors, Karla, the colors!"

"What are you talking about?"

"When we went to the temp agency where Nestor works, the colors there reminded me of something, but I didn't know what. Now I remember. Why didn't I notice it before?"

Karla still didn't understand. Alex took the folder and left the room again, and she jogged after him to keep up.

He sat at the computer, opened an internet browser and began typing.

"Alex, what is it? What are you searching for?

Alex finally looked up at her.

"Do you remember when we interviewed the van's original owner, Pere Franco?"

Karla nodded slowly.

"Well, this was the pen they used to sign the contract," he said, turning the screen toward her.

The browser showed a photo of a blue and orange pen with some writing on the side that said, *Work Job Institute*.

She gasped sharply and covered her mouth with her hand.

Alex nodded.

"I know. Franco will confirm it."

He snatched up his phone, looked up the man's contact and typed a message. The man answered almost instantly.

He asked him if he could identify the pen and sent him a photo.

As he waited for the answer, he looked at Karla, and she smiled. Was she prettier than usual, or was he just imagining it?

The answer arrived.

"I think it was the same pen, or at least the colors were the same."

"That still doesn't prove anything, Alex, said Karla cautiously.

He knew she was right. He let out a long breath, racking his brain for a solution.

"Hang on; just humor me for a moment," he said, opening a graphic design program and superimposing a couple of photographs on each other.

Karla's expression became even more astonished.

"Where did you learn to do this? Are you a graphic designer, too?"

"There are many things you don't know about me!" said Alex, picking up his phone again.

Pere Franco, the farmer, was still online. He took a photo and sent it to him. It was an image of Nestor taken from social media. Alex had superimposed a pair of Ray-Ban aviator sunglasses onto his face.

He pressed "send". A minute passed.

Two blue ticks appeared, showing that Pere had read the message.

A muscle under Alex's eye twitched as he saw Pere was typing his reply.

When Alex saw his answer, he stood up, overcome by rage.

67

Alex barged into the room without even knocking on the door. He wasn't usually so rude, but this was urgent. Rexach was on the phone and glared angrily at him, but Alex couldn't care less.

"Roberto is Nestor," said Alex, followed by an anxious-looking Karla.

The boss apologized to whoever he was talking to and hung up.

"What's the matter, Alex? How about you knock next time you want to talk to me, "Rexach snapped.

"It's him, Boss, it's him!" Alex replied, putting his phone on the desk in front of Rexach.

"What are you talking about, Cortes?"

"Roberto is Nestor. Jesus, how many times do I have to repeat it?"

The Lieutenant raised his hands.

"Wait. What are you talking about?"

Alex explained what he'd just discovered. As he listened, Lieutenant Rexach looked sideways at Karla.

"Ramirez, what do you think?" he asked once Alex had finished.

She nodded. "I'm with Alex on this."

"All right, I'll call the judge and ask her for a warrant," said Rexach, picking up the phone.

"But Nestor has disappeared, Boss," she said, "He hasn't been seen since yesterday. The officer watching Nestor was concerned he hadn't seen him all day and went to look for him. Only then did he spot another exit door at the back of the building. We don't know where he is now. We've got a BOLO out on him but haven't had any sightings yet."

The boss scratched his head and looked at the sergeant.

"We'll start at his workplace. Let's question his colleagues. Maybe they know something we're missing," said Alex.

"In the meantime, send forensics to his house to check it over. They may find something," ordered the lieutenant.

"Okay, but knowing Roberto, I doubt we'll find anything," Alex answered, looking skeptical.

They were going through the door when the boss called out.

"Alex?"

The sergeant turned around.

"Keep a cool head, Cortes."

Alex nodded, gritting his teeth with barely suppressed rage, and disappeared out the door.

* * *

Within minutes, the sirens and flashing lights of the riot vans emerged onto Avenida Diagonal, stopping the traffic and ignoring the traffic lights. At that point in the investigation, there was no turning back.

Alex sat in the passenger seat. He bit his nails and jiggled his leg nervously.

"That's why he gave us those folders and said, '*You can take them with you. We won't need them anymore.*' The son of a bitch!"

"What are you talking about?" Karla asked.

"Miguel and Mauricio's folders. We told him they were *missing*, not dead. But he already knew. Why didn't I think of it before?"

She laughed cynically.

"Nestor knew we'd go to his house. He also knew we'd ask about his boss, which was why he had the phone number ready."

"Exactly. That's why he knew it by heart. And he led us to the agency while the boss was on vacation to confuse us even more."

Images of Nestor swirled through Alex's mind. He recalled their conversation and his gut reaction to him. As the van drove down Paseo de Gràcia, he saw Ana's face reflected in every shop window.

The police vehicles crossed Plaza Catalunya and turned onto Portal del Angel, causing chaos among pedestrians. Alex's car and one of the vans stopped in front of the agency where Nestor worked while the others continued to his house.

They all jumped out of the vehicles, and armed officers barged into the office. The screams of the employees could be heard out on the street, and passers-by recorded the drama on their phones.

Both officers were wearing bulletproof vests: the word *"Police"* was written on the back, and the officer's number, together with the coat of arms of the Mossos forces.

Alex approached the young woman at the reception desk, who gazed at him, her eyes wide with fear.

"Hello, do you remember me?" he asked.

The woman shook her head.

"My name's Alex Cortes. We met a few days ago when I came to talk to the manager. He wasn't here, so we talked to Nestor."

"Yes, I remember now," she nodded, her lip trembling. "Would you like to speak to the manager now? He's back from his vacation early."

Alex ignored her question.

"Have you heard anything from Nestor in the last twenty-four hours?"

The woman, staring blankly into the void, shook her head.

"He said he wasn't feeling well and wouldn't be in today."

"It's vital that I know when exactly you last talked to him. Do you understand?"

"Yesterday."

"Did he call you on your private cell phone?"

She shook her head once again.

"Okay, thank you," said Alex, stepping away from the desk. "Is the manager in his office?"

"Yes. It's the end of the corridor," said the woman.

Alex left the counter and headed to the office with Karla behind him.

"Wait," blurted out the receptionist.

Alex frowned and looked over his shoulder.

"You said your name was…" she said, looking at a piece of paper, "Alex Cortes, right?"

"Yes, why?

"Nestor told me that if a Mr. Cortes came, he'd left something for him."

Alex froze, feeling the adrenalin coursing through his veins. "Where is it?"

"He left it in the meeting room on the right side of the corridor," she said, pointing down the hallway.

Alex rushed to the door, and when he opened it, a shadow caught his eye.

The room was dark. He stepped inside while Karla turned on the lights. Then he saw it. There was no doubt that it was for him.

He stopped dead and covered his mouth with his hand, paralyzed with terror.

His darkest fears had materialized just as he was so close to solving the case. But Nestor, once more, had him in checkmate

He was nothing more than Nestor's puppet, picking up the crumbs he'd left the police to follow. The calculating psychopath was playing with him. Until now, Alex had been trailing after Nestor like a fool.

The package on the table was clear proof of that.

There it was, the sixth package.

What the hell was in it?

Or, rather, *who* was in it?

Inevitably, Ana flashed through his mind, but he clenched his jaw and tried to focus on the job.

Despite his fear, he had no choice but to open it.

68

Fear.
Only fear.

Alex felt it possessing him. The package in front of him left no room for misunderstanding.

Nestor was still killing. The five bodies in the van weren't the only ones: more surprises were in store for the police.

Karla approached him. He was still rooted to the spot, afraid to face the truth. He regretted having entered the meeting room inadvertently obeying Nestor, following the murderer's sick whims.

Alex's eyes blurred with tears as he contemplated that Ana could be in the box.

Karla took a deep breath and moved forward, placing her pistol on the table. There was no label on the bundle, only a phrase written in felt-tip pen:

"To Alex Cortes, with love".

Karla took her house key and stabbed at the brown seal, piercing the tape and running the key down the slot. She pulled the flaps and ripped open the box.

Alex didn't dare breathe. Part of him didn't want to know what was inside. But another part did. Desperately.

Once the box was open, he recognized the porex wrapper.

Karla turned around, but Alex still hadn't moved an inch.

She pulled away more cardboard and then took a deep breath.

She lifted the lid and looked inside.

Then she paused and closed her eyes. Picking up the vacuumed bag inside, she pulled it out slowly and left it on the table. There was more blood than there had been in the other packages.

Alex couldn't face it, so he turned around and walked to the door.

"Wait, Alex," said Karla in surprise. "It's not Ana, thank Christ, it's not Ana!"

Alex felt a surge of adrenalin and came alive again. He turned to her.

"Say that again?"

"Look, it's not Ana. It's a man."

He rushed to the table.

Karla squeezed the grim contents of the vacuum bag with her fingers. The transparent liquid, together with the blood inside, revealed a man's face.

"See, it's not Ana, it's not Ana!" she said, almost shouting, her relief palpable.

A small smile appeared on Alex's face, and his breathing returned to normal.

It wasn't his sister, but it was someone else's son or brother.

Another man had lost his life at the hands of Nestor—another innocent succumbing to the, as yet unknown, rules of the killer.

"Another victim. But wait..." said Alex. "This face looks familiar."

"You recognize him?"

"I don't know why, but I think I've seen him before."

The woman leaned closer to the face and said:

"Look, Alex, he has something between his teeth."

"Of course he does. The asshole has left us another message."

"We can't open it here. We have to take it to the lab."

Karla placed the bag in the white porex box, picked up a piece of black cloth and covered it.

"Let's go to the lab. We don't have much time," said Karla, leaving the room.

69

She was waiting for them.

Dr. Guevara took the package as if it were made of porcelain.

She took it to her kingdom, where everything was possible, and opened it immediately; the fingerprint contamination was no longer a problem.

Alex called Alan, informing him they had new evidence and that he'd let Alan know when he could start work on it. But the forensic IT officer seemed skeptical that the new message could contain the key to deciphering the riddles.

When she punctured the bag, Dr. Guevara grimaced at the smell of fermented blood. She immediately noticed substantial differences from the previous shipments when she removed the plastic.

The head and hands hadn't decomposed.
Nor did the bag contain any feet.
Why hadn't the killer sent the feet?
Had he been in a hurry?

Was he trying to convey a different message?

The saw cuts were the same, but something was new. Alba couldn't tell at first glance. She needed more time to analyze it, but time was the one thing they didn't have.

She picked up the head and placed it on the table. The grim trophy was inside. Her assistant helped her with the process, which was now a ritual.

The assistant grasped the head firmly, and Alba levered the jaw open to pull the object between the teeth.

It was an ID card. It was clear that Nestor was no longer playing for time.

The case had accelerated and taken on a whole new twist.

The coroner turned it over and looked for a written message. Nothing.

She walked over to the window and held it up to the light as Karla peered over her shoulder.

"Maxime Garanger," said Karla. "Who's that?"

"Damn it, I told you I knew who he was!" said Alex. "I've been thinking about his face for the last hour."

"So, who is he?"

"He's a best-selling author," Alex said, slapping his forehead. "I'm reading his book."

"An author?" asked Karla. "How's an author connected to this?"

"I haven't got a clue."

"Come on. We need to go to the victim's house," said Karla.

She snapped a photo of the ID card with her phone and gave Alba the thumbs-up, indicating she could keep the document.

"We have to go to his house right away," Karla repeated as they left the morgue.

"Wait," said Alex. "That's what Nestor wants us to do."

"Of course, that's what he wants us to do, but maybe your sister is there."

Alex looked at the floor and turned around. He walked over to the row of chairs against the wall and sat down.

"What are you doing? Have you gone crazy?"

"Hold fire, Karla. This is exactly what Nestor wants us to do, and so far, we've been dancing to his tune. We need to wait, play him at his own game. Otherwise, it will never end for us or my sister."

Karla looked at him with furrowed brows.

"What's your plan then?"

Alex didn't answer. He was still thinking about it.

"Why an author, Karla?"

"I don't know. Maybe he's got a grudge against him? Maybe the answer lies in the books he's written, and there's something in them he didn't like."

"I think that would be too simplistic. Nestor is more refined, a perfectionist. The reason for choosing an author has to be much more detailed, careful, meditated."

Karla shrugged.

"I think we're wasting vital time."

"An author, an author…" repeated Alex, running his fingers through his hair and pacing the room. "Fuck! I just don't get it," said Alex.

"Are you coming with me, then?"

"No, I need to talk to Alan," said Alex, pulling out his cell phone.

"He can give us a head start on how to surprise this son of a bitch."

70

Distancing themselves and taking perspective: that's what they needed to do to decide their next steps.

Alex had a revelation, although he didn't always trust his brainwaves. It wasn't easy to veer from the usual police protocol. It took courage and bravery. The strength his sister had always tried to instill in him flowed through his body. In his early days at the academy, when he first arrived in Barcelona, Ana had always been his pillar: now it was his turn to help her. *But how?* he asked himself.

"Alan, are you in your office?" he barked down the phone.

"Sergeant, you're calling my landline. Where else would I be?"

Alex cleared his throat.

"Listen, it's very urgent. We're with the coroner in Sabadell. We have the sixth victim's ID. He's an author. I need you to do something."

"What do you want now?"

"Something that I haven't got time to ask the judge for permission to do." There was silence.

"I know it's a big ask, but you're the only one who can do

it."

Alex waited a few moments.

"Sergeant, are you asking me to do something *illegal*?"

"Maybe, but I need to save my sister's life and catch that psychopath once and for all. He's been playing with us from the beginning."

"I'm sorry, Sergeant, I can't do that."

"Wait, wait. Have you got brothers or sisters? Children of your own?"

"No, and no."

"Just imagine that a murderer had taken the person you love the most, and you had the chance to save them. What would you do, Alan? Would you waste hours waiting for a goddamn permit? I need your help to catch him. What do you say? Will you help me?"

On tenterhooks, Karla listened to the one-sided conversation and heard a loud sigh from the other end of the line.

"What do you need?" asked Alan.

Alex punched the air.

"I'll give you the author's address, and I need you to log into his computer and tell me what you see."

"What?" said Alan.

"Listen. The killer wants us to go to the address. I need to know if his house has CCTV, to look through any recordings you can find and tell me what you see. And also check what's on his computer."

"On his computer?"

"Yes, I have a hunch, Alan. Just let me know what you can find out."

"Give me the address."

Alex gave it to him and heard the click of Alan's keyboard

as he typed it into the system.

"Puigcerda… in the Pyrenees."

"Yeah, a long way from here, so we need this information fast."

"Give me five minutes," said Alan.

"We don't have much time; please hurry," said Alex, muting the call.

"Karla, call Rexach and explain the situation to him. Tell him to send the local cops to the author's house. Top priority."

"Okay, good idea. What about us?" she asked.

"We'll need to go by helicopter."

She nodded and dialed the boss's number.

"Alan, are you still there?"

"Yes, I'm getting into his Wi-Fi. In thirty seconds, I'll be inside the network, and I'll be able to see everything that's connected," he said, typing at breakneck speed. "Okay, let me see. Yes, there are cameras. It's a cheap alarm system."

"Tell me what you see."

"Nothing, it's dark, and everything is still. There's a cat in the living room. The cameras in the garden – all still. No movement in the house. Nothing unusual, Sergeant."

"It can't be. Damn it. Look more closely; zoom in. There's got to be something, a body, Nestor, something, damn it."

"I don't know what I'm supposed to be looking for or what you expect to find, but there's nothing here at all."

"Okay. We'll have to go and check it out ourselves. That's all we can do," Alex said resignedly. "Thanks for helping."

His chest felt tight, and his shoulders were rigid with tension. All he could think about was Ana.

Just as he was about to hang up, he heard Alan speak.

"Did you say something?" he asked

313

Alan didn't answer.

Alex thought it must have been his imagination.

"Wait, Alex…" Alan's excited voice came down the line.

"What is it? Alex said, trying to keep his voice even.

"I can see something. I think it's an office," said Alan. "I can definitely see something, but I'm not sure what it is."

"What can you see? Is it a woman?"

"A woman? No, it's a computer. It's switched on."

"Is anyone using it?"

"No, there isn't anyone there, but it's turned on. I'm looking at a desk with a laptop on it. It looks like a study filled with books and documents. It's weird because it seems to have been on for a while but doesn't have a screen saver."

"What are you saying?"

"Hang on; I'll go into the laptop camera. Maybe there's someone in the back."

He logged onto the laptop's operating system, activated the camera and looked to see what was on the other side.

"Alex, there's no one. The chair's empty."

"Damn it!"

"Wait, I'll try to get into the computer and see what's there. Maybe there's another message from the killer," said Alan, his fingers flying over the keyboard.

"See anything?"

"I'm going in," said Alan, "I'm going in now. For fuck's sake. Holy crap," said Alan, letting out a low whistle.

"What the fuck is it?"

"You won't believe this…"

"Tell me what you can see, and that is a fucking order!"

"It's a website. With some books."

"What the hell are you talking about, Alan?"

"It's a product page, a website where this guy sells his books."

"What does that have to do with us?"

"*Everything*, Alex, everything. For fuck's sake, *everything*. It's a book published through Maxime's account, but the author is Nestor Luna, and the title is... are you ready?"

"Alan!" roared Alex, his heart pounding out of his chest.

"Diary of a Suicidal Killer."

"What the fuck?" Alex rubbed his hand over his face and glanced over at Karla.

"I think the guy is going to kill himself."

Blood rushed to Alex's ears as he processed Alan's words. After all that son of a bitch had done, he wanted to take the easy way out by committing suicide. He'd killed six people and possibly his sister. What would become of Ana if the bastard died? He would never see her again. He had to stop him.

Alex caught his breath. He couldn't give up now. They had too much to lose.

"Excellent work, Alan. Now I need something else. Find out there's a car registered to Nestor."

"Sir, I can't..."

"ALAN! We don't have time for formalities. See if he has a car, damn it!"

Alan went back to pounding on the keyboard.

"According to our database, he doesn't own a car."

"Okay, now look up Maxime's name."

"Yes, he has a black Volkswagen Golf."

"Okay, now log into the traffic camera system to see the last time a camera pinged him."

There was silence. Karla approached and gestured to Alex

to ask how the search was going.

Alex muted the phone.

"What did Rexach say?"

"We have the helicopter, but we'll have to wait. It'll be here in twenty minutes, top."

Alex nodded.

"We've got him, Alex. You there?" came Alan's voice.

"Tell me."

"We've got him. He passed through the Cadi Tunnel an hour ago in Maxime's car."

Alex looked at Karla and clenched his jaw: they were so close to catching the murderous bastard.

71

There's a moment when a wounded animal is about to die but surprises its predator by returning to the fight with a vengeance.

That's how Alex felt: that the prey was now hunting the predator.

"Good job, Alan," he said. "Which direction is he going?"

"Toward you."

"Me?"

"Yes, toward Barcelona. Wait," said Alan, "he passed *La Roca del Vallès* thirty minutes ago."

"What else?"

"Nothing else," said Alan and then corrected himself. "No, wait, he's just passed a camera at the exit to the Costa Brava."

"Excellent. Call me when you have more news."

Alex grabbed Karla's arm. They climbed the stairs to the roof of the Mossos d'Esquadra police headquarters, where the helicopter was ready for take-off. The pilot was performing protocol checks and nodded at them as they approached, crouching down.

Alex opened the side door, and the noise was infernal. Karla climbed into the cabin, put her ear protectors on and looked at Alex quizzically.

"Get in," she shouted over the roar of the engine.

"I'm not coming; you'll have to go alone."

She raised her palms and shrugged.

"I need you to go to the author's house. If Ana is there, you have to save her."

"What are you talking about? You have to come with me!"

"No, I need to catch Nestor. I'm not letting that piece of shit get away."

"Please come with me! Your sister is more important."

Alex looked at her, shaking his head.

"I trust you, Karla. I love Ana more than anyone else in the world. Save her for me."

"We can't take off until Rexach gives us the nod. I can't leave yet!"

"Fuck the orders. It could be the difference between life and death for my sister," he pleaded, squeezing her hand.

He reached up and grabbed her ear protectors, and yelled into the microphone.

"Captain, take off now! That's an order."

Alex could feel Karla's warm breath tickling his cheek, and he stared into her eyes. Karla inched toward him and leaned into him, gently kissing his lips. She hesitated and drew back, afraid of being rejected, but the corner of Alex's mouth curled up into a sad smile.

"Take care, Alex," she said, snapping shut her harness. "Let's go," she shouted to the pilot.

Alex stepped down from the helicopter, and as the speed of the blades increased, he covered his head with his arms, watching it rise into the air. He didn't take his eyes off it until it was no more than a tiny dot in the distance and disappeared behind the mountains.

He raced downstairs, jumped into his patrol car and set off, his tires screaming on the tarmac. Gripping the steering wheel tightly, he flicked on his lights and sirens and headed toward the highway. As people returned from work, the highway from Sabadell to Barcelona was heaving with traffic. He sped along the hard shoulder until he reached the highway to Girona. Cars and trucks slowed down, and he had a clear run. The needle on the dashboard read 120 mph, then 135 mph. He reached 150 mph and thumped angrily on the steering wheel

"Come on, you heap of shit. Let's go!" he yelled, frustration getting the better of him.

His foot touched the floor as he pressed on the pedal: the patrol car couldn't go any faster.

In less than ten minutes, he was at the Girona exit. As he headed to the coast, he called Alan again.

"Is there any news?"

"Ok, ok, there's no need to shout," replied Alan bluntly. "You need to take the Sant Feliu de Guixols exit. He's just been caught on camera heading towards Tossa. Have you got that?"

"Understood, Alan, thank you," he shouted again and hung up.

Alex tossed the cell phone on the passenger seat and concentrated on the road, weaving expertly in and out of the traffic as he headed toward Platja d'Aro.

He exited the highway and joined the main road, only

slowing down for the ubiquitous roundabouts. Anxiety tightened his chest, and fear felt like a brick in the pit of his stomach.

He had every faith that Karla would save his sister.

He re-lived moments of his childhood with Ana and Marc as he drove on autopilot, accompanied by the childhood images which pressed down on the brick stuck in his gut.

Cars let him pass, startled more at his speed than the sirens. He reached the outskirts of Tossa de Mar. He knew these streets well, having been a few times with Mary.

The winding road to the town center lay ahead of him, and his tires screeched as he took the curves at speed. He came around a blind corner and slammed on his brakes. In front was a queue of cars held up by something further down the road out of sight. It was too dangerous to overtake them when he couldn't see what was coming from the other direction.

He took his foot off the accelerator and inhaled, blowing out his breath slowly. He hadn't predicted a traffic jam. After waiting idly for a few minutes, an ambulance overtook him at full speed.

He frowned and got out of the car; the queue was longer than he'd first thought.

From nowhere, a chill made the hairs on the back of his neck prickle. He grabbed his phone and started to run.

72

A different world.

From a helicopter, everything looks different.

The distance, the height, the perspective of things.

Karla watched as Alex grew smaller in the distance until he disappeared completely. The helicopter tilted on its side and headed toward the Pyrenees, not quite thirty minutes away as the crow flies. No sooner had they set off than they were making their descent. Rexach had called several times, but she didn't pick up. She wasn't in the mood to argue.

She put her phone on silent and gazed down at the stark countryside and the mountain range becoming closer.

The pilot informed her that they were about to land and pointed to a white dot where they would land.

The helicopter approached its destination, hovering over the tiny red and blue lights on a wooden hut with solar roof panels that guided them down

They looked for a safe place to land.

On one side was an overgrown orchard filled with weeds and shrubs. An old red tractor was parked beside a rusty swing, and a small treehouse looked like it had been abandoned years ago.

The breeze from the blades made the tall grass dance.

Once she received authorization, Karla climbed down from the helicopter to be greeted by an officer from the Puigcerda corps.

She walked away from the helicopter, relieved when the pilot turned the engine off.

"We've searched the house, ma'am," said the officer.

"Did you find anything?"

"You'd better come and see for yourself."

Karla paused for a moment, suddenly afraid. They'd been after this killer for days and hadn't had much luck. Judging by the officer's comment, she expected whatever it was to be bad.

He led her to the house, and she followed him in, stopping to put on an overall and shoe protectors.

Despite the gravity of the situation, Karla felt a frisson of excitement to be among the first to enter Maxime Garanger's house. He'd been a much sought-after best-selling author: a literary phenomenon who had publishers trying to tempt him with eye-watering offers amounts of cash. But he'd turned them all down, staying true to his self-publishing ideals.

The musty scent of second-hand books permeated the whole building.

Karla followed the officer to the open study door. The laptop was still sitting open on the desk, and everything was as Alan had described. Forensics were dusting the computer and the desk for prints.

"Follow me, please," said the officer, beckoning with his hand to a door. "There's nothing there. We just checked."

She nodded.

"The party is downstairs," he said, descending the stairs.

Karla gripped the flimsy banister as they went down into a basement. It felt like a descent into hell. But not like Dante's in the Divine Comedy: this one was real.

Her eyes took a moment to get used to the darkness, and a musty smell with a hint of pine crept through the mask.

They reached the bottom step to see a massive garage with concrete flooring. Officers in white overalls were illuminating the ceiling with Luminol, and at each side of the room hung a myriad of green air fresheners in the shape of fir trees, forming a peculiar forest that clung to the ceiling.

"They've found blood stains everywhere," the officer told her. "The ceiling is covered, even though it looks clean. It must have been a bloodbath."

As she listened, she looked around. It looked like a typical garage, with a wide door for cars that led to the garden. Tools and some gadgets she didn't recognize hung on a wall.

"Is this what you wanted to show me?" said Karla, slightly disappointed.

"No," the officer replied brusquely. He gestured for her to follow. "Here."

At the back of the room was a black plastic door, which looked out of place.

"Are you ready?" asked the officer, raising his eyes and grimacing.

She nodded, and the sergeant opened it to reveal a hidden space next to the garage. She looked at the floor, recoiling as if she'd been slapped and covered her mouth with her hand.

73

Alex ran after the ambulance, but he soon lost sight of it as it disappeared around a curve.

Apart from the cars backed up on his side, he hadn't seen any oncoming vehicles for a while.

He slowed into a jog, scanning the traffic for a black Volkswagen Golf, trying to catch his breath. He wouldn't have made it this far without all the training he did along the Barcelona seafront. Unlike many of his colleagues, he'd managed to keep fit since joining the force, who had succumbed to the practicality of junk food and sodas. Fortunately, he rarely needed his ability to run fast, but it proved extremely useful that day.

The endless line of idling cars was melting under the warm May sun.

He slowed down when he spotted a dark-colored Golf and put his hand on the gun under his jacket.

He stepped closer. The bright afternoon sunshine had tricked him into thinking the car was black, but it was dark green

Gritting his teeth, he resumed his desperate search until, after around a mile and a half, he reached a straight road. In the distance was the ambulance parked beside a fire truck. A police drone was monitoring the area from above. Onlookers craned their necks to see what was happening, and there was a hushed murmur of speculation and excitement.

Alex picked up his pace until he reached the emergency vehicles.

"I'm sorry, but you can't come any closer," said a fireman, holding out his arm to block the way.

"I'm a police officer," he said, pulling aside the lapel of his jacket.

The man saw the badge and nodded.

"What's happened?" asked Alex.

"An accident. A car has gone through the barrier and crashed down the embankment."

"Shit," he said, peering over the steep edge where he saw a mangled mass of burning iron. The smoke spiraled up on the wind. Alex couldn't make out the model or the license plate number. He could hardly even see the color of the vehicle. Forestry officers and firefighters were trying to tame the flames from all angles to prevent the fire from spreading to the surrounding shrubbery.

His worst suspicions seemed to have come true, and Alex needed confirmation.

Amidst the commotion of the emergency crews, he turned to one of the officers.

"Excuse me, do you know what make of car it was?"

"It's not confirmed yet," said the policeman without looking at him. "But we think it's a VW Golf."

Alex felt his chest shrink and threw his hands to his head.
"What color?"
"It appears to be black."
"What about the driver?"
The officer's lip curled in a cynical grin.
"We'll try to recover what's left of whoever it was. It happens regularly on this stretch of road; people are always in such a goddamn rush or think it's a Grand Prix circuit."

Alex covered his mouth with his hand and turned toward the burning scraps of metal.
"You okay, buddy?" asked the officer half-heartedly.
When Alex didn't reply, he returned to his work.
Alex dropped to his knees. The last chance to catch the Cryptogram Killer was slowly slipping away.
Tears of rage and frustration ran down his cheeks, dripping off the tip of his nose into the abyss below as he berated himself for not having arrived sooner. In his pocket, the phone rang.
He pulled it out; it was Karla.
"I hope you have good news," he said despondently.

74

It took Alex less than an hour to arrive at the author's house.
After dropping Karla off, the helicopter was instructed to pick up Alex.
When he arrived, Karla was waiting for him in the tall grass.
"Hey, how you doing?" she asked.
"Any news?"
She shook her head.
"Follow me," she said and led the way.

They went down the basement stairs.
Alex had imagined many endings, but not this one. Fear and shock had tormented him throughout the trip. All he could think about was the moment he would have to call his mother and break the news to her. He would never find peace, much less the words to justify his failure.

Karla opened the plastic door, letting out a blast of cold, icy air and revealing a body lying on the floor.
The hands had been severed at the wrist, and the head was missing. They entered the room and closed the door. The body was dressed in jeans and a blue sweater with a shirt

underneath, and the feet pointed awkwardly up to the ceiling. It was rigid and had been frozen.

It was Maxime Garanger.

Alex looked up. There was nothing else in the freezer chamber apart from blood-stained shelves. Powerful fans injected polar air incessantly.

Alex zipped up his jacket and left the room. Karla took another look at the body and followed Alex.

"There's no trace of Ana," she said gently at his retreating figure.

The forensic team was in the garage, dusting for prints.

"Cortes?" asked the sergeant from Puigcerda, holding out his hand.

Alex shook it.

"Welcome to the bloodbath. We've never seen anything like it," he said in a surprisingly upbeat tone. "Look at this."

Alex glowered at him, but the jerk didn't appear to notice. The case had gone from bad to worse, and everything pointed to the fact that he wouldn't find his sister alive or even her body.

"Look," said the sergeant pointing to a machine. "It's a carpentry saw and is covered in blood. The killer hasn't even bothered to clean it up."

"That's not very Nestor-like," pondered Alex.

"But why bother? At this point, he knew we were onto him and that his master plan had failed spectacularly. There was no reason to cover his tracks. This is where he cut up the victim's bodies," he said, pointing to the floor.

"Why do you think it's right here?" asked Karla.

"Because up here…" he said, shining a Luminol's ultraviolet light onto the ceiling. "It's full of blood spatter. He had the decency to wipe the floor but didn't care about the ceiling."

"Now I understand," said Alex, scratching his chin.

"What do you understand?" Karla asked.

Alex turned around, ignoring her question.

"But how the hell did he manage to do it on his own? A dead body is too heavy for one person to lift," he said, almost to himself.

He moved toward the freezing chamber and checked the thermometer; -4º F.

When he turned around, he noticed the forest of fir trees hanging from the ceiling.

He looked at the saw and pointed his finger at it.

"Something's missing."

"What?" said Karla.

Alex went to the back of the room, where a strange metallic structure was leaning against the wall.

"Have you checked this?"

"No. Why? What is it?"

"Pass me some reagent."

The officer handed him the reagent, and Alex poured it on the metal structure. It was a triangle with wheels, the kind of tool that mechanics used to lift car engines.

Once the structure had been doused in the transparent reagent, they shone ultraviolet light on it. The metal became fluorescent.

"I'll be damned," said Karla.

"I've got it! Nestor put the victims to sleep with a cocktail of drugs. Once they were asleep, he laid them on the floor in the freezer. When they had frozen, he lifted them with this hydraulic crane which gripped the body and allowed him to amputate the limbs and then the head. Once he'd removed them, he stacked them on the shelves, grouped by each victim. Then he returned the body to the chamber as if nothing had happened. And so on, one after the other, in a sequence, like a conveyor belt of death."

Alex paused and reflected for a moment before continuing.

"Now I understand why there was so much blood in the van. Can you remember, Karla? The coroner couldn't explain how there could be so much blood in the vehicle if the killer hadn't cut them up there. When you cut off the head, an average of about two or three gallons should bleed out. Even if the heart had stopped beating, blood should come out when cutting off the limbs. Now I understand why! It's because the bodies were frozen when he amputated them."

Karla was silent, but her expression said it all.

"The lividities: that's why they were in the back part and were almost nil. He froze them when they were unconscious, but their hearts were still pumping."

"He butchered the poor bastards."

"It could have been even worse, Karla. At the very least, they probably didn't feel anything."

"That's how they lasted thirty days in the van: the bodies were frozen and stored inside an isothermal van, just like a freezer," said Karla, agreeing with her colleague's theory.

The local officer had been listening to their theories and occasionally nodding. It was clear he had no idea what they were talking about.

"Now we know why the decomposition seemed much less than a month. Christ only knows when he kidnapped them."

Alex's phone rang while they were trying to piece together the facts.

"Cortes," he replied.

"Alex, it's Alan. I've got something."

Alex froze to the spot.

"Are you still in the author's house?"

"Yes, we are."

"I found something else on the Wi-Fi network."

"I'm listening."

"Your sister's phone, along with a few others."

75

It felt like Alex had been hit by lightning, and it took him a few seconds to react.

Turning to Karla and the officer, he blinked and inhaled deeply.

"Did you find any cell phones?"

Karla and the sergeant shook their heads, looking mystified.

"Negative," Alex said.

"Well, you have to take a better look because they're there somewhere."

"Okay, I'll call you back. Nice work," said Alex. As he was about to hang up, he added, "Hey, did you order a copy?"

"Of the book? I've already downloaded it. I'll show you later."

"We have to look for the phones. If Alan says they're here," said Alex, racing up the stairs.

He began to search room by room, and Karla did the same. The officer hurried to tell his colleagues to look.

The house wasn't very big, and they'd gone through all the rooms in five minutes.

They eventually met on the first floor.

"Nothing?" he asked her.

"Not a trace."

"Nothing here," shouted the other officer from the garage.

"Damn it," Alex hissed.

"Maybe he's wrong, and it's a computer trick?"

Alex shook his head.

"Hang on a minute, I have an idea," he said, taking his phone out of his pocket. He logged on to the messaging app, pressed the phone icon and put it on speakerphone.

He heard the ringing tone.

"Silence," shouted Alex. "SILENCE!"

No one moved a muscle. Just when Alex was beginning to think it had been a stupid idea, he heard something far away, almost imperceptible.

"Can you hear it?" he whispered to Karla.

She nodded hesitantly.

Alex began to follow the source of the sound: it was coming from the first floor. He went upstairs into Maxime's bedroom. He looked around, and the ringing seemed to get louder. It was definitely in here somewhere. He pressed his ear against the wall: the ringing was coming from the other side. He rapped on the wall until he found a hollow spot. There was no handle to open it, but there had to be a secret room. He shoved his shoulder against the wooden panel, which cracked and collapsed.

As the panel gave in, it occurred to him that Nestor might have set a trap for them. One that he had just fallen straight into. Maybe the evil bastard had set a booby trap. Well, it was too late now because he was going in.

"Fuck it!" he said and pushed.

The door started to open while Alex closed his eyes and cringed, waiting for a detonation.

Nothing happened. Alex opened one eye, and his shoulders sagged with relief. Cautiously, he stepped into the hidden office. His sister's cell phone was there, sitting on a shelf and plugged into the wall, ringing.

He was speechless.

Karla appeared behind him, gasping as she spotted dozens of cell phones.

Under each was a label with the owner's name, phone number and PIN code.

On closer inspection, all appeared to be in airplane mode, but the Wi-Fi was on.

Photos of the murdered victims, annotations, newspaper clippings on the case, and maps covered the walls. The whole sick plan of action. In another section were photos of Alex and all his appearances in the media.

Right next to it, he found photos of his sister. A yellow Post-it was stuck on the image with two words: *"Kill her"*.

On the desk were various objects, including scissors, glue and pens. There were purchase invoices for the saw in the author's name, the van sale contract, and several pens from Nestor's temp agency.

"He answered messages from the victims' families, so it looked like they were still alive," said Alex, shaking his head in disgust and horror.

He pulled out his sister's cell phone, and when he turned it over, he realized it was attached to the desk with Velcro.

"You found it," said Karla.

"I haven't found anything," Alex replied. "My sister isn't here. Who knows where the hell he took her."

75

There was a noise behind them.

"I told you to wait for me," said Rexach as he came panting into the room.

Alex ignored him.

"It's all your fault, damn it!" shouted Alex, pointing his finger at the boss.

Rexach remained silent.

"I wanted to go to Tarragona, and you forced me to stay and look," he said, holding his arm out to show the boss the extent of their discovery. "My sister could be dead, and this place looks like the Texas Chainsaw Massacre. I wish I'd told you to fuck off!"

Karla looked down and sat on the double bed.

"Alex, I told you to wait for me with the helicopter. It was an order!"

"Are you serious? My sister's life could be hanging by a thread, and that's all you're bothered about?" he yelled in the lieutenant's face. "I would never have expected this from you," he spat and left the room.

Karla followed him, shooting a glance at their boss.

"Where are you going?" she said as he went downstairs.

"Back to headquarters to work with Alan on the riddles," he said without turning around. "There's nothing else I can do here. Who knows, maybe the killer's book can help us."

335

76

The truth.

Sometimes it's uncomfortable, and we don't want to know it. Other times, we're forced to scrutinize reality until we finally discover it.

But sometimes, the truth stinks of death and fear.

The book Alex held in his hands reeked of *the scent of death.*

The book Alex held was the truth in all its abhorrent glory.

"Diary of a Suicidal Killer" by Nestor Luna.

Alex and Karla were in the meeting room with Alan. It was almost the middle of the night, but that hadn't deterred them. Coffee sustained them as they picked the brains of their favorite computer nerd.

Alan had downloaded the killer's e-book and given the two officers an e-reader each. A photo of the last victim and the code they'd found inside his mouth was pinned to the board

"Life has not been easy for me, and this book is proof of that. May these pages be a testimony to my brief but troubled existence. From

the day I was born until today, this is a record of my life and the lives I have taken to the grave. I will explain my reasons for doing what I have done, as I cannot do it in person".

Alex read the text aloud while the others listened. Their need to know more was greater than the pull of sleep.

"It all started about forty years ago when I used to go to the beach with my grandfather. My parents worked in a shipyard. I was the third child, several years younger than the other two. I was a mistake, a miscalculation. My father didn't kill me because he didn't want to lose his job, but all I remember from him were spankings. My mother, the poor woman, barely showed me affection, only when my father wasn't looking so as not to anger him. My brothers always got the best things: the first spoonfuls of soup, the new clothes, the soccer games, and the best seats in front of the television. If there were any leftovers, they were for me and my mother".

"Looks like a posthumous letter," said Karla.

Alex nodded and continued.

"Until I reached my teens, I believed my grandfather loved me. When you're young, everything seems normal. The old man, useless jettison from the Spanish Civil War. He would talk about the battlefield, what the war gave him, and what it took away from him. Over time, he spoke less about the latter and demonstrated it to me by his actions. He liked to take me to a cave on the coast, hidden among the rocks. He raped me many times there, but I was only a child and didn't even realize it. Back then, getting any attention was better than nothing. However, those experiences changed my outlook on life forever."

"Later, I began working at the shipyard and met Cristina, the company secretary. A girl my age who was already married. Stolen glances turned into forbidden touches, and then we moved on to more. During the breaks, we would hide in a corner and fuck like rabbits. I enjoyed those days until I wanted more from her, and she refused to give it to me. She threatened to leave me. One night, during a building renovation, I got her drunk and threw her into the fresh concrete foundations. No one ever found out. They searched for her at sea and on land. But they didn't look for her in her concrete coffin, and no one ever found her. I liked that. I missed having sex with her, but the pleasure of having taken her life, dismembering and burying her forever, was even greater."

"Cristina was the first of many. Through my hands have passed many men and women who disappeared without a trace. I even tired of my brothers, who ended up the same way. The bodies were never discovered. There are many accidents in a shipyard; one more or one less isn't noticeable. The unions shout a lot but do nothing apart from taking our money."

"It feels as if I were reading Maxime Garanger's writing. It's the same style," said Karla.

"I think that Nestor dictated the story to him, and Maxime wrote it."

"My father died a natural death. My mother remained alone and now lives on a minimum retirement pension. I found a job in an employment agency in the center of Barcelona. All those people were lost souls. They needed a change, and I offered it for good. Nobody noticed. The parents and friends received messages, which I sent by studying the pattern of the previous ones. They would

remain calm, and I would tell them that "I" had gone on a trip, was at a boyfriend's house, or any other nonsense I thought of. People believe anything you tell them. But life is hard, and when far away from home, there's a remote but very real possibility of falling into the hands of an artist like me".

"Then I met Miguel. We went out together several times. One day I decided to kill him, but I bided my time. My mother needed money for the nursing home and medication. Only she didn't have enough, so I devised a plan. I found Maxime, the author, on a dating app. When I saw his house, I knew it was perfect. He's here now, writing, my slave author. My sex slave and my memoirist. Why kill for free if you can get paid for it? Yes, you heard it right. By buying this book, you are paying for my mother's nursing home. It occurred to me that killing five, six, or seven people would get me plenty of press coverage: it would be the best marketing to sell my book. The Monster of Barcelona. The Cryptogram Killer. *Everyone will want to know, and here you will find the reasons, my ways, and the whys. All of it. No more, no less".*

Alex stopped again.

"He's talking about five victims, the ones in the van. Six with the author and," he swallowed, finding it hard to go on, "seven with my sister."

"We don't know for sure yet," said Karla. "Keep going, keep reading."

"I was only missing one piece, a way to get at the police. The case of the kidnapped child came up and granted me a hero I could turn into a villain. Two for one! At first, I liked him, but then

I realized he was too clever. Even so, playing with fire from my hideout was fun. I challenged him. Then I kidnapped his sister. She was pregnant and cried like a scolded puppy. It was easy to take her with me in exchange for leaving her young son alone. She did what I wanted, and then I sedated her. Yes, she allowed me to do EVERYTHING I wanted to her."

Alex punched the table, making the coffee cups rattle.

He closed his eyes and took a few moments to recover.

Then he went on until the end. The last sentence read:

"Alex, when you read this, I hope there's still time... but it all depends on you. I have given you the clues; whether you can interpret them is up to you. Good luck with Ana".

Alex looked up and then glanced at Alan.

77

"This is our last chance," croaked Alex, his eyes blurring with angry tears.

Alan looked at him, silent.

"Alex, this is a message. Nestor is challenging you to find your sister," said Karla.

"But how? Where?" asked Alan.

"I don't know. He might have chopped her into pieces and put the parts into boxes to be mailed to me in the future. Or maybe the son of a bitch buried her, God knows where, and we'll never find the body." His voice broke, and he paused for a moment before concluding. "I seriously doubt she's still alive."

He rested his hand on Alan's shoulder.

"I need your help. Now it's your turn," he said quietly.

Alan sat in front of his computer. He cracked his knuckles and adjusted his glasses.

"Let's see," he said, wrinkling his nose, "Let's review the data again. When Miguel died, the first message we had was on 09.18.06.05.20.21. When Patricia died, it was 21.16.13.24.16.20. Then Mauricio 22.09... If the code just referred to a change of words to numbers, i.e., a Caesar code…"

"Caesar?" asked Alex.

"Caesar, the Roman emperor, sent encrypted letters to distant legions. Each one followed a different protocol and code. Some had one number shifted to the right and another to the left. So the alphabet began with shifted numbers. If this was the key, we could test it, but it would take us all night," said Alan, looking at Alex, unconvinced.

Alex shrugged.

"Only you can do it. I don't understand any of that."

Alan sighed.

"Let's suppose it's a combination of encrypted codes, and then we're left with just one word. Then what? I've been wondering about this since we got the first barcode. I wanted to wait and see if the psychopath finally gave us the encryption key, but he hasn't. It's not in the book, either. But if a standard encryption system was used, the key has to be hidden in the text."

They spent hours figuring out the encoding system, trying multiple combinations.

Dawn broke over Barcelona under gloomy, overcast clouds that promised rain.

Karla had fallen asleep on the couch, and Alex covered her with his jacket.

They tested different variations until daylight found them.

It didn't take long for the heavens to open up and rinse away their hopes, trickling down the drains like a river of tears.

Alan peeled himself away from the screen. He rose from the chair and slowly stretched his scrawny arms.

"I can't do this anymore."

"I know," Alex replied in a resigned tone.

"I've tried every combination I can think of," he protested. "We could spend the rest of our lives here unless we have the key."

Alex thought about his mother. Since Ana had disappeared, she'd been calling him non-stop. He no longer knew what to say to her.

He stared at his reflection in the glass. A week had passed since the bodies had been found. It was old news, and the press had moved on to other stories, no longer besieging the building.

Alex stepped back toward the table, picked up the book again, and turned to the last page.

He reread it:

"Alex, when you read this, I hope there's still time... it all depends on you. I have given you the clues; whether you can interpret them is up to you. Good luck with Ana".

He looked at the others, then at the board.

"*Good luck with Ana*," Alex repeated in a whisper, "*Good luck with Ana*," he said louder. Alan, what if *that* was the key?"

Karla woke up and stretched.

Alan narrowed his tired eyes.

"What do you mean?"

"The password, what if it was the last word in the book,

Good luck with Ana," he said solemnly. "*Ana*, the keyword could be my sister's name!"

Alan frowned, but as Alex's words clicked, his eyes widened.

He sat back down and restarted the computer. He entered the encryption portal and typed the first sequence of letters using the word Ana as the key.

"Nothing. It's not the keyword."

Alex bit his lip.

"What if you make it simpler? Enter it exactly word for word in the Caesar system, the first letter with the first number."

Alan obeyed.

He then entered the sequence of letters "QIFEST" and the keyword *Ana* into the Vigenère encryption system and pressed enter.

The words "*You can*" appeared on the screen.

Alex let out a shriek that resounded throughout the station.

"You got it, Alan! You did it!" he yelled. "Keep going! Keep going!"

Alan got all the words in until he got the sentence:

"You can save your sister in the house."

"She's alive!" shouted Alex, slamming his hand down on the desk.

"In the house? Which house?" asked Karla.

"Maybe Nestor's house?"

"No, we searched it from top to bottom, and forensics checked everywhere."

"So which house?" asked Alan.

"Then it can only be Maxime's."

"But we've searched it from top to bottom. It can't be," said Karla.

"Yes, but I found a secret office, remember? Forensics had overlooked it. They're not infallible."

"Do you think she's there?" she asked, arching her eyebrows.

Alex nodded, watching her intently.

"We only have one card left and have to play it fast. My sister's waiting for me."

78

Bad weather prevented the helicopter from taking off.

Raindrops hammered on the car's windshield; there was no other option but to drive to the author's house.

Karla and Alex hadn't informed the lieutenant of their destination.

Alex drove with the blue light on, and the Mossos convoy weaved in and out of the slow-moving traffic.

Alex's life had changed in only two weeks. He felt like he'd lost everything

Mary was gone. The transfer to Tarragona, although granted, had not yet been executed because his boss had insisted he stayed. A murderer had targeted him, and his sister had suffered the consequences. His life had turned upside down, and he was about to face the final act. He had to find Ana.

The weather was even worse in Puigcerda. The rain added to the constant humidity of the Pyrenees, and the strong winds buffeted their vehicles.

They parked near the front yard. What had probably been

a lawn months ago was now a flooded swamp full of weeds and puddles.

They ripped through the police tape and kicked down the door. The small group stood on the landing, dripping on the hardwood floor, and shrugged off their soaked jackets.

Alex told Karla to head to the second floor while he took care of the first floor.

"Ana!" they called out in unison as they checked the building room by room.

Karla turned the author's bedroom upside down, finding nothing. The bathroom was still untouched, although black fingerprint powder dusted every surface, starkly contrasting against the white ceramic of the old-fashioned toilet.

She entered the narrow office. Forensics had already taken all the evidence from there.

Karla gave up. She took one last look around and then went downstairs, each step creaking as she stepped on them. Alex heard her and came out of the living room.

"Did you find anything?" she asked him.

He shook his head.

"Only the basement left," he said, nodding toward the stairs.

Alex went down first, turning on the light at the top of the stairs. Re-entering this chamber of horrors wasn't easy, and his heartbeat thrummed in his ears.

After the first few steps, the cloying aroma of the air fresheners hanging from the ceiling greeted them

Not only was Alex terrified of finding Ana's body, but he was also wary that Nestor would be down there waiting for them. he inhaled, trying to steady his breathing.

The space was exactly how forensics had left it.

The saw, the tools, the splashes on the roof. Everything was still there.

Before entering, Alex looked at the temperature: it was the same, four below zero.

When he opened the door, a cold blast of air hit him. He stepped inside, scanning the room for something he might have missed earlier. The author's body had been removed. The shelves sparkled with crystallized blood. He banged his fists against the wall and floor but heard nothing unusual.

Karla shivered, but Alex didn't feel anything. He wondered what it would be like to die in a freezing chamber.

He hugged Karla and rubbed her arms to warm her up, his eyes constantly flicking around the basement.

What else was there?

What was he missing?

Where else could Nestor have hidden his sister?

They went back upstairs, at a loss of where to search next.

Where was the *house* Nestor was talking about?

Alex began to cry and allowed all his worst fears to overcome him. Karla put her arms around him, wiping away his frustrated tears with her frozen fingers.

"I've lost her forever. Why the fuck did we even bother to come back here," he sobbed, burying his head into Karla's shoulder.

Karla didn't answer. She cast her mind back to the moment they'd first arrived in the helicopter and tried to visualize the house from above in her mind's eye.

"Wait, Alex. Nestor wrote *house*, but he didn't say *which* house."

"What do you mean?"

"The house. *House.* What if it's a treehouse?"

Alex gave her a sidelong glance, frowning.

"Outside, Alex, I saw a wooden treehouse," she said, pulling away.

"But surely forensics checked the garden?"

"Whatever, let's go have a look."

She opened the gate leading to the garden, which Nestor had used to drive the van in.

The garden was waterlogged and slippery with mud.

They went outside into the heavy rain.

Karla ran to the tree while Alex, rooted to the spot, surrendered himself to the rain.

She scaled the ladder, clinging to the trunk. When she was ten feet off the ground, her foot went through a rung, and she lost her footing. Grabbing hold of the next step, she hauled herself onto the next rung and continued her ascent. She rubbed her dirty hands on her jeans, straightened her shoulders and pushed the door open.

The treehouse was empty. There was nothing, just leaking, weathered wooden boards and mold.

She peered over the edge and shook her head at Alex, then looked toward the main house, wondering if the killer hadn't meant *in the house* but *from the house*.

She narrowed her eyes as she scanned the garden, but nothing else caught her attention—a*nother failed attempt.*

She climbed back down to the ground.

Alex's face was blank as he watched Karla coming down. He had nothing left in him to give. He stared at his reflection in a large puddle at his feet as the incessant raindrops rippled the surface. To his right was an old red tractor, rickety and rusty, with water pooling underneath. Alex stepped toward the tractor, noticing the rain flowing under the vehicle.

He frowned and moved closer, feeling a tiny shred of hope flare inside him.

"Karla!" he shouted at the top of his lungs. "Come here quickly!"

79

Water swirled in a vortex beneath the tractor.

Was it magic, or was it divine intervention? Whatever it was, Alex couldn't care less.

He knelt down and saw the water gushing down a green metal hatch.

"I think she's here!" he shouted.

He showed Karla the lid: they would have to remove the heavy vehicle to open it.

They pushed, but the tractor didn't budge an inch.

Alex climbed into the vehicle. Everything in it was rusty. He could see two long tire trails in the mud. He ran into the garage, grabbed some rope and tied it to the patrol car. It skidded across the lawn, zigzagging whenever it accelerated, but the tractor didn't move.

"If we don't get this tractor out of the way fast, she'll drown," shouted Alex, desperately scanning the garden for ideas.

There was no time to call a tow truck.

Karla went into the garage again, picked up another rope and tied it to the first one, which was still attached to the patrol car. She climbed into the car and inched it into the garage. She pressed down on the gas, and the tires screamed as they gradually caught traction on the dry garage floor. The smell of burning rubber filled the garage, and white smoke, like a fall fog, stung Karla's eyes.

The car inched forward slowly, moving a few inches, then a couple of feet, then a few yards. Karla looked over her shoulder, guessing it had moved enough, but Alex was nowhere to be seen when she climbed out of the car.

The hatch was open, swinging to and fro. Rain trickled into her eyes, and the wind whipped her hair into her eyes, making it hard to see. She crept closer, fear coursing through her veins.

When she peered in, she saw a bottomless pit under the tractor, like a water deposit. The walls were several feet deep.

Water pooled at the bottom of the well, where Alex was crouched, holding his sister in his arms, sobbing and murmuring, his tears mixing with the raindrops. Ana's right hand had been amputated, and a blood-stained bandage was in its place.

Karla stood at the edge, watching the scene. It took her a moment to realize that Ana was moving, and Alex's tears were tears of joy.

They'd found her.

Ana Cortes, the final victim of Nestor Luna, The Cryptogram Killer, The Serial Killer of Barcelona, was alive.

Karla sank to her knees in the mud, her strength almost depleted.

They'd been too late for the other victims, but at least they'd managed to save the only one Nestor had given a chance to live.

PROLOGUE

Travessera de les Corts police station, Barcelona.
The Monday after.

The killer's wish had been granted.

The book, written by Nestor Luna, and dictated to an author imprisoned in his own home, had become a best-seller in Spain.

Diary of a Suicidal Killer was breaking all records.

The media loved news like this, and Nestor had gained notoriety, just as he'd dreamed of. He had devised the sickest marketing plan in history to sell a book that would support his ailing, elderly mother.

A noble end, by ruthless means.

The press distorted Nestor's life to make it seem more horrifying than it was: a simple working-class guy who had turned into a deranged serial killer. It had sold in the millions, and publishers worldwide sought out Nestor's mother, begging her to sign their lucrative translation contracts.

Nestor had achieved everything he had ever wanted. Except for becoming a hero.

But Alex had succeeded again: first, he'd saved the president's son, and now he'd rescued his sister.

The lieutenant patted Alex on the shoulder.

"Congratulations, a well-deserved success once again," said his boss, poking his head around the door into the conference room where a crush of journalists, VIPs and fellow corps members were waiting for Alex Cortes to make a statement.

"With six bodies in the morgue, I don't think congratulations are in order," mumbled Alex under his breath as a round of applause came from the audience.

Rexach cleared his throat and beamed at Alex.

"Have you decided to stay with us, then?" Rexach asked quietly.

"I don't know, we'll see."

The lieutenant nodded.

"You know this will always be your home."

"I don't think I want to stay here, though. Too many memories in Barcelona."

"Well, give it some thought. The most important thing is that this case is over," said the boss from behind his hand. "Or at least that's what we want the journalists and the public to believe."

Alex fell silent and stood on tiptoe, looking toward the opposite side of the room.

"What do you mean, boss?"

"Haven't you read the forensics report about the author's house?"

Alex looked at him, surprised.

"They found someone else's DNA in the freezer and on

the saw and haven't been able to identify it. It doesn't match any of the five bodies in the van," he said, flapping his hand dismissively. "But that doesn't matter today. Just say what we agreed, okay?" said the lieutenant, adjusting his tie

Alex was perplexed, but before he could speak, the chief inspector called out his name from inside the conference room.

Alex took a deep breath and walked out into a barrage of flashlights and shouts of "Turn to the camera".

The applause was deafening, and he couldn't stop himself from grinning as he recognized friends, colleagues and respected journalists who slapped him on the back as he passed.

He went up to the podium and sat in the center of the table. On his right was the chief of the police station, and on his left was Corporal Karla Ramirez.

Karla and Alex exchanged a complicit smile, and she covered her mouth with her right hand, wiggling her fingers at him. At first, Alex didn't understand what she was doing. And then it suddenly dawned on him; she wasn't wearing her engagement ring and wanted to make sure he saw it.

He bit his lip and tried to hide his delight by pretending to fiddle with his mic.

Ana was in the front row, her arm bandaged and held in place by a sling.

He caught her eye and smiled gently; the nightmare was over.

He cleared his throat.

"I want to thank you all for coming today. Before I start, you should know that I'm not very good at speeches."

The camera bulbs popped every time he moved, and furry mics edged closer to his chair.

"Without the help and dedication of Corporal Ramirez and digital forensic specialist Alan Martinez, we wouldn't have been able to solve this case."

A cell phone shrilled loudly in the hushed room, and a red-faced journalist muted it.

Alex continued.
"The Cryptogram Killer will not kill again. His body was recovered from his car after suffering a fatal road traffic accident. No one else was injured in the accident."

Three other cell phones ran, and Alex paused until there was silence.

"I want to reassure the public that this man is no longer a threat and that peace on our streets has been restored. As he glanced around the room, he felt his phone vibrating in his pocket. Like a domino effect, dozens of Mossos' cell phones began to ring simultaneously.

The journalists, witnessing the scene, chattered excitedly, snapping photo after photo to capture the shocked faces of the officers. The attention was no longer on Alex.

At the back of the room, Mario, the forensic, clenched his jaw. When Alex looked at him, his friend pointed at his cell phone and gestured for Alex to do the same.

Alex fished his phone from his jacket pocket, and the screen lit up. It was a standard message sent to the whole investigation team.

The blood drained from his face and the elation he'd felt only seconds earlier vanished. He passed the phone to Karla, who was watching him intently. With a trembling hand, she took the phone and read the message.

"Another package, addressed to Alex Cortes, has just been delivered to the police station in Lloret de Mar. The sender's name is Nestor Luna".

Did you enjoy this book?

Discover "KILLER ON BOARD", Book 2 of Inspector Alex Cortes *Murder in Barcelona* Series.

GET THE BOOK HERE

There's only one thing worse than fear: when it materializes and gives way to the darkest reality one could ever imagine.
A package delivered to a police station reopens a closed chapter.
A charred corpse in the kitchen of a cruise ship.
A clandestine clinic hiding bodies from botched operations.
Three stories intertwine in the second adventure of Inspector Alex Cortes.

Sergeant Cortes embarks on a desperate search for the most bloodthirsty serial killer in the history of Barcelona, tormented by his thirst for revenge after what was done to his sister.

Ghosts of the past resurface when the chief of the Mossos d'Esquadra forces Alex to swiftly solve a murder on a cruise ship. Thus, the previous unresolved case sneaks back into Alex's life, with the discovery of new cryptograms

DID YOU ENJOY THIS BOOK?

from the serial killer, who was thought to be dead.

In their search for the cruise ship murderer, agents Álex and Karla will be dragged to the limits of cunning. In their investigation, they will be helped by an ingenious chef, who will become their assistant in true Watsonian style.

<u>Vengeance, mystery, and blood are the ingredients of this thriller, the second installment featuring Barcelona's finest inspector.</u>

Sergeant Cortés will have to use all his intuition and learn to curb his thirst for vengeance.

GET THE BOOK HERE

ACKNOWLEDGEMENTS

Thanks to my father, my "ace up the sleeve", both when plotting the story and as an alpha reader.

Thanks to Pili, my beta reader: your advice is invaluable.

Thanks to Pablo, who keeps showing me the way from above.

Thanks to Pedro, for making me dream big.

Thanks to my mother, for her sensitivity and creativity.

Thanks to Eva, for your advice, for believing in me and for all the conversations, support, and ideas.

And thanks to you, for making this dream come true.

ABOUT THE AUTHOR

Riccardo Braccaioli (Italy, 1982) is an Italian writer and lecturer. He has written several autobiographical and personal growth bestsellers, including DIARY OF MY BANKRUPCY.

He's the author of two thriller series: The Malatesta Series and the Alex Cortes – Murder in Barcelona series.

If you liked this book, I would be very grateful if you could leave a review.

Printed in Great Britain
by Amazon